LOVE IN MY TEARDROPS

By

Vanessa Hollis

Published by Teardrops Publishing
ISBN 978-0-9767602-0-7

Additional copies of this book are available by mail.
Send $17.75 each (which includes shipping & handling) to:
PO Box 920561
Norcross, GA 30010

Or pay through PayPal on the website @
www.TeardropsPublishing.net Or www.VanessaHollis.com

Printed in the U.S.A. by Morris Publishing
3212 East Highway 30, Kearney, NE 68847

TEARDROPS PUBLISING

ACHNOWLEDGEMENTS

I first would like to thank my maker, for without him in my life this wouldn't be possible.

I would like to thank my two sisters who had a hand in my process. Shalonda Rowland, for her guidance in what she thought the characters should do next, little did she know that I would go in the opposite direction. Terri Rowland, for a couple of poems she contributed. All I had to do was ask and she delivered what it was that I was looking for each and every time. I would like to thank my mom, Margaret Rowland, for her participation in getting me details of certain locations within the city of Tulsa. I also would like to say thank you to a special friend, who is and will always remain dear to my heart. You know who you are.

And for my cheering squad, my entire family who believed in me the most, so much so, that they allowed me to leave the state to focus on my dream of completing my first novel. I would also like to personally thank my brother Joe, for the wonderful picture art designed on the front cover of the original book; that was created especially for me. I would like to thank my handsome model for allowing me to display his picture on the revised cover.

Finally I would like to say a special thank you to my son Termaine Yargee, who has been in my corner from beginning to end. I love you very much.

This comes from your mom, your sister, your daughter, and your friend.

Vanessa 05'

Book one 'LOVE IN MY TEARDROPS' 2005
Book two 'WHEN MY TEARS CRY' 2006
Book three 'TEARS OF KATRINA' 2007
Book four 'JUDGING CHEYENNE'S SHADOW' 2007

A fellow author once said, "Sometimes it's necessary to start close to the end to understand the beginning."

INTRODUCTION

Mekyla entered Bergstrom International Airport through the automatic glass doors. The wheels of her suitcase, humming across the sidewalk a moment earlier, clacked over the metal strip of the doorway, and then fell silent as they reached the brightly patterned carpet. Tired, she led the bag to a window and stared out at the planes coming in to land, and rising fast out of Austin after takeoff.

Sinking into deep thought, she wiped the occasional tear from her face. She had been called back home for a family emergency; one of her sisters had been admitted to the hospital. No one had told her why. And addition to her family's emergency, Mekyla had her on little situation to deal with, maybe sooner than she had hoped. A decision that will not only affect her life, but someone else's as well. She'd made that kind of decision before, but in a completely different context.

Wiping a few final tears from her eyes, she began to think about modern airport security and remembered she'd need extra time before boarding the flight. She looked at her watch, and then began to trot toward the ticket counter, working her way around less purposeful passengers, feeling in the side pocket of her purse, reassuring herself for the hundredth time that she had her ticket. She'd have to make that one last phone call before boarding the flight as well as to confirm her ride upon arrival. Mekyla heaved a habitual sigh – a sigh that would usually have meant that if she could be doing something different, something different would win.

A few hours later Mekyla's plane arrives into Tulsa International Airport.

"Hey it's me," Mekyla said into her cell phone. "I'm here at the airport, about to get on the plane. I've looked at the board and confirmed that it's on schedule, so I should be arriving in about five and a half hours, including the layover in Dallas."

"Are you okay Mekyla?" said Ian. "You sound out of breath."

"Yes, I'm fine now. I had to do a little sprint to the boarding area."

"Should you be running in your condition?"

"I'm fine. I said it was a *little* sprint." She wondered why he was so concerned now anyway.

"Okay, don't get excited. I was just asking. I'll see you in the baggage claim area when you arrive."

"Okay. Hey, they're already boarding the plane. You better let me get going. I'll see you in a little bit. Bye."

Mekyla turned and surveyed the area. She estimated the distance back to the newsstand she'd passed on the way to the gate. She walked across to the gate and leaned an elbow on the counter. "Excuse me sir."

The man in uniform looked up.

"I'm starved," she said. "You think I have time to make a mad dash to the newsstand down there and grab a bag of chips?"

He gave her an official smile. "Sure, but you better hurry. We're boarding the last rows now."

"Thanks." She started toward the newsstand, and then turned back. "Oh! Did you need anything?"

"No ma'am. Thanks for asking."

"Okay." She started off again and called back over her shoulder. "I'm hurrying. Don't close the door on me."

At the newsstand, she grabbed a bag of chips and hurriedly laid some money on the counter. "Here's a dollar fifty for the chips. Keep the change, my flight's boarding."

The woman behind the counter gave her a worried look. "I'm sorry ma'am, but those chips are *two* dollars and fifteen cents. Plus tax."

Mekyla furrowed her brow. "You're telling a tale. You do know this is only the grab bag size." She gave it a little shake. "It only has maybe twenty chips in it. And that's only if the folks at the factory were in a *good* mood that day."

"Yes, ma'am." The counter woman shrugged. "Airport prices are higher."

Mekyla dug into her purse for more money. "These chips better have gold trim and a ticket to Hawaii in there." With chips in hand, Mekyla hurried back toward the gate.

The man in the uniform was motioning to her when she was still twenty yards away. "Today's your lucky day, ma'am. You're just going to make this flight. If you hurry."

"Oh, I'm hurrying," she said. "I'm going to have to write a letter to these chip people. Just as soon as I write the letter to Nike. This is just getting out of hand." She handed the man her boarding pass, then waved the chips at him. "Sorry I'm running late. The chips held me up. Literally."

Inside the pane, she tried not to bump anybody with her carry-on. She checked the seat number on her boarding pass. "Twenty-three B," she said aloud. "I guess that's not first class." She found her seat and had to trouble the woman on the isle to let her in. "Pardon me. Sorry to have to climb over you. I would have been here earlier, but I had to take out a loan to buy these chips." She let the snack dangle from her fingers.

"I never shop those airport vendors."

"I won't be again, if the only thing they can see is up." She settled in her seat. "My mom really brought me up better than this I'm Mekyla Marie Williams." She smiled at her neighbor.

"Natocha Aurie. Nice to meet you, Mekyla."

"It's nice to meet you Natocha."

"Your name sounds very familiar."

"So, are you headed home, Natocha?"

"No, I'm traveling on business. And you, Mekyla?"

"Yes, I'm going home, but unfortunately it's for a family emergency."

"Oh, I'm sorry to hear that."

"Thank you. And *I'm* sorry to be so disorganized." Mekyla gestured toward the mess creeping out of her small carry-on book bag. She began to gather all the unorganized papers as she could. She hadn't had time to pack correctly because of the suddenness of her trip. "I'm sure if we weren't getting ready for take off, they would probably ask me to leave." She said as she struggled to get a grip on a thick handful of papers and photos.

"Here Mekyla, let me help you with that," said Natocha, reaching over to lend a hand.

"I'm usually not this clumsy, and this is such a small space to be clumsy in."

"It's okay." Natocha's attention was drawn to the photographs she had taken hold of. "These are nice," she said.

"Thank you."

"Is that you and your husband."

"No, they're two different guys and they're both friends, well maybe one more than a friend. Excuse me, I rambling."

"You have yourself a couple of very handsome looking men there."

"Pictures can speak volumes. One of them was a romantic fairytale meeting, which turned out to be anything but a fairytale-like ending. Have you ever had a fairytale beginning or ending Natocha?"

"Most definitely, I have a wonderful husband and two daughters back home, whom I adore. I would not trade them for the world, even when my husband teeters around that last nerve of mine."

"You sound like one of my sisters," said Mekyla. "She would say the same thing to me and I would think she was in denial, that life couldn't be that wonderful with one man, one commitment, and one lifetime partner. And on the other hand in a lot of ways I envied what she appeared to have."

"I take it Mekyla; you have had some problems with the whole concept of one man." Natocha smiled.

"How could you possibly have known that? You've only known me now five minutes or so."

"I think repeating the number one three times was somewhat of a give away."

"Having some problems with it; would be putting it mildly. I was completely terrified of committing to one man. So I would always make sure I had a backup man. So I wouldn't have to deal with the heartbreak of my inevitable personal condemnation of the relationship." She sighed. "You could say I'm a very confused young lady. It would terrify me to be alone or fathom the possibility of growing old by myself. And on the other hand it would also terrify me when I started to believe I wouldn't be enough for my partner. It terrified me to think that he would also look elsewhere for the things he didn't find in me. In turn, my mind allowed me to be my own worst enemy as far as happiness was concerned. I started to believe I was not worthy of happiness." She looked out the window for a moment then turned back to Natocha. "You know the old saying, 'Anything worth having is worth waiting for?' Well, I never viewed it as ever pertaining to me."

Natocha nodded. "Therefore, you would personally make sure that you ruined, somehow, any possibility of the relationship being a success. Mekyla, I think we were all like that at one point and time in our lives, but maybe not to the degree you've managed to take it to."

"Here I'm telling you all of my problems, and you're just my flight partner."

"It's okay. Sometimes you have to vent with someone you don't know. It makes you feel like they won't be, or are unable to be, so judgmental of your situation. It minimizes our need to use the psychiatrist couch." She giggled.

"That's very true Natocha, thanks for listening. You're saving me a fortune."

"Sure. You have two more hours to borrow my ears."

"Okay, thank you. But if you don't mind, I'm going to listen to a little Nora Jones for the first hour or so. I need something to relax my mind before this flight lands."

"Nora Jones? I don't think I've ever heard of her."

"She hasn't been around long, but the two CDs she's completed so far, to me are very nice."

"I'm not going to continue to disturb you Mekyla. I'm sure I should be going over my presentation for this business meeting I'm having tomorrow."

"I wish you well on your presentation, Natocha. I'm sure you'll do well."

"Thank you, Mekyla."

Mekyla adjusted the headphones on her head. But out of the corner of her eye, she noticed Natocha looking toward her. She turned.

"Mekyla," said Natocha. "I know if you could, you would kick me off this plane, but one more thing." She nodded toward a stack of papers lying on top of Mekyla's book bag. "Is that a manuscript?"

"Yes it is."

"Is it a film, play script or a novel?"

Mekyla laughed. "Well, I'm not certain yet, but I'm hoping it will become my first romance novel."

"So you're a writer. Would you mind if I read some of it?"

"No, not at all, but excuse all of the possible errors. I just completed the first draft a week ago and this is just a few of the chapters, the rest is on disc."

"Okay, sure. I'll keep that in mind."

'Okay girl,' Mekyla thought to herself. 'Don't get nervous because someone is getting ready to possibly comment on your writing. Just remember, you don't even really know this person. After the plane lands, you will never see her again. She can tell Cousin Willie it was a piece of crap for all I care. Anyway, that's just one person's opinion. Who am I kidding, I'm about to pee my pants, because I truly care what this lady is going to think. Okay, I wonder what she thinks so far, because I'm sure she should be crying, laughing, or something by now. Okay it's going to appear obvious if I try to get a peek at her expressions. This is going to drive me crazy. Maybe if I look out of the window and try to figure out what the clouds remind me of, I won't look so nervous.' She couldn't help but fidget in her seat, and with Nora Jones singing sweetly in her ears, she tried to concentrate on the clouds. 'I swear that one looks like a lady trying to throw something out the window. I wonder how my sister is doing. I hope everything turned out okay. If this woman only knew the road I traveled she would think twice about that psychiatrist comment. Instead, she'd tell me she knows a friend who knows a friend who could see me immediately. Two weeks ago, I would never have thought I'd be in this situation. But here I am on a flight home still with no answers to my situation. Leave it to me to always take the road less traveled. In times past I know I said I would not change a thing in my life, but if I could have done anything different, I would have done *everything* different in this case.'

As Mekyla, attempted to get comfortable for the long flight, she began to think about how the events of the last two weeks had led to her present situation.

CHAPTER TWO
A COMFORTABLE MESS

TWO WEEKS EARLIER:

"Good morning Mekyla. What time did you actually get in last night?"

Mekyla turned from the mirror, both hands still working an earring in. "It was probably around 11:00," she said quietly.

"Is that all?" Ian stretched and yawned. "I must have been very tired. I felt you get in the bed but I couldn't raise my head up. It felt like a ton of bricks was weighing me down."

Mekyla turned back to the mirror and checked her makeup and hair, smoothed the front of her suit jacket, turned a little to the left, then back, admiring how the lines of the jacket cut in sharply from the broad shoulder pads.

"So, you went ahead and drove straight through. What was that, a seven hour drive?"

She shrugged. "Six and a half, I guess."

"I didn't think you would go in today, but you're obviously not dressed for a picnic." Ian looked at the clock next to the bed. "We'll talk about your trip later, okay? I know you have lots of stuff to share with me, and I will be all yours tonight." He said as he smiled that 'you know what I mean' smile.

Mekyla pick up the cup of tea she'd brought in and set on the dresser. She took a sip and realized too late that it was still very hot. "Ouch," She shouted.

"Be careful with that tea," said Ian. "See you tonight sweetie."

Mekyla fanned her tongue and let that serve also as a wave goodbye.

CHAPTER THREE
MY LITTLE TAX DEDUCTION

Mekyla set her teacup down on the kitchen counter and heard footsteps behind her. "Good morning, Termaine," she said, as she turned around. She was always impressed by the sight of him. It seemed like only last year he was an awkward little boy, and now he was a handsome twenty-one-year-old man.

"Hey, Mom. How was your trip?"

"It was wonderful, absolutely wonderful."

Termaine was about to open the refrigerator door, but he stopped to look at his mother. He smiled. "Wow, you sound very happy. You know a different kind of happy. So did you get a lot of information from the book convention?" He pulled open the refrigerator and grabbed a bottle of water.

"It was a really good experience, very informative. And how's everything going with you. Is everything okay?"

"Everything at the house is the same way it was before you started spending all your time at Ian's, but I was thinking about making a few changes."

"Changes in *my* house? Like what?"

"I'll tell you later. I'm on my way out." He started for the door. "Love you, Mom."

"Love you too son," Mekyla said, as she looked at the clock on the wall.

CHAPTER FOUR
I PREFER MY DOG WITH CHILI AND CHEESE ONLY

"Ms. Smith, I'm sorry to say that there is no coverage for that situation based upon your current policy," Marie said into the phone. "I would like you to stop by the office very soon so that we can go over your coverage's to make sure that this doesn't happen again. Sorry we weren't able to help you today."

That's Marie, Mekyla's number one in her office; she knows how to run Mekyla's office the way Mekyla's requires it to be ran. She's a single mom that moved in from Mexico to raise her son here in the states. Mekyla sat on the edge of the desk as Marie wrapped up the phone call.

"Hi, Mekyla," said Marie.

"Good morning Marie. I'm expecting a phone call from Mrs.

Tidwell, so if I'm on another line please have her wait. I really need to speak with her."

"I sure will," said Marie, making a note of it on her notepad.

"It seems as though time is standing still. That says it's only 11:30 in the morning," she said, pointing at the clock on the wall.

Marie glanced at the clock, then at Mekyla. "It seems pretty slow everyday to me. Then again I don't have anything to rush off to. Other than going by McDonald's on the way home and playing ball with my son. Good morning to you, by the way. And how was your trip?"

"It was good. But, you know, Marie, we're going to have to work on getting you a guy in your life, girl. McDonald's and playing ball with your son?" She gave her a sideways look.

"Yes Mekyla, that's what you said last year."

"It's been a year? And you still haven't found you a good man?"

"Nope. And you haven't introduced me to anybody either."

They both laughed.

"Mekyla, are you going out for lunch today?"

"No, not today. Ian put some dogs on the grill last night, so I'll be having leftovers. I'm trying to cut back on eating all of that fast food; I need to shed this second person from off my hips for my sister's wedding."

"I wish I had those hips and butt."

Mekyla stood up and twisted to get a look at her rear end. "No you don't girl. You just wish you got the attention from the brothers."

Marie laughed. "You might just be right about that, Mekyla."

"You know your Spanish brothers won't have that." She turned to leave, but stopped dead in her tracks and lowered her voice. "Oh my, what do we have here?"

"What, Mekyla?"

"Look at this tall caramel piece of work coming towards the door."

"I can't see him!"

"You will, but only his back, because his front belongs to me."

"Mekyla, you know its little phrases like that that will label you as being selfish."

"Selfish doesn't have anything to do with this. That's what you call confidence, but very low key."

"Hello, I'm looking for Ms. Mekyla Williams."

Mekyla gave the man her best smile. "Hello, I'm Mekyla. Can I help you?"

"My name is Brent Elliott, I just recently moved into town from Louisiana. I'll be here for a few months and I'm looking to transfer the insurance on my truck to Tulsa, Oklahoma."

"There's no need to add Oklahoma when referring to Tulsa. We pretty much know what state we're in. Nevertheless, you've chosen the correct door."

Mr. Elliott laughed and Mekyla was pleased to see that he had a sense of humor as well as a fine body.

"Come on back into my office and have a seat, Mr. Elliott." She turned and began leading the way. 'Oh my goodness,' she thought, giving Marie a quick wink. 'This man is even more gorgeous up close.' "Are you with another company or are you just transferring from another City Farm office out of Louisiana?" She gestured toward a chair and went around the business side of her desk.

Mr. Elliot settled into the chair. "No, I've had my white ghost insured with your company for a while now."

"White ghost? That's an interesting way to refer to your vehicle. Is there a story there?"

He chuckled. "Yes, but it's a long one."

'If he only knew. I'd make time to hear that story in remix version.' "Well you're going to have to tell me about it one day," she said.

"I will."

'Oh my, look at those lips. I could just lick those lips until he says to stop.' Mekyla picked up a pen and started taking notes on a pad. "Are there any other drivers I need to list on your policy, such as your wife?"

"Right now, no."

"Okay sir, there shouldn't be any problem getting your insurance transferred from Louisiana, but if there is, I'll personally take care of it."

"You're very kind. You're the first lady I've seen in a long time whose teeth are prettier than mine." He gave her a big smile.

"Well thank you. Do you always give yourself a compliment like that when giving a compliment to someone else?"

"Sometimes."

"And we're modest too," said Mekyla with a chuckle.

"No, I'm just confident."

"I see. Okay, well here's a list of the things that I would need for you to bring back in order to complete this transfer." She reached across the desk and handed him a list of the items necessary to complete the transaction.

Mr. Elliot took the list and gave it a quick glance before looking Mekyla directly in the eye again. "I'm free tomorrow."

Mekyla smiled at his use of the word 'free,' allowing herself to believe that he might be trying to send her some kind of signal. She liked that idea. "Tomorrow would be just fine. Because when City Farm Insurance put my name on the door, the underlying message was that I should show up everyday. Shall we say 11:30?"

"You're smart too, huh?"

"Mr. White Ghost, I'm going to take that to be a compliment."

The man rose from his chair and extended a hand to Mekyla. "Madam, it has been a pleasure and I'll see you tomorrow."

"It was a pleasure meeting you as well, Mr. Elliott," said Mekyla, shaking hands with her new customer.

"I love your laugh; it's very pleasant."

"Why thank you. I'll see you tomorrow."

"I will be here with bells on."

'He knows I'm going to watch him walk away,' she thought. 'So I hope he shows me something that would make me smile.'

"You're also a very charming lady. You know that could be viewed as sexual harassment?"

"I aim to be pleased, with or without the jury watching."

Mr. Elliot laughed as he walked to the door. He glanced over his shoulder and caught Mekyla watching him and waved before he stepped outside.

"Wow," said Marie.

"Mm, mm, mm, do you think it can get any better than that? The thought of my favorite Lemon Meringue Pie being sliced in nice little triangles and perfectly arranged on each muscle of that six pack; I imagine he has hidden up under all of those clothes. That would satisfy every sweet tooth in my mouth just fine. Girl, he looks and sounds scrumptious! I want to find out if he tastes the same."

"Mekyla, girl you're too much."

"Marie, that man that just left, I guarantee you that he will be coming around here again for no reason."

"Yes, he's going to be coming around again: to ask for another transfer to another agency, because you're acting like a woman who has just been asked, if she had a wish what would it be? And just as a reminder, have you forgotten about your significant other?"

Mekyla waved her hand. "I don't think he would want me to talk about this with him, seeing that he doesn't like to share."

"Mekyla, how do you switch up your feelings like that?"

"I don't. I'm just flirting."

"Tell me something Mekyla. Didn't Ian ask you to move in with him?"

"Yes, but I still haven't given him a firm answer. I have most of my clothes there anyway."

"Then, why choose him?"

"What?"

"Why are you holding onto him?"

"I really like the way he makes me feel physically, we connect mentally and he's very caring."

"Mekyla, I know I don't have a real history of dating, so maybe I don't really understand men, but it seems to me that Ian's the dream date, husband and friend."

"I know but it still feels like something is missing."

"Like what, Mekyla? Like I said, I know I don't have as much experience as you. I mean, it's been three years since I've even had a date. So pardon me if I'm crossing the line, but are you crazy?"

"Sometimes I know that I am Marie, but hold on. Three years it's been?"

"Yes, three years and he was my first and we didn't date very long."

"But you're over thirty years old, right?"

"Yes ma'am."

"So, that would mean that you were a virgin all the way up to thirty-something years of age. Come on now. Give up the juice."

"Well, there's not that much to tell. I lived with my mother until I was thirty and I lived a very sheltered life. Mom and I were like sisters and I was the middle child. I was left to watch over her, because her husband was very abusive. And when I discovered that I was losing my life worrying about her, I decided to move in with my sister and that's when my sister introduced me to a friend of her boyfriend. He was a police officer in the little town I was from near the border of Mexico in Texas. He took me out on a few dates. I had a real good time. Until one day, he convinced me to go all the way and I did. We connected maybe a couple more times and that's when I became pregnant."

"Does your son get a chance to see him?"

"No my son has never met his father. The man wanted me to have an abortion. I chose not to and he then chose not to be a part of our lives. And I haven't seen him since."

Mekyla raised her eyebrows. "You mean he's never seen his son?"

"Nope, never has. I took him to court and now I get child support and besides, he recently got married."

"Sorry things didn't work out for you two. But he does pay his child support?

"Yes he does, but he doesn't pay regularly and I can't afford to continue going back to court to make him pay. So, I just wait."

"One of my sisters waited it out also. Not for child support I mean, but for sex. She wanted to be married before she gave a man that special part of her. I take it that's why you waited, right Marie?"

"Partly, yes, and the other was that I just wasn't interested in it."

"Wow, I would have to think back to have that innocent feeling. I mean aneurysm back."

The phone rang and Marie started to reach for it. "Thank you for calling City Farm. This is Marie." She paused, and then smiled. "Oh, hey Termaine. How's everything going for you?" Another pause. "Good, good. And how's that daughter of yours?" She picked up a pen and started to write. "Okay, yes and I will tell her. Bye Termaine."

"Hey Mekyla that was your son. He said that he will be by to borrow your car, because his is running hot."

"Girl, I'm going to have to file bankruptcy to keep that boy out of my car and my pocket." She started into her office, but stopped. "And you better brace yourself, Marie, because your son is going to do the same thing to you."

"I don't know Mekyla."

"Yes, it's going to happen, Marie. Especially the direction you're going. Tell me if I'm wrong, but didn't you say that you only buy your son name brand clothes?"

"Yes I did Mekyla, but he's only three years old."

"That's a sure sign of baby debt and the word 'baby' is defined as any male child between the ages of one and twenty-one. And what you're doing is sending him a message at his young age that everything's got to be top of the line or nothing."

"You know, now that you said that, when we're in the store shopping, he says, 'Mommy, that's not Tommy.'"

"Don't get me wrong Marie, its okay to buy what you want sometimes, but just don't overwhelm yourself and forget about the things you really need."

Marie nodded thoughtfully. "Yeah, you may be right. And right now my other need is to go to lunch."

"Okay Marie, see you in an hour and have a good lunch."

Mekyla sauntered back to her desk. It seemed like it was going to be a pretty slow day, which was fine with her. After Mr. Elliot's visit, any additional business would be anti-climactic. Besides, she wanted to squeeze in a couple of hours of work on her novel.

Settling into her desk chair she slipped her new favorite CD into the CD player of her computer. It was a suggestion she'd picked up at the writing seminar. And Nora Jones definitely relaxed her mind and put her in a creative mode.

She pulled up the novel on her word processor and scanned the document to find the point where she'd left off.

'Okay here we go,' she thought. 'Lisa was about to write the letter to her husband, Trevor, explaining to him why she needed some time to herself. So how would Lisa start that letter?'

"Hello my darling Trevor. As I sit here and stare out that big bay window in my office, watching the people as they go by with their big warm coats on, some scraping the frost off their windshields while they wait for their engines to warm up, I think of us. This is a time when couples get closer to keep each other warm. A time when the snot runs down their little kids' faces and their parents are constantly wiping their noses. I have always found that winter could be a bittersweet season. You should see the plants now. Remember the one I started a year ago? You know, from the cutting I took from your boss's violet? You would be amazed at how it has grown. I'm constantly getting compliments on all my plants. They bring such a sweet and wholesome feeling to this office. When I look at that particular plant, you always come to my mind. Here, lately I have found myself thinking of you more often than usual, and my body then begins to ache. I remember the long walks we used to take in the park, and how at the mall people would be staring at us as if they knew how much in love we were. Those are experiences I long to have again. The last time has spoiled me. I'm writing this letter to say that I must go away for a little while to try to put my life back in perspective and try to find out what it is I'm really looking for. I feel lost here, I feel ignored and alone.

I know that you would do anything to take away what I'm feeling right now and replace it with something better. It's almost as if nothing that I can do for myself is enough anymore. It's like putting a Band-aide on a wound that won't heal. I know that we belong together, because I can feel it burning in my soul. I've waited for you all of my life; I know that there's not another one for me. But it's like I've lost what brought us together in the first place and now I'm struggling to find it again.

All I'm asking is that you allow me this time to find myself and to think. I made you some dinners that I have put in the freezer for you to have for the next two or three days. I don't know how long I will be gone, but I will call you when I arrive at the hotel where I'll be staying."

Love,
Lisa Brazile

"Mekyla!"

Mekyla was jolted from her reverie by the sound of the voice. She looked up to see the bewildered face of her sister. Schonda is Mekyla's sister whom has always been the mother hen of the family. The God fearing child of the family, but yet has had children out of wedlock with her fiancé' Deon, who has finally asked her to marry him.

"Oh, hey Schonda. I didn't hear you come in."

Schonda nodded. "I noticed. Is that the artist Nora Jones playing? She has you all intense and preoccupied. Because I walked in like a minute ago. So is that your new theme music for when you're writing now."

Mekyla laughed. "You've got me all figured out."

"So how's the book coming along?"

"It's coming along just fine, but enough about me." She pointed at Schonda's tummy. "How is my nephew or niece doing in there?"

Schonda sighed. "I'm ready for this little person to get out of there."

Mekyla laughed. "I know you are. And what about your big day? How is the wedding plans coming along?"

"That's what I wanted to come in and talk with you about." Schonda cocked her head and wrinkled her nose. "Do you think the colors that I picked out are right for a wedding?"

Mekyla raised one eyebrow. "This is kind of like a late hour to be changing colors, don't you think?"

"Well, Deon said something about the colors a few months ago and now I'm wondering if he was right."

"Months ago, huh? And you're just now getting around to asking your big sister?" She laughed. "Don't worry about it, darling. You're going to look beautiful in anything that you decide to wear. It's not about the outfit; it's about the two people uniting. Focus on that okay."

Schonda heaved a sigh. "I knew that if I came in to talk to you about this, that I would leave feeling much better. Thank you for that, sis."

"Glad I could be of help. Now I have a question for you. How many more pounds will I have to lose, to look good in that maid of honor dress?"

Schonda shrugged. "Big sis, you know you look good. Lose however many pounds you feel comfortable with, as long as it's at least ten pounds."

They both began to laugh.

Mekyla turned serious and crossed her arms over her chest. "I really wasn't looking for you to comment on that. That was just one of those things you say that didn't really require feedback."

"Mekyla, you know I was just kidding. And remember, we're meeting right after my baby shower to fine-tune everything, okay?"

Mekyla nodded and smirked. "I remember."

"Love you sis, and I'll see you tonight at the baby shower. Yes, that's right, tonight."

"Schonda, kiss those kids for me, and I love you too.

"I will." Schonda turned to leave.

"Hey Schonda," said Mekyla.

Her little sister stopped and turned back to her.

"Read me that poem of yours again."

"Right, now?"

"Yes, right now. It's such a beautiful poem."

"Okay." Schonda smiled and dug the poem out of her purse. She cleared her throat and began to read.

"Wow, I didn't know you carried it around in your purse." Mekyla said, as she laughed to herself.

"When I first laid eyes on you, your beauty perfect to me, me without you or you without me, I thought it could never be. You promised me you would love me, you said we would never part. How could your love, let one night of pleasure, hurt my tender heart? What happened to our relationship, where did we go wrong? I find myself now spending almost all of my time alone. Questioning my love is it not enough or too much. What I would do to hear your voice or feel your gentle touch. When you say I love you, are the words you say real? When your lips touch mine, is it love that you feel? Your words express love, but your actions show hate. When will I have all of you, how long must I wait? In the midst of our relationship, we created beautiful life. Maybe that's why they say before family, become a man's wife."

Schonda looked up from the page. "Don't start sis. You cry every time. Now you're going to make me cry right here in your office and I wrote the darn thing."

Mekyla wiped the tears off her cheeks. "If anybody sees us they'll just think we're crying because you're not insurable and you have nowhere else to go." She looked into her sister's eyes. "I love you Schonda. You're going to make a beautiful bride."

"I had the best big sister for my model," Schonda said as she put her arms around Mekyla to squeeze her tight.

"Thank you for that," said Mekyla as they parted. She pointed to the paper still in Schonda's hand. "So are you going to recite this to Deon in front of everyone along with your vows, or are you going to save it for the reception?"

Schonda looked down at the poem and thought for a moment. "I haven't decided yet. So, you're going to have to wait and see along with the others."

"Well," said Mekyla, "It's an idea." She smiled and nodded.

"I need to make a few more stops today, so I'll see you later, okay?"

"Okay. Love you, sis."

"Love you to Mekyla." Schonda started to leave again and remembered to say. "Oh, and I think Deon is bringing Termaine by here to borrow your car. Something happened to his."

Mekyla chuckled. "I know. He called a little while ago. I do need to get caller ID for this office."

Schonda laughed. "Tell Ian I said hello."

"I will."

CHAPTER FIVE
AND THIS TOO SHALL PASS

From her desk, Jennifer glared at Nicole and Zoë. "Please don't stand in front of my door," she said. "You're blocking my view."

"What is she talking about?" Nicole asked Zoë in a low voice, then she turned to Jennifer. "Block your view of what?"

"My view of whatever I want to look at outside of my office door."

"She needs to get a life," Zoë said under her breath as she began to walk away.

"I heard that," said Jennifer. "Just step away from my door, please, except you Nicole. Would you come into my office for a moment, please?" Jennifer was a young lady with a big hole in her heart that is constantly being filled by guys that don't care anything for her. It's such a waste. She's such a beautiful and smart girl that happens to have a personality that resides at residence evil.

"Sure Jennifer, give me just one second." Nicole tossed the papers she had in her arms onto her desk and then strolled into Jennifer's office. "Hey what's up girl?"

"Could you type up a proposal for that property up in Gilcrease Hills?"

"Sure. You're about to close on another one?"

"Somebody has to pay the bills at home, since my mother decided to retire at the age of fifty-four with no savings. I don't know what she is going to do when Junior goes off to college, because that's going to be my last day as well."

"I totally understand. You did yours backwards. Usually Mom moves in with you when she becomes disabled. You've helped your mom through her good years."

Jennifer shrugged. "That was the hand dealt to me, but he did give me a vision that this was not going continue for much longer."

Nicole furrowed her brow. "He who?"

"Never mind, Nicole. Can I just get that proposal? Thanks."

'I wonder what my girl is doing this afternoon,' thought Jennifer. 'What is today? I believe there's a game tonight, so I guess that's where we're going.' As she began to dial Mekyla's office number, she looked out her office door and gave her co-workers a look that could have burned a hole right through them. "Mekyla Williams, please," she said into the phone.

"May I tell her whose calling?"

"Sure, tell her it's Jennifer Holiday."

Mekyla chuckled. "To what do I owe the pleasure of this phone call, Ms. Holiday?"

"Hey what's going on, Ms. Williams?"

"Clearing my desk of some paper work that's been sitting here too long."

"I hear you. Looks like we're at a basketball game this evening, yes?"

"Yes, I'm going to be there to support my man. Even though I really need to stay home and write."

"That's why you're taking off for a week, right?"

"Right, but I probably still need to leave the planet to concentrate."

"I hear they're attempting another flight to the moon."

"Very funny, Jennifer. I tried, you know, but Michael Jackson got the last million-dollar seat."

Jennifer laughed. "Oh well. You still have the basketball game to look forward too."

"Yes, and you know I have my baby sister's baby shower to go to after the game."

"Your family sure is country. Who has a baby shower around 8:00

PM? Only people who are planning on partying until midnight. But that's why I love your family. You guys are so close."

"We are that, Jennifer. I'll see you at the game."

"I'll be right there on the bench with my, 'I would invite you over after the game; if I had my own house outfit on'."

"You're so crazy. Bye."

CHAPTER SIX
JUST SAY NO

"Hey Mom," said Termaine as he strolled into the City Farm office. Termaine, is a spoiled, only child, handsome, and well-dressed young man with everything to live for. Aside from his short-comings of being a father too soon, the mother of his child is not letting him forget who has control of their child, by giving him the baby mama woes. He has every intention of doing the right thing when it comes to his daughter, but it seems as though that's never enough in the eyes of his daughter's mom.

"Hey baby. Where's Deon?"

Termaine shrugged. "Oh, he just dropped me off."

Mekyla cocked her head and smirked. "How did you know if I was going to say yes?"

"Mom, you always say yes. Besides, you know I need your help right now. You wouldn't let me down."

"Yes, right *now* you need my help. And, I'm afraid, *from* now until Jesus comes again. Have my car back here no later than 5:00."

"Hopefully I'll be back before then. The Expedition does have gas in it, right?"

"Wrong. Even though the gas gauge says almost full, I need you to put what you use back in there."

Termaine smiled and nodded deeply. "Yea, and that reminds me to ask if I can get thirty dollars until."

"No you're not going to say 'until.' Until when, Termaine? You need to goon with that, 'I will pay you back' stuff."

"I had to get my daughter some stuff with the little money that I had. Oh, and what I was going to surprise you with this morning when we were talking was that I switched our rooms out."

Mekyla narrowed her eyes and looked at him askance. "What do you mean, you switched out our rooms?"

"Since you have moved in with Ian, I thought that it would be okay for me to have the master bedroom."

She crossed her arms over her chest and raised an eyebrow. "To have a master bedroom, you would need to pay master bills. I'm not going to have this conversation with you right now Termaine. How is my granddaughter anyway?"

"Cheyenne's growing like wild flowers."

"Give her a big sloppy kiss for me and don't forget to be here no later than 5:00."

"Okay. Thank you and I love you."

"Yeah, I love you too."

CHAPTER SEVEN
LOVE HAS NO FURY ON A WOMAN'S SCORN

Mekyla picked up the cell phone and punched two on her speed dial. Her middle sister, Christy the next to perfect wife and mother with very expensive taste and low self-esteem, but will do anything for you, answered on the second ring. "Hey Christy, it's me Mekyla."

"Hey girl, what's going on?"

"I was just thinking about the game tonight. Will Trey be playing?"

"Yes, I believe so."

"Are you going to be there for support tonight?"

"You know that I'm not really into going to those games, but if you're going and want some company, then I'm there, Mekyla."

"I'm there, because Jennifer just called me to make sure I was going to be there, she didn't want to be there alone."

"Jennifer! Huh! I don't know why you hang with her. And she must be on the prowl."

"Because she's one of the branches from my tree of people that I love and that are dear to me."

"Well Mekyla, sometimes you need to trim those tree limbs back or just break them off."

"Jennifer doesn't bother me. She just annoys the mess out of you, I suppose. I think it has more to do with you feeling better than her, because you guys didn't have the same type of spoons growing up. You know, silver versus regular?"

"Whatever Mekyla. It's not like you didn't eat from the same spoons as me. There's something about Jennifer that still rubs me the wrong way."

"Maybe she wants to go out on a date with you."

"Very funny! Instead of trying to become a writer, you probably need to think seriously about becoming a comedian. You always have a funny little remark for everything."

"Loosen up my darling Christy and I will see you tonight."

"I'm serious, Mekyla. And don't forget we're going to the baby shower afterwards."

"I know you're serious Christy. And you know you're probably going to have to remind me again about that baby shower."

Christy clicked her tongue. "I don't know why people aren't taking me seriously these days."

Mekyla laughed. "See you tonight, Christy."

Mekyla hung up the phone, but immediately dialed the number for Dowell Welding. "Hello Swayla, this is Mekyla. Can you connect me to Ian's office, please?"

"Sure Mekyla, one moment," said the receptionist.

Ian, a very quiet and polite, hard working, and sometimes borderline boring man, whom Mekyla has loved for many years, "Hey, what's up?" said Ian with a smile in his voice.

"Hey sweetie, you miss me yet?" Mekyla said as she propped her feet up on her desk.

"I missed you the moment I left the house this morning and not a second longer."

"You're so sweet. That's why I'm going to keep you for awhile."

"Well Mekyla, *I* was planning on upgrading in a couple of years myself."

"Good luck with that, because there's not a grade higher than me. Anyway, Big-head, I just wanted to hear your voice. How is your day so far?"

"There were a couple of guys that didn't show up, so I had to fill in. You know how that can go."

"You didn't get too dirty, did you?"

"Very funny, Mekyla. I don't mind a little dirt every now and then, just to remind me where I come from. Now, you remember I have a game this evening, so I'm going to be late coming home for you to tell me all about your trip."

"Yes, sweetie, I remembered. And the trip, it was nothing, we can talk about that whenever."

"Tonight is good for me. Were you coming to the game?"

"Yes, the girls and I will be there with our rusted bells on. See you tonight and I miss you much. And remember I have that baby shower to go to afterwards."

"The baby shower, oh, yeah. Okay, well I miss you more, Mekyla, and I'll just see you at the game and more importantly I'll see you in our bed sometime tonight."

CHAPTER EIGHT
FOREVER MINE

"Hey, guys," said Christy, addressing her children as she surveyed the living room. "How many times have I asked you to put your stuff away when you're done with it? You know your father doesn't like seeing your toys and shoes strung out everywhere in this house. So let's get cleaning. I'm cooking your auntie Mekyla's specialty for dinner. Spaghetti and meatballs. Anyone opposed, speak now, or forever hold your piece." She paused and cupped a hand to her ear. "I don't hear anything, so I take that to be a yes."

She left the kids in charge of cleaning up and headed into her bedroom. She opened the closet door and started looking through her wardrobe. "Okay, now what am I going to wear to this baby shower tonight?" She pulled an outfit out and held it up to herself in the mirror. "Oh yeah, I've always looked good in this little number. Let me go put this gift for the baby shower in the car, because if I don't do it now, I will forget. Get the kids ready for mammas before the game and I will just bring them back home after the baby shower. I'm all set."

CHAPTER NINE
ANOTHER DAY, ANOTHER NICKLE

"So Marie, are you ready to close it up for today?" Mekyla was leaning in the doorway of her office, looking at her watch. "I have a full schedule this evening and for some reason I'm already exhausted."

"I'm ready to call it quits, but is there anything I can help you with before I go, Mekyla?"

"No, but thanks anyway. You have yourself a good evening and I'll see you tomorrow."

"Oh no, here comes a policyholder."

Mekyla sighed as she saw the woman outside reaching for the door handle. "Don't worry about it Marie. I'll help her. You go on and have yourself a good evening. Besides, Termaine hasn't shown up with my vehicle yet."

"Yes, that's right. Well, okay, see you tomorrow Mekyla." Marie grabbed her purse and headed for the door, nodding to the customer as they passed each other in the entryway.

Mekyla gave the customer a professional smile. "Hello, Mrs. Crenshaw, how are you this evening?"

"I'm doing just fine, Mekyla. Sorry for holding you up from going home, but I really needed to get this bill paid today."

"Oh don't worry about me," said Mekyla taking the check. "It will only take a few extra minutes. How is Mr. Crenshaw?"

"He's fighting that arthritis again."

Mekyla sat down at Marie's desk and prepared the payment receipt. "Just rub him down with some of that old fashion remedy stuff and that should take care of it." She handed the receipt to her customer. "Well, I thank you for your payment, and you take care of yourself as well."

"Thank you Mekyla, you're always so kind to my husband and me."

"You're very good people and I appreciate your business very much."

"The church is having a bake sale next Saturday; you should stop by and get a pie."

"They say those church pies are the best. Is that true?"

Mrs. Crenshaw nodded emphatically. "The ones I bake are."

Mekyla laughed. "I'm sure they are. I just might do that if I'm in the vicinity of your church on Saturday."

Mrs. Crenshaw patted Mekyla on the hand. "I'll put one aside just for you my dear."

"Thank you again Mrs. Crenshaw and you have a good evening."

"You do the same Mekyla. And when are you going to get you a husband, nice looking young woman like yourself?"

"I'm working on it Mrs. Crenshaw. Goodnight."

"Goodnight."

Termaine appeared in the doorway and held the door for Mrs. Crenshaw.

"Hey Mom," He said, strolling into the office. Here are your keys and thanks for the use of your vehicle."

"You're welcome. Does my key to the house still work, son?"

"You're straight. Since you're paying the bills at the house."

"Thank you for allowing me to keep my house keys."

Termaine smiled.

"I'll see you later sometime," said Mekyla. "And don't be having a lot of company at the house. Please wait until I'm completely out."

"Mom, you know I don't have that many partners that I'll hang with."

"Alright, love you, son."

"Love you too. Well I need to go. Ol' girl in the car is waiting on me."

Mekyla rolled her eyes as she began to shut down the computers. "I dare not ask who this one is. You change them the way you change your underwear."

With Termaine gone, she picked up the pace on her closedown

procedure. Before she turned off the last light at the front door, she looked at her watch. She just had time to swing by Ming Palace, pick up some Chinese food, and wolf it down before heading to this game.

CHAPTER TEN
OUR LITTLE ATHLETES

The squeak of the shoes and the thump of the ball on the wood floor echoed through the gym. The men shouted back and forth to each other and danced their macho ballet.

Mekyla's concentration was broken as Jennifer approached. "Hey guys, sorry I'm late. What did I miss? Has my sweetheart played yet?"

"Sweetheart, you don't have one," said Christy, with a hard look on her face. "Well, not in here anyway."

Jennifer put a hand on her hip. "Christy, don't hate, just because you conceived Trey's first child in his dorm room and later married him on the basketball court. Don't go pretending you weren't the typical groupie of lust."

"Jennifer thanks for the recap. The key word is 'groupie,' since we were young back then. Now that we're in our thirties the appropriate words for your kind of activity would be 'promiscuous' and 'unfaithful.'"

Mekyla looked up at the heavens and shook her head. "All right ladies, now that Ms. Jennifer Holiday has made her grand entrance, can we watch the game?"

"Mekyla you know we never come here to watch the game," said Jennifer, shaking her head slowly. "Besides, it's not like they're playing professional basketball. It's just city-league ball. You know something for them to do to keep *in* shape and *out* of denial." She tilted her head one way, then the other. "We come here to catch up on each others lives and gossip." She scanned the gym for guys and gossip. "Hey, you see that lady down there with the powder blue cashmere sweater on?"

"Leave it to Jennifer to describe the material of the sweater the lady is wearing," said Christy.

"Girl, I know my materials."

"Okay, what about her, Miss Country Make Over?"

"I'm going to pretend I didn't hear that Christy. She was here a little over a week ago, also wearing a cashmere sweater but in a different color, she must have a gang of those sweaters."

"Other than I-spying on folks and what they're wearing," said Christy in a clam, unconcerned voice. "And note to self: two doesn't represent a gang. What is the point of this story?" Then she leaned a little closer to make sure she didn't miss a word of Jennifer's answer.

"Rumor has it that she's having an affair with one of the ball players and may be pregnant."

"Jennifer, is it an affair because *she's* the one married, or *he* is?"

"What difference does it make, Christy? An affair is an affair. However, *she* is married." She paused. "But not to one of the basketball players. And I'll tell you what else. I've never noticed her before a couple of weeks ago. Apparently, she just moved to town."

"From where," said Christy, almost challenging Jennifer's talent as a gossip?

"I don't know where she's from yet, but I will, Miss I thought you weren't interested."

"Jennifer, how do you get this information on people?" said Mekyla.

"No one outside of us really tells me anything. I usually over hear a lot of my information." She looked at the other two girls and recoiled as if startled. "Why are you guys sitting here all serious looking? I'm sure it's not either one of your men."

"I'm going to get something to drink," said Mekyla. "I'll be right back."

"Mekyla, bring me a Snickers back and a drink," Said Jennifer as she watched her walk away, then leaned towards Christy. "What's wrong with Mekyla? We both know it's not Ian, even though he *is* fine and has a body that would make you feel like you need a cigarette just from brushing up against him. We all know he loves him some Mekyla. It has to be love; because she's so low maintenance, and has such simple requests of men."

"Okay, since you feel you have this psychic knowledge, what about Trey? Do you think Trey's the type to have an affair?"

"I don't know, Christy. And I'm probably not the person to ask. Nothing personal, but shouldn't you have that psychic ability, because he is your husband?"

"I'm just asking for a simple observation, Jennifer. It's not like you're having an affair with him. So give me an overview, the way you did Mekyla and Ian."

"Trey, he's a different type of challenge."

"What do you mean?"

"He has more to lose; he has you as well as the kids to make him feel guiltier. This is a simple observation as you requested." Jennifer looked out onto the court as Trey passed the ball to Ian. "He looks as though he has the potential to creep." She nodded toward Ian. "See Ian, he'll feel guilty, but a different type of guilty. He would have less to lose of course, since Mekyla is a non-wife. Also, with Ian, you'll never know he cheated, because he's so low key. However, with Trey, he'll probably confess."

"Why do you feel he would confess?" asked Christy.

"He would confess to free himself from his own guilt, and also because he probably wouldn't be threatened by you. No offense."

"Why wouldn't he be threatened by me?"

Jennifer shrugged, as if the answer were obvious. "He wouldn't, because, you're not that aggressive."

"Jennifer, you can bring a cold chill into a hot basketball gym."

"Don't hate the messenger, Christy, only the message, if you're feeling threatened. That boomerang stuff is pretty scary huh? You know the not knowing when or if it would ever come around because you had your little secrets, back in the day."

"That was before I got married. Jennifer, I'm secure and very faithful in my marriage."

"Okay." She shrugged again. "Then why are you bugging, Christy?"

"Let's just watch the game okay, and what's taking Mekyla so long?" Christy looked up to the end of the court, then around the bleachers. Mekyla was coming from the side. "Oh, hey Mekyla. I was just asking about you. What took you so long? I don't see Jennifer's snicker. And where's your soda?"

"I decided that I didn't really need a soda. I'm going to head out early."

"But we just got here. And what does you leaving early have to do with my candy bar"

"No, Jennifer, you just got here."

But Jennifer wasn't paying much attention. Something in the crowd had caught her eye. "Look Christy, I think the cashmere sweater woman is looking at Trey."

"That's enough with the games, Jennifer. Mekyla, I'll be over around seven o'clock. Don't forget."

"No, I won't forget our little sister's baby shower. All right, take care and I'll see you girls later, if you don't kill each other with all those kind words first."

"See you, Mekyla." As Mekyla walked away, Jennifer turned to Christy. "What's she all bummed out about?"

"Jennifer, let's just watch the game, okay?"

"Christy you should be watching Ms. Cashmere."

"I'm not going to respond to that Jennifer."

At home, Mekyla powered up her computer and tried to focus. She checked her watch to calculate how much time she had to finish the chapter. She had to get it done before Christy and Jennifer arrived, since whenever they entered a room, everything else had to cease.

"Okay, focus, Mekyla," she said to herself. She scanned through the document on the screen and found her last stopping point. Lisa had just arrived at the hotel and was about to check in after the long drive from Tulsa.

"You should have a reservation for me, under the name Lisa Brazile."

"Yes, Mrs. Brazile we have you for the next two weeks in suite number 1207. The Doubletree is very happy to have you as our guest and we hope you enjoy your stay here in Austin, Texas."

"Thank you very much. What I've seen of Austin so far has been very impressive. Although, the sun set on me back in Waco, leaving me with only the beauty of lights shimmering off the buildings and the headlights on the roads. I'm sure it's even more beautiful in broad daylight."

"Yes ma'am. I think you'll like it."

"Would I be receiving valet parking with my stay here at the hotel?"

"Yes ma'am, that's part of the package you booked."

"Thank you very much. My vehicle is the white Cadillac Escalade parked right out front."

"Yes ma'am, we'll take care of that for you and we'll bring up your copy of the valet ticket."

"That will be fine. Which elevators do I use?"

"The bellman will show you the way and here are some of our fresh and hot Doubletree cookies. Thank you again and have a nice evening."

After settling into her room, Lisa placed a call.

"Hello," said the voice.

"Hello Trevor. I made it to Austin."

"Austin? When you said you needed space; I didn't know you were going to leave the state. Are you okay?"

"Yes, I'm fine. I'm staying at the Doubletree Hotel here. If you like, you can take down the number?"

"Yes, of course, I'd like to have the number Lisa."

"Its 512-555-1234, and I'm in suite 1207."

"Honey, how long do you think you will be gone?"

"Well, I reserved the suite for a couple of weeks."

"A couple of weeks? That seems like an awful long time, baby, to be gone away from home, away from me."

"Trevor, please understand that I don't know how long it's going to take, all I know is that I need this time to think."

"Lisa before you began to make any serious decisions, please let's take the time to talk about it. That's all I ask."

"That's a fare request Trevor. I'm very tired from the drive. I'm going to take a bath, go down and have some dinner, and then pretty much turn in for the night. We'll talk again soon."

"Okay, Lisa, I miss you baby."

"Goodnight Trevor, and I miss you too."

"Goodnight."

Lisa hung up the phone and tried to think about going downstairs to eat, but she was just too tired. She picked up the phone and asked for room service.

"Room service," said the voice. "How may we help you Mrs. Brazile?"

"I would like to have a nice Caesar Salad with baked chicken and a diet Dr. Pepper, please. I'm in suite 1207 and just charge it to the room thanks."

Lisa ran a hot bath, knowing that dinner wouldn't be up for a while yet. She sat on the edge of the tub and tried to imagine what Trevor was doing. The truth was she missed him, but she wasn't nearly ready to let him know how much. She believed that in order for a man to fully realize what he had, it was necessary for him to miss it every now and then. She knew the same was true of a woman.

With the water still running, she slid into the bath. She moaned as she immediately felt every muscle in her body relax. If she could just manage to get a five-minute nap there in the tub before her dinner arrived that would be the icing on the cake.

'No,' she thought. 'The icing on the cake would be for my husband to come in and start rubbing my feet, or massaging my back with his big strong hands. But no, I needed to drive all the way to Austin to make my point, to find myself.'

She wondered if she'd packed anything other than clothes. She'd left in such a hurry, trying get out of the house before Trevor made it home from work. She might need to pick up a few things, but maybe not for a couple of days.

There was a knock at the door, startling her out of her reverie. "One moment, I'm coming," she said. She stepped out of the tub and slipped on her white terrycloth robe. "Who's there?" she called through the door.

"It's room service ma'am."

She opened the door with a smile. "Come in and put that right over here, please." She gestured to the table.

"Would there be anything else for you ma'am?"

"No thank you, sir, but please add fifteen percent to that tab. That should take care of it."

"Thank you ma'am, and have a good evening."

The room service waiter let himself out of the suite and closed the door behind him.

She grabbed the television remote and sat down at the table. Turned on the television and uncovered her dinner. The scent of the baked chicken drifted up to her nose. Her mouth began to water and she suddenly remembered how hungry she really was. She drizzled Ranch dressing on her Caesar's Salad, because it was her favorite. She took a bite of the salad, cold with fresh lettuce, crunchy and overflowing with croutons. Then she tried the chicken. It was so tender; it almost melted in her mouth, and seasoned just right. "Compliments to the chef," she said out loud. "He put his foot in this one." She paused with a forkful of chicken half way to her mouth. "No, that doesn't sound very nice. Let's say he put his magic touch into this meal."

Mekyla giggled at what she'd written. "Lisa, Lisa, Lisa," she said, getting up from the computer and going into the kitchen to grab a quart of butter pecan ice cream and a spoon. "It may not be seasoned baked chicken," she said, as she pulled off the lid. "But this is really going to hit the spot."

Mekyla returned to the computer with the ice cream and looked over the last couple of pages she'd written. She was satisfied she had Lisa exactly where she wanted her to be at that point. And she had some great ideas about what her heroine was going to do a few days later, so she decided to skip the transition for the moment and forge ahead. "Just keep the momentum, Mekyla." In the text she made the simple notation, 'qqq develop transition,' so that she could go right to that spot again by using the 'find' function in her computer's word processor. Then she set up the Wally World scene.

Feeling very refreshed after days of total relaxation and quiet thought, Lisa decided to go to Wally World to pick up some cooking items. She'd begun to feel a little guilty about eating in the restaurant almost everyday and charging it to her husband's charge card, since she was use to cooking. She decided it was time to get acquainted with the suite's kitchen.

She found her purse on the dresser and glanced into the mirror as she did. She couldn't go out in public with that head. She decided she could just throw a scarf over it. After all, it wasn't like she was trying to catch anyone.

Down in the car, she checked the directions once again. It looked like a simple enough drive: Mopac to 1325 and then cross over I-35. Nothing to it.

As she drove, all she thought about was what a beautiful city Austin was. She could do without the expressways, though. She found Wally World without any trouble. Everybody seemed to be going there. She just followed the traffic.

Once inside the store, she tried to ignore everything she passed. "Dish rack," she said to herself. "That's all I need. Stay focused. Housewares, focus on housewares." She knew the store could suck a person up like a good Hoover vacuum. And then the food section caught her eye. She *did* need some Cheerios for breakfast, but that was all in the food section. Just get Cheerios and maybe a jar of pickles too. No harm in getting a jar of pickles. The baby sweet and crunchy ones are to die for. Lisa made it out of foods with a minimum damage. Now onto housewares for that dish rack, but a saucepan would be good too. After all, if she had no saucepan, what would she put in the dish rack? If she bought a saucepan, she could *use* it first, *then* put it in the dish rack. She grabbed a saucepan and continued. She made her way up one aisle and down the next, looking high and low for the dish racks. Since the suite has a mini kitchen, I might as well use it, right.

She was so preoccupied with finding them that she didn't see the man she ran into. "Oh, pardon me."

"Hello," said the man with a smile.

"Hello," Lisa said.

He wasn't bad looking, but she practically broke her neck trying to see his left hand. She couldn't tell if he was wearing a ring. She looked down at her own left hand and cringed. What was she thinking? *She* was wearing a ring. Finally she stumbled upon the dish racks. No wonder she hadn't been able to find them all that time. There were only two of them. Not only that, they were seven dollars and butt ugly. Well, maybe *they* weren't butt ugly, but the price was, especially when added to all this other stuff she now had in her basket.

"Head for the register and just look strait ahead," she told herself. And when she got to the register she was still looking straight ahead, right at Mr. Maybe-Married-Man's butt. 'That reminds me,' she thought. 'I needed to pick up a couple of apples for my guilty snack. Well dang, I barely qualify for the express lane. I need some therapy.'

"How are you today, ma'am?" said the cashier.

"I guess I'm fine. I'm certainly feeling charitable now that I've decided to donate my last dime to Wally World. I wouldn't have a clear conscious if I didn't do my charity work." She looked over at the next checkout lane where her new almost acquaintance was checking out. 'Well that's a nice looking mirror he has in his basket,' she thought. "But, why did he get that one? It has the big sticker price on the glass part. And halogen lamps. He must be single or recently divorced."

"Ma'am, your total is $43.62."

"All I came in to get was a sink rack, and now I cannot even afford that. Okay, here is three dollars and sixty-two cents." Lisa dug around in her wallet until she found what she was looking for. "And here's my bankcard to charge the balance. I have this thing about charging even numbers on my card."

The cashier looked pained. "Oh, I'm sorry. I thought you would be using all cash. I'm going to have to call customer support to come over and void this out."

Lisa sighed. "Okay, I'm sorry. I would give you the rest in cash, but I don't have enough on me."

"I'm sorry for the inconvenience, ma'am, but I'm going to have to re-ring your items."

"Not a problem. Let me help you take them out of the bags that you so neatly put them into."

As she took her purchases out of the bags, she glanced over at the next checkout lane. Mr. Put-Out-Of-the-House, single person was still over there. There was something peculiar at the bottom of his basket. It looked like some type of bug or rat bait. A pest problem? Maybe, but he certainly didn't seem to be living badly. In fact, she wondered why he was so neatly dressed on a Saturday afternoon. 'He makes the rest of us look like a whole store full of someone's stepchildren,' she thought. She looked at his leather sandals, probably Birkenstocks, and his shirt so perfectly pressed with the sharp crease on the sleeves. Whoever he was, he seemed to be finished with his purchases and ready to take his housewares to his new house or apartment. And as he gathered his bags together, she saw that he was bopping his head. He wasn't wearing headphones. She tried to figure out what he was listening to. And then she realized that it was the music on the store's sound system.

"Hello," a voice said. "Excuse me, ma'am."

Lisa realized the cashier was talking to her. "Yes?"

"May I have your credit card again?"

"Sure." She handed the card over.

The cashier started to say something else.

"Shush. I can hardly hear the song that's playing."

"Excuse me."

"I'm sorry. Do you hear that song that's playing?"

"No," said the cashier. "Oh wait. Yes I do.

"Who is that singing that song?"

"I believe that's Nora Jones."

"Nora Jones? Well, I've never heard of Nora Jones, but that song does sound special. But not bopping head special, but more of a groove special."

"Are you still talking to me, ma'am?"

Lisa looked at the cashier who looked pained again. "I'm just thinking aloud. Can we just listen to the song?"

An announcement came over the PA system, breaking into the song.

"Okay, now why do they keep interrupting the song with all those announcements? Please make them stop, at least until the song goes off."

"Ma'am, I can't do that."

Now why is he coming back into the store? He must have forgotten to get the toiletries for his new bathroom or maybe it could be his credit card. Look at him. He's just jumping the line. He must have stolen something, then felt guilty, and decided to come back and pay for it, as Lisa thought to herself. "Let me stop it. Are we done?"

"Yes ma'am," said the cashier, looking at Lisa like she might be crazy. "All of your bags are in the basket."

"Thank you, Miss, and have a nice day."

Lisa picked up her bags. As she walked out the door, so did the man she'd been watching. It almost looked like he'd planned on leaving at the same time as her. Outside, she hesitated on the sidewalk; she'd forgotten where she parked. She surveyed the lot and tried to remember. She didn't want to look like she was waiting around for the man to say something to her. But then it looked like he remembered where he was parked, because he started to move away from her. She looked in the opposite direction and saw the Taco Bell on the side of the parking lot where she'd come in. That was the side she'd parked on. She started off in that direction. Then she heard a man's voice.

"Excuse me."

Lisa turned and found herself face to face with the man from the store. She tried to maintain a nonchalant look, all the while thinking, 'I can't believe he turned around and came back to say hello to me.' "Yes?"

"My name is Jonathan Baize," said the man. "I just wanted to let you know that I was not stalking you in there."

"What do you mean, stalking me?"

Well, it seemed like every time I started down an aisle, you would just be leaving it.

"I'm sorry; but I didn't pay attention to that. I was so involved in trying to find a dish rack."

"Well, I felt I better explain that to you, otherwise I would have gone home wondering if you thought that. To tell you the truth, I got kind of lost in there trying to find the light bulbs."

"Oh yeah, I did seen those in your basket."

"I know. I saw you looking in my basket."

"How is that, I never saw you turn around."

"I saw you in the mirror I just bought. That was the other thing you were scrutinizing."

Lisa laughed and put a hand to her face. "I'm not embarrassed."

"You should be," said Jonathan with a wry smile. "May I have your name?"

"Name – uh-Lisa, my name is Lisa Brazile. Jonathan, are you from here? I detect some type of accent."

"Yes and no. Born in California and raised in a little town here in Texas. But I've been here in Austin for a couple of years now."

"Oh, I was thinking somewhere else."

"What, like Jamaica?"

"No." Lisa said with a squint that screamed 'yea or an African with a proper/country accent' that's what I thought.

"Are you from around here Lisa?"

"No, I'm here for – well, let us just say, vacation."

Jonathan shrugged. "Okay, let's say vacation. But listen, I'm not going to stand here and talk you to death in the Wal-Mart's parking lot. Is there a phone I can reach you on?"

"Yes, I have a number."

"Would it be too pushy to ask you for that number?"

"No, not at all." She got a business card and a pen out of her purse. "I'll give you the hotels phone number. Just ask for suite 1207." She wrote it all on the back of the card and handed it to Jonathan.

"I'll give you a call tonight, if that's not a problem."

"Okay, that'll be nice. I haven't had a chance to see your city. Maybe you could do the honors, Jonathan. In the meantime, you have a good day, okay?"

"Okay, and you do the same." He turned and started to walk away.

"Hey, Jonathan?"

"Yes," he said, turning back.

"Never mind."

"What was it Lisa?"

"It will keep Jonathan. Talk to you soon."

CHAPTER ELEVEN
LIFE'S LITTLE LESSONS

The ringing of the phone broke Mekyla's concentration. Suddenly she was back in the world of her own life, leaving Lisa and Jonathan in the parking lot of Wal-Mart.

She grabbed the phone, a bit disoriented. "Hello?"

"Hey, girl, are you ready?" said Christy.

"Yes, I'm ready."

"Okay, well open the door then."

"What do you mean open the door?"

"We're right outside your door, so open it please."

"What? Hang on." She hung up the phone and jogged to the front door. "Hey guys."

"Don't 'hey' us," said Jennifer. "What took you so long?"

"Very funny. Did you two ride together?"

"You know we didn't ride together. We just left at the same time."

"You've been doing nothing but writing this whole time, haven't you?" said Christy.

"I have a deadline, Christy, and this is what I do in my spare time. All the rest of my time is nothing but people pulling me here and there. I don't have the luxury of being just a housewife."

"Ever since you began writing this book, you haven't really had enough time for me and my problems," said Christy. "So, get dressed, Mekyla, so we can go to our little baby sisters baby shower and enjoy our mother."

"I am dressed."

Christy rolled her eyes. "Please put something else on just this one time. You're always wearing those sweat suits."

"That's not a very nice thing to say Christy. I think my feelings may be hurt"

"Yea, okay whatever. It wouldn't hurt you to dress up a little outside of the office. We may be going out for drinks afterwards. I think I really need one. I'm going to take advantage of this time. No kids and Trey thinking I'll be with my family for most of the evening. Besides, you owe me.

"Why do I owe you?"

"Well, you *did* leave me at the basketball game with Jennifer."

"I heard that Christy," said Jennifer from across the room.

"I don't know. Ian may have plans for us."

"Girl, please. When was the last time my husband and Ian ever had plans for us after a basketball game."

"You may be right, Christy. Girl, I keep confusing myself with the character that I'm writing about."

"So, Mekyla," said Jennifer. "Tell us about what you've written so far."

"I can't do that. It will throw me all off balance, and I'm not sure I'm ready for constructive criticism." She looked at Christy and thought. "Christy, did you go home and change? Both of you ladies look very nice this evening."

"Ha!" said Christy. "Someone was distracted at the game." She tugged at her pantsuit. "This is what I was wearing. And thank you. I *do* look nice, don't I?"

Mekyla smirked. "I said you *both* look nice, and yes, you do."

"Yes, I do. And you could too, Mekyla."

"There you go, Christy. Let me ask you something. You feel like you stepped out of *Vogue* every day when you leave the house, don't you?"

"I used to. But now, a husband and several kids later, I look like I shop Dillard's and very well, I might add."

Mekyla raised an eyebrow. "I do like the way you put stuff together, but that's your look, not mine."

"Okay, but you didn't use to dress like that back when we were younger. So what's your look now? What do you call your variety of sweat suits and the one pair of designer jeans you own?"

"I have suites and dresses that I wear to work everyday, what are you saying?"

Jennifer sighed. "Hello! Did you guys forget that we're supposed to be somewhere, because I can use a drink right about now?" She turned Mekyla around, took her by the shoulders and pointed her toward the bedroom. "Now, Mekyla, you go in there and put on one of your ankle long denim skirts and a nice blouse."

"Thanks, Jennifer, for appreciating my style." She started to walk to the bedroom.

"Mekyla, I was being sarcastic."

Mekyla came to an abrupt halt and spun around.

"Christy's right, but we don't have time for this right now. Ian likes it. He's an athlete. Sportswear is all he knows. But of course that doesn't mean that's all he ever wants you to wear."

"Someone's cell phone is ringing," said Mekyla.

"Not mine," said Christy.

"Then it must be yours, Jennifer, because mine is on vibrate."

Jennifer pulled her phone out of her purse. "Hello." There was a pause, and then she smiled. "Hello, Daddy."

Jennifer frowned into the phone. "Which hospital, Daddy?"

"What?" whispered Mekyla.

Jennifer waved her off. "I'm on my way," she said, and ended the call.

"What, Jennifer? What's wrong?"

"It's my grandmother again. She's had another heart attack. They took her to St. John's Hospital."

"Okay change of plans," said Mekyla. "Let's go."

"No, guys, you go ahead and I'll catch up with you later."

"We can't let you go by yourself."

"It's really okay. She's survived this heart attack stuff before. I know she will do it again. So just go for me."

Mekyla hung her shoulders. "Jennifer, only if you promise to call us, if you need anything."

"I will, Mekyla, and Ian is with you because you're a beautiful person inside and out. That's why he's with you and the reason why I have remained your friend for all of these years."

"Thank you, Jennifer, but you go and make sure your grandmother gets better and give her a kiss for me."

"That goes the same for me, Jennifer," said Christy.

"Thanks, Christy. See you guys and I will call."

"If you don't, we will."

Mekyla watched Jennifer go then heaved a sigh. "Christy, I'm going to stay here to wait on Jennifer's call, just in case she needs me."

"I understand. I'll see you later, Mekyla."

"Tell my brother-in-law I said hello and kiss those kids for me."

"I will Mekyla." Christy put her hand on the doorknob, but hesitated, then turned back. "Mekyla?"

"Yes?"

"Did that bother you about what Jennifer said at the game?"

"It's not so much that it bothered me, but that it made me wonder for a moment. Just for a moment. Christy, if you really look at me and my situation, I really don't have the right to judge Ian or suspect him of anything. I'm doing dirt. Dirt I believe is going to catch up with me if I don't get a handle on it. You, on the other hand, shouldn't be worrying so much. But, did it bother you, Christy?"

"The sad thing is it didn't bother me so much that my husband may be having an affair, but that the lady who's supposed to be having an affair with *someone's* man was very beautiful. I found myself comparing our appearances."

Mekyla drew her head back and frowned. "You're jealous of her looks?"

"Mekyla, I workout everyday to keep in shape and I watch what I eat so my skin stays blemish-free, and I never say no to my husband. So why do they still look when they have something that's not sore on the eyes at home?"

"Christy, we all look. That's not the problem. It's whether we touch or not. What is it that you get in return from Trey?"

"What do you mean? My family means everything to me."

Mekyla shook her head. "Christy, you've gone beyond that point."

"What point?"

"We'll talk again later. You're going to be late for the baby shower."

Christy looked at her watch. "Okay," she said. "But we *will* talk again later. And keep me informed about Jennifer's grandmother."

"I will."

Christy put her hand on the doorknob again. "Alright. I'm headed for Schonda's for some drinks and family drama."

Mekyla smiled. "Yeah. I'll give her a call before you get there to let her know that I won't be coming."

"Okay. Love you girl."

"And don't worry so much, okay? Love you, Christy."

Christy walked out the door and Mekyla immediately picked up the phone.

"Hello, Schonda, this is Mekyla."

"I don't want to hear it, Mekyla, you're going to be here, right?" Schonda said with that squeak in her voice.

"Well I have a little bad news."

"What? What's wrong? Is Termaine okay?"

"There's nothing wrong with Termaine, my granddaughter Cheyenne, or myself."

"What then?"

"Jennifer's grandmother was rushed to the hospital and I wanted to stay close to the phone in case she needed me."

"But don't you have your cell phone?"

"Yes, but you know."

"I know that I'm probably sounding selfish, but I really wanted you to be here. You're my big sister."

"I know, but I'm definitely not going to let anything stand in the way of me being there for the delivery of my nephew or niece, since I'm the one that's going to get to do the big snip."

"Okay, Mekyla. I'll let you off the hook this time, even though I know the real reason you want to stay home is that you'd like to get more writing in. But I know you love me and your unborn niece or nephew."

"Thanks, Schonda, for understanding and I'll see you soon, okay? Give Mom a kiss for me. Oh, Christy will be bringing Jennifer's gift and her apologies for not being able to make the baby shower."

"Tell Jennifer that I will say a little prayer for her grandmother, okay?"

"Okay, Schonda. Love you, bye."

CHAPTER TWELVE
I KNOW YOU IN NAME

'I can't stand hospitals,' Jennifer thought as she made her way towards her grandmother's room, feeling like she needed to be wearing sterile gloves. 'They're so creepy and sickly.' Oh, there's dad. "Hello, Daddy."

"Hey baby," said her father. "She's been in and out consciousness. They have her heavily sedated."

"Are they going to operate, Daddy?"

"No shugga, they won't be operating this time."

"So what's going to happen? What did they say?"

"They said that her heart can't take another operation."

Jennifer sighed. "So that's it?"

Her father nodded solemnly.

"I'd like to go in and see her."

"Sure, Jennifer, she's just around the corner in 3-B."

Jennifer rounded the corner and entered the room. She stood looking down at her grandmother for a moment, listening to the beeps of the monitoring equipment. "Grandma Bee," she said. "I'm not sure if you can hear me, but I'm right here."

"Hello," said a voice from the corner of the room.

Jennifer turned, startled. A man and a woman were sitting in chairs in the corner of the room. They both stood and came toward her.

"Sorry if we scared you. I'm Pastor Smith and this is my wife, Mrs. Smith."

"Oh, okay. I'm Jennifer, her oldest granddaughter."

"You look just like your father."

"Yes sir, I get that a lot."

"Well it was nice to have met you."

"I'm sorry. I didn't mean to rush you out of the room."

"No, we were just leaving."

"Well, it was nice to have met both of you. Take care of yourselves and thank you for coming to see my grandmother." Alone with her grandmother now, Jennifer pulled the reclining chair closer to her grandmother's bed and settled into it.

CHAPTER THIRTEEN
OH, WHAT A TANGLED WEB WE WEAVE

Mekyla began to squirm in her chair. She knew Ian would be coming home soon.

She forced herself to focus on the novel. She wanted to get a few more pages in before Ian arrived, knowing that when he did, he would want all her attention.

She paged down through the manuscript until she found the place she was looking for. Jonathan had just called Lisa on her cell phone and given her directions to a spot called Midtown, off of Cameron Street.

Lisa walked into the bar from the bright sunlight and let her eyes adjust for a moment. Then she saw Jonathan and walked toward him. "I'm glad you called," she said. "The directions you gave were on the money. But your highways still make me almost pee my pants."

Jonathan laughed. "Well, I have a confession to make. So that I wouldn't steer you wrong, I drove it and wrote it down as I went. Austin can be a little confusing when it comes to our highways and streets. Each one has at least two names. And if I could lower those expressways, I would just for you. We don't want to have you peeing your pants."

"This is a nice club," said Lisa, taking in the plush interior. "And I love the paintings."

Jonathan pointed to his favorite. "I tried to buy that one, but the owner wanted too much for it."

"Mm, I especially like that one. That's a big picture, though. Were you going to have enough space for it?"

"I would have dedicated a whole wall to it. What would you like to drink?"

Lisa took a seat and looked at the drink in front of Jonathan. "You're having Michelob? I will have the same."

"Are you sure? You can order anything you like."

"I'd like to have what you're having." He motioned for the waitress, pointed to his beer and then to Lisa. The waitress nodded from a distance. "You have beautiful skin, Lisa and your eyes are so inviting."

"Thank you." 'Inviting, huh? What are they saying now? Because what my eyes were actually saying is that your company is nice, and that's all.' Lisa said to herself.

Jonathan smiled and nodded.

"The band, do they play here often?

"They usually play here once a month."

"They're good," said Lisa as she began to get into the beat.

"Are you hungry, Lisa?"

"No, not really. Are you?"

"Yes, can we get out of here in a little bit and head for Bennigan's, if you don't mind?"

"No," said Lisa, flattered but a little nervous at how fast things were moving. But after all, she was a big girl. It would only be dinner. She could handle that. "Just as long as I'm back in my hotel room at a decent hour, then I'm good."

"They're finishing up this set. You'll just follow me in your car." Jonathan said and he finished off his Michelob.

Following Jonathan around all the overlapping expressways, Lisa noticed that they had just passed a Bennigan's. That seemed odd, but she didn't know her way around. Maybe they'd have to turn around to get to it. But after a couple of minutes she realized they were not turning around. She wondered why they had passed Bennigan's, and more importantly, why she was still following him.

After another ten minutes of driving, they pulled into the parking garage of a condo building. Lisa followed Jonathan to the parking area and parked next to him. As she sat in her car waiting for Jonathan to come and open her door, she thought of a few more questions she wanted to actually ask him instead of asking herself.

"Hey, what happened to Bennigan's?" she said as soon as her door was open.

"I decided to put something together here at the condo. Please come up."

"I don't know, Jonathan. You're kind of throwing me a curve ball here."

"I'm not going to bite, and I promise when we get inside I'll tell the bellman that you're coming up with me, and that if you're not down by daybreak to come up and rescue you."

"Daybreak? You're that sure of yourself, huh? And, by the way, if you didn't notice, I have a ring on?"

"I'm sure that you're here right now and that you're a big girl."

She thought of telling him that he'd better take a second look, because this was all woman right here.

"Come up with me."

Lisa followed him through the lobby and onto the elevator. "Where's that bellman?" said Lisa as she watched what button Jonathan pushed. "Penthouse, huh?"

"Must have the best. You only get one life, and this is how I choose to live it."

Inside the penthouse, Jonathan gestured to the floor to ceiling windows.

"This is very nice," she said, strolling over to the windows. "And you can see all of downtown Austin. And there's a lake. What lake is that?"

"That's Town Lake. It stretches from one end of Austin to the other." He backed away from her. "Excuse me while I start the fireplace. Would you like something to drink?"

"Yes, I'll have what you're having."

"Please make yourself comfortable."

Lisa turned from the window and took in the interior. "I'm admiring all of your art. It's beautiful. Did you have a decorator come in?"

"No, I did it all myself," Jonathan said over his shoulder as he started the fire.

"You're kidding me."

"No, I did it. I love picking out my own decorations."

"So, Jonathan, is there an ex or present in your life?"

"There is a soon to be an ex," He said, going to the bar and pulling down a couple of glasses. "We separated a few months ago after ten years of marriage. Now, I guess you could say I'm enjoying the single life." He returned with two glasses of wine. "Lisa is that a booger on your face?"

"What?" said Lisa, feeling around her nose? "You're kidding me, right?"

"Yes, I am." He handed her wineglass. "Relax and take your shoes off. Would you like to listen to some Nora Jones?"

"That's what you were bopping your head to in Wally World, right?"

"I don't think I was bopping my head, maybe grooving a little. I like her style." He put a CD on the disk changer and pressed play.

"Look, Jonathan, it's starting to rain."

"Well Lisa, I guess someone is playing in my favor."

"I'm not afraid of a little rain. Brown sugar takes a little longer melt, but is equally sweet."

Jonathan laughed. "I like that Lisa. You're a very interesting person. Maybe you'll tell me the real reason you're in Austin and not at home with your husband."

"Maybe we can swap stories," she said, smiling. "You know fiction and non-fiction versions in remix."

Mekyla heard Ian's car pull up and decided she was at a good stopping point. She clicked "save," but left the document open and went to the front door to greet him. "Hello, sweetie," she said, as he came through the door.

"Hello, Mekyla. Are you okay?"

"Sure," she said. "Why wouldn't I be?"

"Because you left the game early," said Ian, putting his arms around her.

"Yes, I'm fine, baby. Just wanted to come home and write."

"Ah," said Ian, releasing his grip on her. "How's the book coming along?" He began to strip down to his briefs.

She sighed. "Well, I can be doing very well one week, and then the next week it's like my brain just stops."

"Well, I thought you were going to your sister's baby shower anyway."

"I was, but I didn't feel like laughing and celebrating under the circumstances."

Ian furrowed his brow. "What circumstances?"

"Jennifer's grandmother was rushed to the hospital again. I thought it would be better for me to stay by the phone."

"Is everything going to be all right?"

She shrugged. "I haven't heard anything yet. I'm going to give it another thirty minutes or so, and then I'm giving her a call."

"Good idea," said Ian.

"Ian, how was the game? Did you guys win?"

Ian laughed. "Yes, of course we won. But you know those guys are still knuckleheads."

"Your game ended hours ago. Did you and the guys go out afterwards?"

"Yes, me and a couple of the guys went and had drinks at Friday's."

"Was Trey with you?"

Ian shook his head. "No. Why do you ask?"

"No reason."

"Mekyla, I'm going to head for the shower; would you make me a nice ham and cheese sandwich with lettuce, tomato and mayo with a tall glass of ice tea?"

"Sure, Ian."

"Thanks, baby. Then we can talk about your trip."

"Sure, but we have plenty of time to talk about my trip, no rush." Mekyla said as she was going into the kitchen to pull out fixings for Ian's sandwich. As she was putting the bread on the plate, the phone rang.

"Oh, I got it," she called out. Then she heard the shower running. "Of course I got it," she said to herself. She picked up the phone. "Hello."

"Mekyla, this is Jennifer."

"Hey, Jennifer. How is everything? How's your grandmother?"

"I saw her, but she's still asleep from the medication. Mekyla, I don't know what to say to her. It's been so long since the last time I saw her."

"Jennifer, I don't know what you and your grandmother are at odds about, but just be truthful in your response."

"Mekyla, you know I can't do that. That would surely kill her."

Mekyla tucked the phone between her shoulder and her ear as she spread mayo on the bread. "Kill her, what could be, you know what, do you want me to come down there?"

"I don't know yet. Let me just give you a call back."

"Okay, Jennifer, I will be waiting right here for your call."

"Thanks, Mekyla."

"Love you, Jennifer."

"Love you too, Mekyla."

She hung up the phone as Ian strolled into the kitchen.

"Well, that was good timing. I'm just putting the finishing touches on your sandwich."

"Good. I'm starved. Did I just hear you on the phone?"

"Yes, that was Jennifer."

"How is her grandmother?"

"Still heavily sedated. Jennifer's going to call back."

"Call back?" said Ian, looking at the clock over the stove. "It's already late, Mekyla."

"I know, Ian, but she needs me." Mekyla put the top on the sandwich and set the plate on the kitchen table.

"*I* need you," said Ian as he picked up the plate.

"What do you need?"

"I need for you to come to bed and lay next to me." He turned toward the bedroom with the plate in his hand, looking over his shoulder at Mekyla. "It's only been a week."

"In a minute, baby. I'm going to do a couple more pages and I'll be right there. Besides, you shouldn't be eating in the bed anyway."

"That's why you need to come up with the invention of a bed vacuum so that when I do decide to eat a meal in our bed, in the bed that we paid for, you can just come in suck the crumbs right away." Ian stood and looked at Mekyla who seemed deep in thought. "Mekyla, are you listening to me?"

"Yes, I hear you Ian. I just figured out a direction I want a character to go."

Ian cocked his head, as if listening for something. "Nora Jones? That's the same CD you were playing this morning."

"Yes, I know."

"Baby, there are other CDs on the rack."

"I know that we have other CDs. This is the one I like to play when I'm writing now. She relaxes my mind."

"I have something that will relax your mind also."

Mekyla laughed and shook her head. "I just bet you think you do. I'll come to bed in a little bit, okay?"

"Okay, but don't stay up too late. It's hard for me to sleep when you're not lying next to me now."

"Then why are you already snoring by the time I come to bed?"

"That's just substitute snoring, the real snoring happens when I realize you're safe and warm next to me."

Mekyla furrowed her brow. "How sweet and sickening at the same time is that? I guess you hold all the little gas bubbles in until I get in the bed as well?"

Ian smiled. "Only for you, Mekyla. Only for you, baby."

"Thank you, Ian; I have always wanted to have little holes blown out of my back every night."

Mekyla sat down at her computer and let Ian wander off to bed. She read through the last few lines she'd written and tried to get back into the spirit of Lisa. She had to get at least another hour of writing done.

"I swear I'm going to have to leave earth to get this done," she said out loud. "But I don't need what happened before to happen again, I think. I wonder why he never called. What am I saying, that's so over." She shook her head to clear her mind and settled back into the life of fiction.

"Jonathan, what are you cooking in there?" said Lisa. "It smells very good."

"I thought you weren't hungry. I hope you weren't lying when you said that, because I'm just making enough for me."

"Ha! I'm not hungry, but I'm not going to sit here and stare at you while you eat, either. And by the way, I love your spiral staircase."

"Would you like to see what's at the end of the staircase?"

"No, I can see all I need to see from here. This wine is very good. Do you mind telling me who makes it?"

"Rosso Villa Monticelli. It's from the big Sangiovese, Merlot, Cabernet Sauvignon, and Cabernet Franc grapes. It has a brilliant red ruby color, and an intense and penetrating perfume with a balanced persistency, a mature fruit and mulberry scent."

"Jonathan, now that was a mouthful."

"I was reading from the bottle."

"Good. All I can remember from that was Rosso."

"That was the first thing I read."

"I had to hold onto something while you kept going on and on."

"Lisa, I like that you have a sense of humor."

"Thank you. You need any help in there?"

"No, you just keep snooping through all of my things like you've been doing."

"I'm not snooping. I'm admiring your stuff. There is a difference, you know. Do you mind if I open your balcony door? To let the sweet smell of the rain, come in, to say hello to us?"

"Please, go right ahead. Lisa, may I ask you something?"

"Sure."

"Are you really married, or just wearing the ring?"

"I have been married five years now."

"Is everything okay back home?"

"Yes."

"What compelled you to say 'yes' to my invitation?"

"One, I was getting pretty bored, and two, curiosity, I supposed."

"Curiosity of what it would be like to cross the line?"

Lisa frowned. "No, but yes. I wanted to know that I could sustain."

"If you were to fail, would you have any regrets?"

"To be honest, I never saw myself going past the meeting at the nightclub. And, no, there would not be any regrets about something that I'm aware is happening."

"Well I'm glad that you were snooping in my basket, and checked me out up and down and made the decision that I was possibly a good risk."

Lisa took another sip of wine and felt its warmth in her throat and chest. "If I forget to say it, Jonathan, thank you for tonight. I have had a wonderful time. I made an excellent choice in picking this city to come to and relax."

"Austin embraces you, Lisa, and so do I."

Mekyla pushed back from her computer screen, bleary-eyed. She was satisfied that she'd written enough for one day. Tomorrow, she could pick up where she'd left off. She saved the document, closed it, and shut down the machine.

She stood up stretching. "Okay, let me go and get my back blown out and my ears overwhelmed with his snoring," she said. "Maybe I'll even fondle him a little to make him think that something happened, and then I can get me some sleep."

CHAPTER FOURTEEN
WHAT WAS DONE IN THE DARK WILL COME TO ME

Christy was curled up on the couch when the door opened. "Hello, Trey," she said over the top of her magazine. "Your dinner is in the oven."

Trey, the hard working husband and father; who is known for believing that the world revolved around him and that his wife was to do everything that needed to be done around the house and for their kids and him, no exceptions. Trey tossed his keys on the table and dropped his gym bag in the corner. "Would you grab my dinner for me, Christy?"

"Sure," she said, getting up from the couch. "You're late getting in. Were you hanging out with the guys afterwards?"

Trey dropped into the recliner. "What's with the questions, Christy? Do I have a curfew?"

"No baby, it's just that we're not spending that much quality time here lately."

"Are you not satisfied with what I'm providing for you and the kids?"

"I'm very satisfied." Christy said as she took the plate from the oven and set it on the coffee table in front of the recliner.

"Then what's with the nagging?"

"Trey I don't believe this is nagging. I'm just having a conversation with my husband. What would you like to drink with your dinner?"

"Please bring me a glass of milk."

As she poured the glass of milk and sat it on the table, she replied. "Trey, I'll be upstairs if you need me."

"I'll be up after awhile. I'm going to watch a little ball downstairs; I don't want to disturb you."

"Please be sure to kiss the children goodnight when you come up."

"I will. I always do."

CHAPTER FIFTEEN
SECRET LOVER

"Hey, what are you doing?" Jennifer said into the phone.

"I'm just getting my clothes ready for work tomorrow. Hey, it's late and I'm not alone. And you know you're not supposed to be calling me this late. Come on now."

"I was just thinking about you. Sorry. I didn't realize I had a curfew on my phone calls to you."

"Don't start. This is not the right time. Call me at work tomorrow. I really need to hang up now, okay."

"Keep your cell phone on. I hate leaving messages with your secretary."

"I will. Goodnight."

"Goodnight."

'Why am I waiting on this man?' Jennifer thought as she ended the call. 'He's not all that good to me anyway. Why is the loving always so good with someone you can't have?'

She turned out the light and curled up in her bed, alone again.

CHAPTER SIXTEEN
AND THE EMMY GOES TO . . .

"Hey you!" said Mekyla, as Ian came into the kitchen

"It's a good morning, Mekyla." Ian sat at the table and thumbed through the paper, finally pulling out the sports section. He looked up at Mekyla. "What's with the Cool-aide smile this morning? I know it wasn't anything I did last night, because I was too tired."

"I know," said Mekyla emphatically. "I took care of it myself. Sorry. But at the game last night, Jennifer pointed out a woman in the bleachers. She said she overheard the woman was having an affair with one of the ball players. And then an hour or so later her grandmother had a heart attack. All that, plus the fact that I still have car lag from the long drive from the night before, and then working a full day. ... I tell you, I'm just beat."

Ian folded down the paper and looked at her across the table. "I understand. Hey, baby, we haven't talked about your writing in a few weeks. Give me the latest on Trevor and Lisa."

'Okay, I guess he didn't hear what I just said,' thought Mekyla. But that was okay. For the time being. She gathered her thoughts and picked up from where she'd left off from the last time she and Ian had talked about her book.

"Okay, well remember I said she left Tulsa and headed for Austin?"

"No, I don't remember that part. I think you may have left off right before that when she decided she needed a break from Trevor, but start from there."

"Well she drove to Austin, checked into a hotel, and decided to go out and see some of the town a few days later. She stopped at Wal-Mart and ended up meeting this guy."

"Hold on. This lady just left her husband to think and she's already meeting someone else?"

"Yes, baby, but remember, this is just fiction."

"Is that something you would do?"

"That's a crazy question to ask me?" Mekyla said with a look of surprise on her face.

"Well you know what they say. You write about your life experiences or dreams."

"Who said that?"

"You know, those people, Mekyla. I don't know exactly who they are. I just heard it said before."

"Well 'those people,' whoever they are, aren't always right, and very wrong in my case, because I don't believe I'm writing about things I wish would happen to me."

"What do you mean, you don't 'believe' you are? I hope you're not writing about you as well, Mekyla. And why would you even make a statement like that, knowing it's bound to bring some type of curiosity to my mind?"

Mekyla rolled her eyes, then gestured at her breakfast. "I'm having toast and tea. Would you like some breakfast?"

Ian checked his watch. "No, baby, I'll grab something on the way to work." He stood up and started for the door. "See you tonight. I need to get going, but I made a note to myself to come back to that question you thought you avoided."

"See you tonight, baby. Kisses." 'Hmm,' she thought when he'd gone out the door. 'He can catch that, but didn't have anything to say about what I said earlier. Mr. I'll-remark-to-the-ones-I-want-to-remark-to, but-leave-this-house-with-a-note-to-self-remark. Who does he think he is? Who am I kidding? I will avoid that question like the plague.' But as she got up from the table and carried her tea into the living room, she did wonder why Ian didn't respond to what she'd said earlier. All he wanted to focus on was the fiction. And maybe some non-fiction stuff as well.

As Mekyla reclined in her favorite chair, she adjusted her T-shirt over her favorite pair of granny panties. She tried to forget about her relationship troubles as she sipped her cup of hot tea, staring out their bay window with its view of the azaleas arrayed with her favorite colors: billowy white; red, which represented love; and pink, which told the outside world there's a girl on board. When in full bloom, they would stand taller than the bay window itself. But try as she might to forget about her troubles, Mekyla's mind kept drifting back to Ian. She began to try to come up with another way to ask him if he knew which of the men in his circle might be having an affair with the lady with powder blue cashmere on. But she'd have to do it without stirring up that question that he'd made note to himself to come back to. The phone was ringing.

"Hello."

"Good morning, Mom," said Termaine.

"Good morning, baby. To what do I owe this morning call?" She crossed her fingers and looked up into the heavens, as if praying that her son wouldn't need to use her vehicle again.

"I just want to call and tell you good morning. And thank you again for letting me use your car yesterday. I love you, glad you're back home, missed you and have a nice day."

"Thank you, baby. You have a nice day as well," Mekyla said, trying not to sound too obviously relieved. She smiled at her son's thoughtfulness.

"Okay bye, Mom."

"Bye." She hung up the phone and then sat back in her recliner and just stared at it, waiting for it to ring again and to hear her son's voice saying, 'Oh Yeah. I forgot to ask you something.' She then checked the clock on the wall to see how much more lounging time she had before it was time to head to work.

CHAPTER SEVENTEEN
A QUIET STORM

As Christy went about her preparations for breakfast, she let the pots and pans clang against the stove. It was her way of saying she still had some unanswered concerns on her mind.

"Good morning," said Trey as he entered the kitchen.

"I've started some breakfast. Are you eating this morning?"

"Christy, I've eaten breakfast every morning for as long as I can remember. Please pour me a glass of orange juice, and without the attitude you apparently have."

"I just wanted to talk with you last night and you cut me off," said Christy, jerking open the refrigerator door.

"I didn't cut you off, Christy. You just came at me wrong, and when you do that, you know I don't want to be bothered. I prefer to have a conversation in which we're going to speak with some sense."

Christy set the glass of orange juice on the table with a little too much emphasis.

Trey sighed. "I tell you what, can we finish this conversation when I come home this evening? I have a meeting this morning and I don't want to go in there with other things on my mind." Trey furrowed his eyebrows.

"Sure, Trey," said Christy. "Tonight will be just fine." She recognized the look on his face. She knew he'd had enough of her pouting.

"Now, may I have my breakfast please?"

"Sure, darling."

Later, as she cleared the breakfast dishes from the table, Christy wondered why she was so upset with her husband. She wished Jennifer had never mentioned the lady in the cashmere sweater. It probably didn't mean anything. I'm sure it hasn't anything to do with Trey.

CHAPTER EIGHTEEN
OUR SKELETON STORIES

'What is this, grand central phone station?' Mekyla said to herself as she went to answer the phone again.

"Hello."

"Good morning, Mekyla."

"Oh, Jennifer. Good morning to you. How's your grandmother?"

"I didn't get a chance to speak with her last night, but she did open her eyes and saw I was there."

"Jennifer, you never did tell me what the big suspense was between you and your grandmother," Mekyla said as she tried to continue getting dressed while talking on the phone.

"I know, Mekyla, and this is something I've been dealing with for a long time."

"Would you like to talk about it?"

"I believe it's time for me to talk about this with someone. Maybe that will allow me to really deal with what I've been hiding all these years. Can we meet later? Around six o'clock when I get off work?"

"Sure, Jennifer, would you like to come here, or should I meet you somewhere else?"

"Would Ian be home?"

"No, he'll be at the gym for a couple of hour's right after work, so we'd have time."

"Then I'll see you there around six, Mekyla. Could you have something for me to eat; when I get there?"

"Sure, Jennifer, I'll make enough dinner to feed you as well."

"Mekyla, hold on. Junior, are you ready to go?" said Jennifer away from the phone. "We need to leave right now, okay?" She spoke directly into the phone again. "Sorry Mekyla, I go through this every morning with Junior."

Mekyla shook her head to herself. "Jennifer, when are you going to move out of your mother's house and get your own apartment? Hell, your own house? I know you can afford it, and you can definitely find the best deals in town. You're a realtor, for goodness sake."

"I can't leave right now. Junior will be going off to college pretty soon and then I can leave."

"I tell you one thing, Jennifer. I wish I had a big sister like you. You are definitely unique."

"Thanks, Mekyla. So I'll see you tonight."

“After I leave the office I'm going to stop at the grocery store. I should be here around five-thirty, so I'll have everything ready by six. Have a nice day, Jennifer.”

“Thanks again. And don’t work too hard, not that you ever do.”

“Jennifer, I work smart, not hard. See you tonight.”

CHAPTER NINETEEN
AS DEVIANCE IS, DEVIANCE DOES

After arriving at the office late that morning, Jennifer placed another call. “Hello, my tall caramel treat,” she said when the phone was answered. “Can you talk?”

“Yes, but only for a minute. I'm on my way to a business meeting.”

“I was wondering if you were available for a late dinner. Around nine o'clock tonight?”

“Not tonight, Jennifer, I’ve already made plans this evening.”

“I would like to receive the same amount of attention she receives.”

“What do you mean, Jennifer? You know that can never happen right now.”

Jennifer huffed impatiently into the phone. “Well just call me when you’re ready to satisfy my appetite again.”

“Sure, Jennifer. I’ll call. I have to run. I have a meeting in fifteen.”

“Okay. Goodbye.”

“Click.” The phone sounded without even a goodbye from him. ‘I’m not going to give up on you yet,’ thought Jennifer. ‘You’ll be mine one day, and we’ll be a family.’ She said as she stood there listening to the dial tone in her ear.

Usually Jennifer would skip lunch and just work on closing deals, because her goal was to sell at least one house every week, a goal she had met for the last three years in a row. But now her grandmother was in the hospital. She knew it was going to be a little more difficult to reach her sales goals *and* be there for her grandmother at the same time.

She looked at her watch. She had time for a quick dash over to the hospital to see how Grandma Bee was holding up. She hoped the hospital would be releasing her soon. She didn’t know how long she could keep up the juggling act. After all, she had bills to pay and a lifestyle to maintain.

“Nicole, I’m going to take an early lunch,” She said, getting up from her desk. “Did you need me to sign anything before I leave?”

“No, Jennifer, I think everything that’s on my desk can wait until you return.”

“Okay then,” She said, heading for the door.

“Have a good lunch and tell your grandmother I hope she gets better soon."

"Thanks, Nicole. See you in a little bit."

CHAPTER TWENTY
I COULDN'T HAVE SPOTTED A BETTER PAIR

Mr. Elliot stood before Marie's desk as she asked if she could help him.

"My name is Brent Elliot and I was in yesterday and Ms. Williams asked me to bring these items in today."

"Yes, sir, Mr. Elliot," said Marie. "You can go on back. She's expecting you."

Mr. Elliot strode confidently back to Mekyla's office. "Hello," he said as he poked his head through the door.

"Hello to you," said Mekyla with a smile. "Come on in and have a seat."

"I'm sure you remember my name."

"Oh, do I?"

"Oh, I'm sorry. I just assumed you would. I was just here yesterday, and you should have my paper work in front of you with my name on it."

"Well, aren't you just all over my desk, looking and assuming and presuming stuff? And, you presumed right. I have your name right here, Mr. Elliott, or Mr. White Ghost."

They both gave a nice warm laugh to that statement.

"Did you bring in the papers I asked you for?"

"Yes, I did. You can just call me by my first name."

"No thank you. I only use last names with certain people."

"Well, maybe one day I can hear you say my first name in a different setting."

"Okay, all I need now is a signature right here and $165.00 to complete the process." As she leaned across her desk to push the paper toward him, Mekyla could smell the scent of his cologne.

"I think I can handle that, Ms. Williams."

"Is there anything else-any other needs I can help you with today, Mr. Elliott?"

'Mm,' thought Mr. Elliot. 'Not only yesterday, but also today, this young woman still intrigues me with how she speaks to me. She knows how to apply those pearly whites at you in a way you cannot help but be mesmerized by.'

"Mr. Elliott?"

"Yes. I mean, no you have been very helpful and I'm glad I chose this door."

"Mr. Elliott."

"Yes."

"You have a nice day."

"I will, thank you, Ms. Williams. Goodbye." 'I wonder would it be too pushy to ask her out on a date,' he thought. 'I didn't see a ring on her finger, but maybe I should wait. Yeah, I'll wait.'

"Okay, goodbye again." She could tell he wanted to say something else, but he didn't know how to say it. But he'd be back. She was sure of that. She watched him slowly get up from the chair. Her eyes took in his build, the confidence in his walk.

He stopped and turned back. "Ms. Williams?"

"Yes."

"Are you watching me; walk away again?"

Mekyla laughed and raised her right hand. "I'm guilty."

"Good," he said. "I wouldn't have it any other way."

"I wouldn't *think* to look any other way, Mr. Elliott."

"Oh, my goodness, cut it out," said Marie.

"Marie, what are you talking about?"

"I'm going to the ladies room, Mekyla. If Mr. Smith calls me back before I return, please just have him hold the line, okay, thanks."

"Sure, I can do that Marie. Well, okay again Mr. Elliott, you have a nice day." She watched him start to leave again, then decided to keep the conversation going just a little longer. "I really like your outfit. May I ask the designers name?"

"Sure, this outfit is by Dolce and Gabbana, a couple out of Milan, Italy."

"Somehow, I've only imagined you in sports clothes, you know, since you are an athletic coach."

"Oh really, and what else have you imagined about me?"

"Actually, a few minutes ago I imagined that you wanted to ask me something, but decided not to."

Mr. Elliot smiled. "You know you're right. I would like to ask you out on a date."

"Okay, go ahead and ask me."

"Would you like to go out, maybe this Saturday, for dinner?"

"I do have a guy in my life."

"It's just dinner."

"Let's say lunch to start with."

"Say around one o'clock?"

Mekyla held up a finger, and then looked at her calendar to make sure there weren't any other plans her family had for her. After a moment she nodded. "That will be fine. What you can do is call here later this afternoon, and I will give you directions to my house." She handed him a business card from the cardholder on her desk. "Here is the office number."

"Okay, that sounds like a plan. Again, thank you very much Ms. Williams."

"You are very welcome. Like I said, I aim to be pleased."

Mr. Elliott laughed. "You're very interesting, you know? I'm looking forward to seeing you tomorrow."

She nodded. "Goodbye again, Mr. Elliott," she said as she extended her hand, prompting a handshake.

Marie came around the corner just as Mr. Elliot was walking out the door. "Okay, Mekyla, what happened?"

"He asked me out."

"Girl, I have got to give it to you. You know how to work that mouthpiece. The route you take, I know it makes them wonder if you are even going to say yes. You have a southern girl charm, with a seductive approach."

"What do you mean seductive? I'm not being seductive."

Marie cocked her head. "You know how you . . .? You know the way you . . .? Heck," she said, with a wave of her hand. "I cannot explain it. I'm still taking notes. I don't come here just for the paycheck anymore."

"Marie, you are a strange character."

"Okay, one more question Mekyla."

"Just one more question, Marie?"

"Where did you say you lived, or are you going to meet him somewhere?"

"When he calls, if you must know, I'll give him my home address. I still have my own place, remember?"

"Oh, yeah."

"You think we can get some work done, or at least change the subject, because you don't know me like that and I'm not sure you should. If you're going to study someone, make sure it's someone who can teach you something that you can apply in you life in a smart and positive way. Because I can be this manipulating killer, you know? Like a black widow spider."

"Mekyla, a killer? Now that's far fetched, don't you think?"

"I just don't want to be a bad influence on you."

"Hey Mekyla, that reminds me, would you like to go see the Fighting Temptations tonight?"

"Sure, sounds like fun. We'll leave right after work."

"That's too early."

"I'm not your date, okay? It's cheaper if we get there before six, right?"

"Yes, that's true. I guess I did forget I was paying for this one."

"You probably paid for the last one too."

"Forget you, girl, and yes, I did. Is that pitiful or what?"

"Not, or what." Mekyla put her hand on her cheek. "Hey, you know what? I can't tonight, Marie. And I already have too much on my plate this week. Let's shoot for next week sometime."

"Okay, that's fine. I was probably going to have to bring my son anyway. Oh, and I need your signature on these two checks."

"Okay, bring them in and lay them on my desk. I'm going to step outside for a minute."

Mekyla strolled down the sidewalk with no particular purpose. "Big Money," she said to the man in uniform. "How are you doing? How is security work these days? Have you had to pull out your gun on anyone lately?"

The big man smiled and shook his head. "No. Hope I don't ever have to either. Where are you going, down to the bank?"

"No, I was just stretching my legs. Sometimes you just need to take a walk and breathe some different air."

"I know what you mean. I wish I could just breathe my air at home and retire, but I can't, I've gotta keep working."

"It will happen one day. Take care of yourself, and tell your wife I said hello."

"I will, Mekyla. You take care of yourself too."

"I will," she said.

CHAPTER TWENTY-ONE
I WONDER HOW THOSE SHOES FEEL

Marie looked up from her desk and smiled. "Hello Mr. Johnson. How can I help you today?"

"I would like to have Ms. Mekyla help me this time."

"Sure," said Marie, getting up from her desk. "Let me go see if she's available." She walked down the hall and into Mekyla's office. "Mekyla, Mr. Johnson is out front and requesting your service."

"He only wants to speak with me?"

"I don't know why, but he asked for you."

"Tell him to give me a minute and I'll be right out."

A few moments later, Mekyla found Mr. Johnson relaxing in a chair in the reception area.

"Hello, Mr. Johnson," she said with a smile. "How can I help you today?"

"I'm here to make a payment on my Dodge."

"Alright. Come on back with me and I'll take care of that for you."

As he entered Mekyla's office, she gestured to a chair and went around to her side of the desk.

"May I have your first name, Mr. Johnson."

"Robert," said the man. "It's here on my payment slip." He handed the payment slip to her.

"Oh, okay. And will you be paying with cash or check?"

"Cash. I always pay with cash."

"Oh, is that right?"

"That's the only way to go. I'm glad you were able to help me this time, seems like every time I come in, you're either with another customer or you are not here."

"Oh, I'm sorry to hear that, but was there some particular reason you needed to speak with me?"

"No, I just wanted you to help me so that I could ask you face to face if you'd like to have lunch with me."

"Lunch, hmm. I don't think so. I have someone in my life at this time."

Mr. Johnson smiled and sighed. "Well, my loss, huh?"

"Alright, Mr. Johnson," she said, handing him his receipt. "You're all taken care of. Is there anything else I can assist you with today?"

"No, not at this time, but hopefully soon." Mr. Johnson rose from his chair and nodded.

'Okay,' thought Mekyla. 'He's a very handsome man. I guess I never really looked at him before. I don't know why not. He's very tall, one of my requirements in a man.'

She glanced down at the paperwork on her desk. "From what I see in your policies, it looks like I'll see you in a couple of weeks."

"I'll see you in a couple of weeks."

"Okay, repeating me is not good. Now stop that." Mekyla looked at the man askance. "See you later, Mr. Johnson."

'Why do I look at other men?' she thought as she watched him go. 'What is wrong with me? Why was I even considering dating him? I should not be dating policyholders anyway. Hell, not just policyholders. I shouldn't be dating other men. News flash: I have a man. I really need to see a couch doctor.'

'Sneeze.'

"Bless you Mr. Johnson." Ewe, wiping his nose on his shirt sleeve, that's why I've never noticed him.

Marie answered the phone and heard a familiar voice on the other end of the line.

"Hello, Marie, may I speak to Mekyla please?"

"Sure, may I tell her whose calling?"

"Yes, I'm sorry. I was again assuming you knew my voice. Please, tell her it's Christy Love."

"One moment please, Christy, and yes, I do recognize your voice, but I can't assume. It's against company policy."

"Oh, I understand Marie. Have a nice day."

"Thanks, Christy," said Marie before transferring the call to Mekyla's office.

Mekyla picked up the phone with a smile in her voice. "This is Mekyla Williams, Mrs. Christy Love. What's up?"

"I was calling to see if you were free for lunch today."

"Oh, I like the sound of that, because usually the inviter has to buy lunch for the invitee."

"I'm sure those are not words, but I can handle that."

"They are so words. So where are we eating, at my darling sister?"

"How about S and J Oyster? Our usual spot there on South Peoria."

"That sounds good to me. Say around one-thirty."

"One-thirty works for me. I just have to arrange my babysitter, but that shouldn't be a problem. Between both sets of grandparents, someone has to come through. So I'll see you at one-thirty."

"See ya, Christy."

CHAPTER TWENTY-TWO
A TIME TO FORGIVE

Jennifer took a deep breath and steered herself in the hallway outside her grandmother's room. 'I know this is a test of my patience,' she thought. But I'm going to fool everyone. Because, I going to stick this one out. Okay, here goes.'

She rounded the corner and saw her grandmother propped up in bed, fully awake. "Grandma Bee, how are you feeling?"

"I'm okay, Jennifer," said the woman. "So you finally decided to stop by and see me."

"Grandma Bee, I was here last night. You were heavily sedated at first so I guess you didn't know I was here."

"I don't remember that, Jennifer. I remember your father and my other grandchildren being here."

Jennifer sighed, but continued to smile. "Okay."

"How do I look, Jennifer? I guess I won't win any more beauty contests, huh?"

"Grandma Bee, you look just fine. Why don't you take that wig off. I like your natural hair."

"It does feel better when I take it off," said Grandma Bee. She pulled the wig off and fluffed her natural hair a bit. "It allows my scalp to breathe and not itch so much."

"There you go," said Jennifer. "I tried to see your doctor, but he was with a patient. What is the latest on you having the surgery?"

"Well, they're not going to give me the surgery."

"Did they tell you why they wouldn't?"

"They said it's not going to make a difference and that it will be too risky anyway."

"So what do we do now, Grandma Bee?"

"The doctor told me I needed to get my house in order. That would mean to me, prepare to die?"

Jennifer held her breath for a moment, as if the whole world had just stopped. How could her grandmother prepare to die? Her eyes began to fill with tears, and when she blinked, they spilled down her cheeks. As she tried to see through her tears, she took her grandmother's hand and held it as if this were the last time she would feel the warmth of her skin.

Suddenly, Grandma Bee jerked her hand away. "Where is Junior? Jennifer! I want to see him."

"He should be at the house, Grandma. Was there a particular reason you're asking for him?"

"I feel it's time for him to know. And if it's the last thing I do, he will know what you and your mother have done."

Jennifer put her hands on her hips and bowed her head. "Okay, Grandma Bee. I can see it's time to get back to work now. I'll come by again soon. Take care of yourself and do what the doctors tell you to do. Okay?" She turned to leave.

"So tell me, Jennifer. Why is it that you never loved me the way you loved your other grandmother?"

Jennifer spun around, brows furrowed, mouth open. "Grandma Bee, what do you mean?"

"Ever since your mom's mother passed away, you've always given me the impression that you had lost your only grandmother."

Jennifer shook her head in frustration. "I really don't have time to get into this right now, Grandma Bee. I have to go back to work."

The old woman jutted her chin defiantly. "And I, Jennifer, may not be here when you return. So if you would be so kind as to give me this time I need right now, I would appreciate it."

Jennifer paused, and then nodded. "Give me a moment, grandma, while I make a phone call to my office."

"You can use this one right here," said Grandma Bee, gesturing to the phone on the nightstand.

Jennifer rolled her eyes. "Sure, Grandma Bee. That would pretty much eliminate the possibility of me running for the hills, huh?"

She picked up the phone and dialed. After a moment, she said, "Hello, Nicole, this is Jennifer. Would you close my office door? I'm going to be just a little late getting back to the office. I'm here with my grandmother and it's going to take a little longer than a lunch break for sure."

"Sure, Jennifer. Is everything okay?"

"Oh yeah. The heart attack didn't affect her mouth at all. Thanks, and I should be back around three o'clock." She hung up the phone and took another deep breath, preparing herself for the conversation she didn't want to have.

"Jennifer, did you need me to repeat what I asked you before you tried to get out of here so quick?"

"No, Grandma Bee. I remember the question. I'm just trying to find the words to answer."

"No need to get smart with me, Jennifer. I'm still your grandmother."

"I'm not trying to get smart with you. It's just that you're asking me a question about something that goes back close to twenty years."

"I know when your mother's mother passed."

"It's not that I loved her more," Jennifer said, shaking her head. "Just differently. You have to understand, Grandma Bee, I spent a lot of time with my mom's mother, and that's what allowed me and her to become closer than I was with you."

"But Jennifer, I also lived in the same town. What really kept you from coming to visit me on your own?"

"To be honest, it was you, Grandma Bee. I never really had a connection with you. Every time I went to try to connect with you, you'd pull away. I always felt you were very secretive, in a way that kept you from sharing with me who you really were, or are." She furrowed her brow, confused. "Whatever."

"Hmm!" said Grandma Bee, indignantly.

"For example, I have asked you about my dad's father, because he doesn't know anything it seems. Simple things like, where did, or does, he live. And how about what his name was. I've even asked you what *your* real last name is, and I get nothing. Except that I'm being nosy. How is that being nosy, wanting to know who my family is?"

Grandma Bee looked away, her chin raised.

"So, don't you even think about coming at me with the Junior crap, because it's beyond Junior. You have no idea how far beyond Junior. I don't want to hear it, or feel that I have to deal with it from you. When I was a little girl trying to find my way, that was when I needed you. And when I was in college trying to better myself, I could have used some encouragement from you. Now that I'm all grown up and have weathered so many storms and look out on the horizon and see all the storms still to come, I need you to just be supportive of me instead of sitting in judgment."

Grandma Bee was silent for a moment. Then she looked at her granddaughter. "Jennifer, I just want to help you break the cycle of deceit."

Jennifer extended her hands, pleading. "Help me by starting with you. Help me to know my family on my father's side. Who are you? Where were you born? What is my grandfather's name?" Jennifer knew she was asking tough questions. She felt like an interrogator. But these were things she'd wanted to know for as long as she could remember. She looked at her grandmother with the questions burning in her eyes. Her grandmother just stared back. "I thought so. What are you afraid of me finding out? What kind of skeletons do you have in your closet that you don't ever want to get out?"

Grandma Bee began to squint her eyes and grabbed her chest.

Jennifer grabbed the bed railing with both hands. "Grandma Bee," she said, and she could hear the panic in her own voice. "Are you okay?" She turned and ran into the hall. "Nurse, nurse," she yelled.

A nurse came running down the hall. "What's wrong? What has happened?"

Jennifer followed her back into the room. "We were having a discussion and I think I may have upset her."

The nurse busied herself checking all the monitoring equipment.

"Well, I *know* I upset her," Jennifer continued. "And I should be ashamed of myself. But you have to understand. I have so many questions inside of me and she holds all of the answers. I love my grandmother and I truly don't want her to leave me. Not like this."

"Everything looks okay," said the nurse, relaxing. "She probably just needs to rest now."

"Would it be okay for me to just sit here and not say a word?"

"I'm sure your grandmother wouldn't mind, but promise me you'll just let her rest for a little while."

"Yes. I promise. Thank you very much, nurse, and I'm sorry for the disturbance."

Jennifer pulled up a chair near the bed. "Grandma Bee, I'm just going to sit here and not say a word. I just need to know that you're okay." She stood up again. "Actually, I'm going to go out and find something to drink. Did you want me to bring you something, like some ice or some of those good graham crackers?" She paused and waited. "Okay, the silent treatment. I'll take that as a no, for now."

Jennifer left the room shaking her head. 'I can't believe she's so upset with me,' she thought. '*She's* the one who started the whole thing. I tried to leave the room, but no, she blurts out this accusation and locks hold of me like a pit bull and then pretends she's having a heart attack when none of the little monitor gadgets confirms it. So what do I do? Do I pass the vending machines and just keep going, or go back in there and finish what we have started?'

She stood at the vending machines for a minute, pondering what to do. Finally, and with a sigh, she dug some coins out of her purse. If she was going back in there, she was definitely going to load up on caffeine and some of those graham crackers, in the employees-only room. 'Ooh, these are the name brand grahams crackers and look at the small cans of sodas just sitting there waiting to be picked up. Things usually taste better when you sneak them anyway.'

"Hey, Grandma Bee," she said, walking back into the room. "Are you feeling better?" She sat back down in the chair. "I'm sorry for raising my voice, if I did. It's not that important for me to know about my grandfather, because I had Grandpa Sam." She began opening a packet of graham crackers. “He was my grandpa for thirty something years before he passed and you have been my grandmother all of my life. So, all of that stuff I said earlier is irrelevant. I have loved you all of my life because of who you are. I loved you just based on the quality of time spent. I have always told myself that if I had just hint of your grace and knowledge, I’d be halfway there.” Jennifer took a bite of her graham cracker and chewed for a moment before talking again. “Just because I wasn’t always around, didn’t mean you weren’t always in my heart and my thoughts. I think what our problem has been in times past was that there was no connection. We were disconnected in the sense of keeping in touch with each other.”

“Jennifer.”

“Yes, Grandma Bee.”

“Can I get that cup of ice now?”

“Most definitely,” said Jennifer with a smile. “I’ll be right back.” She started for the door. “Did you want me to bring you some crackers as well? Because these I have are mine.”

“No, but I insist you get a couple more for yourself. They seem to have calmed you down to say what was really in your heart.”

Jennifer paused for a moment and thought. Maybe her grandmother was right. “Okay,” she said. “I’ll be right back. I love you Grandma Bee.”

“I love you too Jennifer.”

Once outside the room, Jennifer placed a call on her cell phone. “Hello Nicole, this is Jennifer again. I’m not coming back to the office today. Please, lock my office door and I’ll see you on Monday.”

“Good for you Jennifer. See you on Monday.”

CHAPTER TWENTY-THREE
A BOND LIKE NO OTHER

Christy slid into the chair across from her sister. “Sorry I’m late,” she said. “I had to get the kids all settled in at their grandmothers, and of course I had to visit with her for a while. You know how that can go. So did you order for me, Mekyla?”

“Wasn't sure what you had a craving for today. You have several favorites here at S and J Oyster.”

“Well, what are you having?” she said, opening her menu.

“I’m having their famous gumbo.”

“That sounds good. With some of that good, mouthwatering bread they make from scratch. Actually, add a Caesar Salad to mine.”

They spent most of their lunch talking about Christy’s children, what was going on in the schools, clothes, shopping and traffic. The whole time Mekyla could see there was something else Christy wanted to talk about. Finally, she could wait no longer. "So tell me, what's on your mind Christy?"

"Well, I'm probably just being paranoid, but that's still bothering me. You know, what Jennifer said about the girl in the powder blue cashmere sweater."

"Is that seriously bothering you or just nibbling-on-your-mind bothering you, Christy?"

"I don't know. I'm snapping at Trey for no good reason."

"What are you going to do? How can you ease your mind about something that's just a rumor?"

"I don't know. I can't really just come out and accuse him. Or ask him if he's having an affair with the girl. I mean, there haven't even been any real signs that I can think of."

"Well, Christy, you have just solved your own dilemma. You said there aren't any signs, so don't create any."

"Mekyla, I'm not going to lose my family to anyone."

"I'm sure you won't, Christy. You're a good mother and wife. However, I'm beginning to wonder if this is what's really bothering you. Or are you looking for something that will justify some feelings that you've already been having. You guys have been married for a long time."

"I'm not going to lose my family to anyone."

"I understand, Christy. You already said that. So how is Trey doing?"

"We're supposed to talk this evening about this."

"What do you mean? You just said you hadn't told him?"

"I didn't, but I did have an attitude last night."

"Last night?"

"Yeah, well, it carried over into this morning."

"Christy you need to get yourself together and not let this take over your life."

"Mekyla, did that not bother you at all? Ian does play for the same team."

"Just for a brief moment, it crossed my mind. But then I thought about myself and what I'm doing and not doing. In addition, you have to consider the source, even though a lot of the gossip she digs up does turn out to be true."

"Have you given Ian an answer about moving in with him permanently?"

"Not a complete one, but I do have some of my things over there."

"He seems to be a very good man, Mekyla. Do you still have some major doubts about him?"

"To be honest with you, Christy, I have major doubts about myself as to whether I can commit or not."

"Having the wisdom that I now have the advice I can offer you, that has proven to be true with anyone, is that you should always follow your heart and don't do anything you are not completely ready to do. Otherwise, you're going to open yourself up to regrets, and that will be a total disaster."

"Thank you for that, Mama Christy."

The sisters laughed.

"Will you be coming to the game tomorrow?" said Mekyla.

"Yes, I'll be there. I'm not going to say anything to Trey this evening, but I do need another look at what's going on at the gym."

"So I will see you there, okay?"

"Yes you will. But right now, you need to see what *I'm* seeing."

"What?" said Mekyla, as she turned her head in the direction of Christy's eyes.

"That waiter is so fine. What you think?"

Mekyla rolled her eyes. "There you go flirting and accusing your husband of something you haven't seen him do."

"Girl, this is minor compared to what I know my husband can do. Besides, I'm not going to touch the little dumpling, just look at him. Hey, I get this crap from you; you're a bad influence on me. I'm out of character right now."

"Christy, let's go, actually hold on." Signaling the waiter, "Waiter can you bring over more ice, she's hot."

"Mekyla, you need to stop it."

Mekyla stood up and grabbed her purse. "I'll see you, Christy."

"See you later, sis."

Mekyla turned back to the table where her sister was still sitting. "Christy, you better go out and buy you one of those cashmere sweaters for tomorrow."

"Sure, Mekyla, I will meet you in the check out line."

CHAPTER TWENTY-FOUR
THE MESSAGE

Mekyla sat in her car and called her office from her cell phone. "Hello, Marie, was there any messages for me?"

"Yes, Ian called to see if you were free for lunch, and your mom called to see if you would go by the store and pick her up some items after work."

"Did she say items or item?"

"I'm sure it was items. Because, in fact, I wrote down the list she dictated. You'll find the list is on your desk."

"That's my mom. Are there any policyholder phone calls I need to return?"

"No, I have taken care of everything and your desk is clear of all work except the shopping list."

"Okay, I'll be making a couple of stops on the way back to the office. If I'm not back before you have to leave, just lock up and I'll see you tomorrow. You have my cell if you need me."

"All right, Mekyla. Talk with you later."

CHAPTER TWENTY-FIVE
TILL DEATH DO US PART

When she heard the front door open, Christy looked over her shoulder from her dinner preparations. "Hello Trey," she said, as her husband came into the kitchen. "How was your day at work?"

"The meetings went well today. We submitted the marketing proposal to the company I've been trying to snag for a while now. I believe they're finally ready to negotiate and offer us the contract. I'll be meeting with them again on Monday to hear their final decision."

"That's wonderful, darling."

"Oh, and I invited them to come see me play tomorrow."

"Play what? The basketball game you play?"

"Yes. You say that like it's a kiddy game."

"No, I didn't mean it that way."

"Christy, they know it's something I do to pass time and keep in shape. They realize I'm not going to be playing in the NBA. Besides, I invited them to dinner afterwards."

"What should I wear?"

"No, Christy, it's more like a working dinner. You'd be bored."

"Oh, okay. Are you ready to eat your dinner, Trey?"

"What are we having this evening? Mekyla's special, huh? I want you to sit down and join me, Christy."

"Well, I've already eaten with the kids, but I can have more of that salad."

The invitation to join him was a pretty good indication that he had not forgotten about her attitude that morning. He intended to iron that out now. But Christy couldn't think of how she was going to explain herself at the moment. She needed to think of something else to talk about, and quickly. "Trey, would you like a drink with your dinner?"

"Whatever you're having Christy."

'Whatever *I'm* having?' she thought. He was in a good mood. Maybe he really had forgotten about her attitude.

"The kids spent some time at your parent's house today."

"Oh, yeah?" said Trey. "Mom called and asked you to bring them over?"

"No, I called her and asked if it was okay for the kids to come over for a couple of hours."

"Why? What did you have to do?"

"I went and had lunch with Mekyla."

"You girls had lunch? Where did you go for lunch?"

"We went to S and J Oysters, on South Peoria. I thought about stopping by your office to see if you wanted me to bring you something for lunch, since I was so close. But I got a call from the kids just as I was getting ready to call you. They wanted to know if I would take them to Chucky Cheese for pizza."

"Oh, okay. Were you girls planning any more lunches any time soon?"

"No, that was just a last minute thing."

"Well, you know I don't like surprises, so just call me before you come by my office, okay."

"Sure, Trey."

"Dinner was very good as usual and I know I promised we would talk this evening, but if you don't mind I would like to catch some of the basketball game. The Lakers are playing the San Antonio Spurs tonight."

"Oh, sure," said Christy.

"I promise when I come up to bed we will definitely talk, all right?"

Christy's mind raced as she loaded the dishwasher and put away the food. What did he mean, 'call first?' She'd never called before coming by his office. Maybe he thought she was a fool, but as far as she was concerned, he'd just validated her curiosity. She poked her head into the living room. "Can I get you anything else before I go up?"

"Yes, bring me a Michelob from the freezer, thanks."

She brought him the beer and started out of the room. "I'll be up tucking the kids in."

"Okay, let them know I'll be up in a little bit to give them their kisses."

She turned around and leaned against the doorframe. "Trey, you think you can keep Sunday open for the kids and me? I thought we might go out for dinner and maybe a movie. It's been a while since we went out as a family."

"I don't believe I have anything on my schedule. Remind me on Sunday morning."

"Good. See you when you come up."

CHAPTER TWENTY-SIX
A CONSPIRACY THEORY

Upstairs, Christy placed a phone call. "Mekyla. It's me, Christy."

"Hey Christy, what's up, and why are you whispering?"

"Would you believe this man said for me to call his office ahead of time if I planned on stopping in?"

"Okay, what's wrong with that?"

"I'll tell you what's wrong. I have never had to call ahead of time before, so why is he asking me to do it now? Would you like to know why?"

"I'm sure you're going to tell me, Christy. Please share with me what he was plotting when he told you to be sure and call first."

"Because he's seeing that cashmere sweater wearing, cheating on her own husband and messing up other people's family's woman."

"Wow! That was a mouth full, Christy. Calm down and think about what you are accusing him of with no evidence. Did you piss somebody off in his office playing that wife role?"

"I don't know. So what, if I did?"

"You know this is how marriages can end in divorce unnecessarily."

"Mekyla, I pray to my maker that I'm wrong, but my gut feeling is that he's having some kind of communication with Ms. Cashmere."

"Now Christy, I have never been one to go against the gut feeling, but double check to make sure this time."

"They're having their little basketball game tomorrow afternoon. I definitely count on you being there, because I need to have some type of conversation with this lady."

"You're spacing out. We've already agreed that we're both going to game, but I will not let you make a fool out of yourself, or your husband."

"I won't. A little girl-talk is not going to hurt anyone."

"I'm going to be there, but I'll be running a little late because I have a lunch date. So just sit on your hands until I get there."

"Ian isn't playing tomorrow."

"Yes, he's playing. This is with someone else."

"Say what. Who is this man, please say he's a client Mekyla?"

"You've never met him. He came in from Louisiana to coach a football team here, and he asked me out."

"No! And you just said yes? What about Ian?"

"He'll never know, and I already told this guy that I'm dating someone else."

"Dating? You guys live together! I thought you got that out of your system after Austin, Texas."

"I don't know why I keep acting on these requests made of me. I want to be faithful, but for some reason I still don't feel complete."

"You're going to have to find your way, and stop being so scared to commit. That's all it is. Do you love him?"

"Him, who?"

"Now that's a shame Mekyla, when you have to ask who. I'm talking about Ian."

"I honestly don't know Christy. And you know the sad part is that I know I'm going to have to go through the test of almost losing him before I realize my feelings for him. I don't know if I really know how love will feel when I feel it. All my adult life, the only thing I've been in was lust and strongly liking someone."

"What about Termaine's father, Mekyla?"

"That was definitely puppy love. But it turned into a very strong friendship."

"I guess you can say Trey is my first and only love. Mekyla, do you think it's even possible for a man to have a monogamous relationship with his wife?"

"Of course! There is no doubt in my mind that there are men out there with happy homes, and will never stray."

"Then what are you so afraid of?"

"I'm afraid that I'll be the one whose husband strays. But you know, I can ask you the same question. Why are you being so curious when you know you have a happy home?"

"I'm sure you are right, and I understand where you are trying to take me, but this time, Mekyla, I need to act on my feelings."

"As long as you know that it's not a game. A real decision will have to be made if you were to find what you don't want to see."

"It almost sounds like you're condoning cheating as long as the person never gets caught."

"No, what I'm saying is, are we really ready to deal with what we pray for never to happen? The things we think we most want or most want to know. And do you really want to know something hurtful when you know you're only going to forgive the person who might hurt you? Because if you do learn something like that, it's going to put you all the way out there on the emotional edge. And that's when the thoughts of suicide come into mind."

"Mekyla, you are too deep for me right now."

"No, Christy, the point is that you're not deep enough in your thoughts to understand the consequences of accusing your husband of something. You said it with your own lips. Your family is everything to you."

"They are, Mekyla."

"So my understanding, Christy, is that you will go to great lengths to keep your family, so why dig for something that would possible cause you to lose your family?"

"I don't know. I think the not knowing could be worse than the knowing. And I know what you are going to say. You're going to pull out that old wise man saying that what you don't know won't hurt you. But what that old wise man failed to realize is that the stress of not knowing *will* kill you."

"Well, on that note, Christy, the defense rests. I need to do some writing tonight. I'm starting to get behind."

"Am I in that book of yours, Mekyla?"

"I'm trying to write a bestseller, not a sleeper, Christy. I'm trying to go big-screen, writing about a housewife who sets out to murder her husband because she heard a rumor that there was this lady in a cashmere sweater after her husband. See, now that's some Lifetime channel stuff."

Christy laughed. "You're going to be looking funny if it's true Mekyla?"

"No, you're going to be looking funny, and not 'ha, ha' funny. Love you girl, but I need to do some writing."

"Okay, thanks for listening to me. You're a good friend and sister."

"I know. I hear that a lot. And that's another thing, Christy. Why is it that most people can give good advice, understand it, but never follow it? It was just a thought. And there's no need to answer that question. Love you, bye."

CHAPTER TWENTY-SEVEN
LIFTING MY BURDENS

Mekyla looked at her watch and realized she didn't have time to get immersed in her writing before Jennifer came over, so she decided to cook something for her guest. Twenty minutes later, the women were sitting at the kitchen table.

"The reason why we connect so much is because we're in the same place," said Mekyla.

"What do you mean the same place?"

"You know, somewhere floating beyond the tears."

Jennifer nodded. "Thanks for having me over, Mekyla. I really needed to speak with someone about this. I've been holding it all inside for a long time now. And when we're, we will address your issues, you obviously have."

"I'm all ears, Jennifer, but before we get started would you like to eat while we talk?"

"Yes, I'm starving. What have you got?"

"I made something simple, quick, and filling."

Jennifer smiled. "No need to tell me. When you begin like that, it can't be anything other than your famous spaghetti with ground beef and meat sauce."

"How did you know that?"

"Mekyla, everyone knows that's the only thing you know how to cook well."

"Forget you girl, are you eating or not?"

"You better put me some of that famous spaghetti on a plate."

Mekyla got up from the table and started dishing up her specialty. "So, Jennifer, what's on your heart?"

"There's so much going on with me that I truly don't know where to begin?"

"How about the beginning, I believe we have enough time left in our lives to discuss this."

"Mekyla, do you remember when we worked for the Holiday Inn downtown?"

Mekyla set a plate of spaghetti in front of Jennifer and another at her own place at the table. "Yes, of course I remember that. I could never forget our first jobs."

"You were hired on through your mom and I was hired on through my aunt. Boy did we have fun. We would have our work done by eleven, just in time for *The Young and the Restless*."

Mekyla laughed. "That's right. And do you remember that one guy? I can't remember his name, but you know the one I mean. That guy who was so creepy?"

"No, Mekyla, I don't remember the creepy guy's name."

"But anyway, do you remember when he broke all of the vending machines and gave us the candy and cakes and he took all of the money?"

"Yes I remember that, but you're getting off the point of this conversation."

"Yes, but those were the days Jennifer. Those were the days. And you did ask me if I remembered us working there. And I'm just saying, the answer is, I totally remembered that time. Yeah, working at the Holiday Inn. It was such fun." Mekyla's smile grew even broader as she remembered something else from the old days. "Okay, one more thing, Jennifer. Then we'll get back on the subject. Do you remember when the Bar-Kays and Confunction use to come and stay at the Holiday Inn? Boy, if we only knew what greatness we were in the midst of. We could probably be rich from all the souvenirs we received back then. I still have some of my autographs, what about you?"

"Yes I do, Mekyla. But do you also remember the guy I was dating back then?"

"You're asking me to remember one name out of at least ten guys a year that you dated back then."

"It wasn't quite ten a year, maybe around seven."

"Maybe a dozen, Jennifer, but what's the difference?"

"We were fifteen. I believe that was normal behavior. Anyway, the one I was referring to this particular time was Brent."

"Oh, yeah, I remember the name."

"Okay, where I'm going with this is do you also remember when I suddenly developed the flu for two weeks?"

"Yes, I vaguely remember that."

"Well Mekyla, I didn't have the flu. I had the case of soreness and postpartum syndrome."

Mekyla's fork stopped halfway to her mouth. "What do you mean postpartum syndrome? Doesn't that only occur when you lose a child?"

"Yes Mekyla, that's what happened, I was no longer pregnant."

Mekyla set her fork down with a clank. "Wow, Jennifer! I never knew that. So what happened?"

"Long version made short. This was when we lived out in Turley. Mom worked the graveyard shift and he use to come over every night almost. Well for sure the days she was at work. He was my first, believe it or not, and I was totally in puppy love with him. I used to always bake him chocolate chip cookies." Jennifer smiled at the memory. "Well, this particular evening instead of the usual rug-burning, he touched me in a whole different way."

"Jennifer, before you get past the rug-burning. I just wanted to say, I remembered the rug burning very much. And I remembered when me and this guy I was so into, we use to rug-burn all the time. I was faithful to him, because you know when you made it to that level; it was like you were definitely girlfriend and boyfriend."

"Mekyla, can I finish telling my story, please?"

Mekyla's smile turned to an embarrassed frown. "Sure. I'm sorry, girl. It's just that you're bringing back so many memories. But go ahead Jennifer. I'll be quiet. I promise."

"Okay, where was I?"

"Rug-burning, you were talking about the rug-burning."

"Anyway, he had convinced me to take off my pants, and because I was so into this guy I took them off and he then began to take his off."

"Is this whole thing with your grandmother about your first time? She's still upset with you because of that?"

"Yes and no, but please listen. I need to say this to get to where I want to end up at."

Mekyla nodded and began eating again, slowly, listening intently.

"And so, now that you figured out I was about to embark upon my first sexual experience, I didn't know then, but of course I know now, that that was my cross over from girl to woman."

"I remember my first experience as well. Wasn't that exciting to me. But then again, it may have been because I for sure didn't know what I was doing, and I can't really say if he knew what he was doing." Mekyla laughed, and then stopped abruptly. "Jennifer, why are you looking at me like that?" She put her fingertips on her chest. "Did I make this about me again? I'm sorry. Please continue." She leaned a little over the table. "But, by the way, if you keep scrunching your face up like that it's going to get stuck."

"Mekyla, you are such a goofball. I don't even know why I continue to utter the words of you being my oldest and dearest friend."

Mekyla twirled her fork in her spaghetti. "Because I'm your *only* friend and you think you're in my will. But, Jennifer, please continue with what you wanted to share with me." She took a bite of her food.

"Thank you, Mekyla, for all of your consideration, attention, and kind and comforting words. Okay, so we did the do, and then we did it again, and again, and again. And during one of those 'agains,' I became pregnant with his child. And how I found out that I was pregnant was from that horrible trip to the grocery store when I was run off the road by this man, who I later discovered was stalking me."

"What? What?" As she began to squint with a look of total confusion, Mekyla blurted again. "What happened with this man that caused the loss of your child? And what's this about a car accident? I never knew about that?"

"I didn't have my license yet, but Mom would let me drive, just to the grocery store and on short errands for her. I was like her little errand person. But she would never let me drive to Skateland. How messed up was that? Okay, but this particular time I asked could I drive the car to Wells Grocery store, because for some reason I was dying to have some fruit."

Jennifer paused.

Mekyla gestured with her fork. "And, go on."

"You're going to have to give me a minute with this Mekyla, because this is the first time I've told this story since it happened, other than to the police and my mother at the time it happened. So, like I was saying before, I went to the neighborhood grocery store in Turley. And to this day I don't know why they didn't just call it Tulsa because the only thing that divided the town and the city of Tulsa was 56th Street North. And from 56th Street, Turley was what, a minute long."

"I know Turley, Jennifer, please continue with the story."

"I traveled the back road which was the quickest route to the grocery store. I noticed a dark-skinned man following me around in the store, but I didn't read much into it. Heck, I was only fifteen years old at the time. I didn't have that stalker instinct yet. As I was finishing up at the register, I noticed that it had already become a little dark outside. So I debated about whether to take the same route home, or take the longer route with more lights. As I began to leave the parking lot, I noticed several other cars going the short way back, which was the way I really wanted to go, because it was faster. So, I began to follow them and one by one they either turned off onto side streets or their driveways. So then I was all alone on the road except for one other car that was behind me. You remember how dark some of those back streets in Turley could get."

"I remember," said Mekyla.

"There were hardly any light posts lit up. Some streets there were none at all. The only lights I remember being on the road that night was the headlights on my mom's car and the ones on the car behind me. And all the while, on this deathtrap of a road, I'm telling myself, 'okay you're a third of the way there. Okay, now you're halfway there.' And I kept checking my rearview mirror, and that car was still behind me." Jennifer paused again.

"Yes," said Mekyla. "I'm listening. You can't stop now."

"Okay. Then all of the sudden I looked in the rear view mirror and there were no more headlights behind me. The only thing I could see back there was darkness. But the thing was, I hadn't passed any side roads just before that. The other car couldn't have turned off."

"Wow!" said Mekyla. "That's scary."

"Girl, you don't have to tell me that. I was there."

"So, what happened next?"

"Then there was this bump to my moms little Chevy Nova. That's what we had at the time. You remember? It was a reliable little car. That car got us back and forth from Houston, Texas every year. We have family there, you see."

"Okay, Jennifer, you're now straying away from the story. Please stay focused."

"Oh, sorry. Now you're rubbing off on me. Okay, now where was I? Oh yeah. I was on that dark road. I'm thinking, 'Oh my God! What's going on here?' Then I could see this huge car in my rearview mirror because it was right upon me. I mean pushing me. And it kept pushing me until I lost control. Just before I did, I remember I looked down at the speedometer and I was doing eighty and holding the steering wheel so tight I'm surprised that either it or my fingers didn't break. The next thing I knew, the Nova went flying up an embankment and then flipped and started to roll back down. I lost track of the number of times I flipped, but when I finally came to a stop, I was right-side-up."

Mekyla shook her head. "Girl, I never knew anything like that happened to you, any injuries from that?"

"Well, I collected my thoughts and took stock of my condition; I noticed that the windshield was completely gone. I felt all over my face and arms and when I realized I had no cuts on me, my only thought was to thank him for sparing me."

"I'll say an 'amen' to that," said Mekyla. "And you know I'm not too much of an 'amen-out-loud' kind of person. But go on."

"Then I noticed this person coming toward my mom's car. When I looked again I realized that it was the man who had been in the grocery store."

"Hush your mouth, girl!" Mekyla said, with a crack in her voice.

"So, I went to grab one of my shoes. Clog mule shoes. You know the ones we use to wear, the wooden shoes? They were the best, but they don't make long-lasting shoes like that any more."

"Jennifer! I know about the shoes. Please continue with your story. I need to know what happened next."

"Okay, yes, so, I went to grab one of my shoes and noticed I only had one. I don't know for the life of me why I remember pausing for a moment and saying to myself, where could my other shoe be. Well, when I sat up from getting my shoe in my hand, this man was at my car window. Except the window was gone just like the windshield. I freaked out and took my clog shoe and commenced to hitting this man. I mean I was out of control. Well, he reached in and tried to pull me out of there, so I opened the door and just kept beating him like I was his match in the ring. I have always called that my Jesus strength. And I guess it must be pretty strong, because after a while the man must of gotten tired of fighting with me, so he just got into his car again and drove off."

"So what did you do?"

"I got back in the Nova and spent a long while trying to find my other clog. But I never found it. So I started walking down that dark and lonely road crying a flood of tears with one shoe on. I remember a car stopping and the people in it asking me if I needed a ride. I don't even recall if I looked at them or their car. I just kept looking straight ahead and I kept walking. All I could think of was getting home. I passed a lot of friends as I walked into the neighborhood we lived in. They were all asking me if I was okay. To this day, I couldn't tell you which of my friends they were, and all I remember is looking straight ahead with now dried up tears on my face. When I finally made it home, my mom had already called the police. She'd called the store and spoken with the cashier who told her I'd left the store long ago. My mom took me to the hospital to get me checked out and that's when I discovered I was pregnant."

"So you lost the baby from that accident. I'm really sorry to hear that."

"No, there was something else I believe God felt I needed to learn. When my mother discovered I was pregnant the next thing I knew there was an appointment made for me to have an abortion. I didn't have any say so in the matter. Even though I was young, I still felt a decision like that should have been made between the two parties who created the situation. And not only did my mother force me to get an abortion, she didn't even allow me to share what happened with the father of the unborn child. My mom said, it was something that only she and I were to know. From that day on, I felt differently toward my mom. I felt as though she allowed a piece of me to be removed without my say so. To this day, Mekyla, I still hear the sound of the suctioning of my child from my body. It's something I wouldn't wish on my worst enemy. There were a number of girls there at the time. The room was filled with all this sadness and the comforting that should have come afterwards was definitely not there. Some of the girls didn't even have family there to pick them up."

"Jennifer, I know today you've talked about something you've tucked away for a very long time. Isn't it possible that the experience has had an indirect effect on your life in ways you don't know about?"

"Unfortunately, it doesn't end there, Mekyla."

"What do you mean? The man came back and found you again?"

"No. I became pregnant again a few years later."

"You had to have another abortion, Jennifer?"

"No, not this time."

They heard keys rustling at the door and Mekyla hung her head. "Oh no, Jennifer. Not the door!"

"We can finish another time, Mekyla."

"No, we're going to finish tonight," said Mekyla standing up. "You're not going to leave me hanging like this."

"It's okay, Mekyla. I'll come back tomorrow, if you're not doing anything."

Mekyla sighed. "Oh, all right."

CHAPTER TWENTY-EIGHT
A TIME TO BOND

They could hear the front door open and close, and then Ian walked into the room.

"Hey, baby!" said Mekyla.

"Hello, sweetie. What are you girls doing? More bonding?" He started to turn away, but did a double take. "Mekyla, you look like you've been crying. Is everything alright?"

"Yes, baby, Jennifer and I were just reminiscing."

"Oh, some of that sentimental girl talking stuff, huh?"

"Hello Ian," said Jennifer as she stood up and gathered her purse and keys.

"Hello Jennifer. Are you taking off?"

"Yes, it's been a long day."

"I know what you mean." Ian turned back to Mekyla. "Sweetie did you cook?"

"Yes, I'll have your dinner for you in just a moment."

"Okay, Jennifer, be careful driving home."

"I will Ian."

As Ian walked toward the bedroom to change, Mekyla leaned close to Jennifer. "I can have Ian's dinner on the table within a couple of minutes and we can resume our conversation."

"Let it go Mekyla. I'll see you tomorrow."

Mekyla tilted her head and smiled. "Okay girl. Love you."

"Love you too, Mekyla."

A few minutes later, Ian was sprawled out on the couch, browsing through *TV Guide*. Mekyla finished fixing Ian's plate and set it on the dinning room table.

"Hey, Ian, your dinner is ready."

"Would you bring it to me in here, please, please?"

"No, it's ready for you on the table. Please come in and eat."

Ian groaned as he got up off the couch. He came into the dinning room with a smirk on his face. "What do you think you're doing, house breaking me?"

"I didn't think we shared that same view of it, but yes dear."

"That's very funny Mekyla. Can I get my kiss now that Jennifer is gone?"

"Sure, you could have taken one when she was here." She kissed him briefly on the lips.

"The air seemed really thick when I walked in," said Ian as he sat down. "So what were you girls talking about?"

"Oh, just remembering our teenage years."

Ian took a bite of cornbread and followed it with a forkful of spaghetti. He looked at the piece of cornbread in his left fingers. "This isn't going to be enough. Baby can you grab me more cornbread, please."

"Yes, of course. How does it taste?"

"You know your spaghetti with cornbread is always good. But you're going to have to explore a little more, sweetie. This isn't the only thing I like to eat."

"I know, I know. And I will, Ian."

Mekyla's mother was a simple cook. Mekyla was trying to put a little variety into her menu for Ian's sake, but simple food was all she'd ever known and she knew she was never going to get too fancy. The family tradition seemed to have been broken with Termaine, though. Somehow he'd become a gourmet cook. She loved his cooking, but the sad thing was that she wouldn't eat anything he cooked unless she watched the whole process from beginning to end. As far as she was concerned, there was no telling where his hands or mouth had been unless she kept a close watch on him. She made a mental note to ask Termaine for a couple of his more simple recipes.

"Ian, I'm going to get a couple of hours of writing in. Did you need anything else?"

"No I'm fine, sweetie. Don't stay up to late. You know how I like to feel your body next to mine. It helps me sleep better."

"I won't be too long, Ian."

CHAPTER TWENTY-NINE
DINNER WITH A LITTLE BIT OF CHOCOLATE

Mekyla found Lisa and Jonathan right where she'd left them: in Jonathan's penthouse condo, about to have dinner.

"Lisa, would you mind lighting those two long candles there on the dining room table?"

"No, I don't mind at all," said Lisa. She used the closest thing at hand, one of the long fireplace matches. "Can I help with anything else? So long as it's not anything major, because a sista is now relaxed and enjoying this moment. My husband doesn't cook. If I'm not cooking, then it must be a special occasion or something."

"Well I'm glad I was able to provide a sista with a nice home cooked meal that she sit back and enjoy," said Jonathan, as he settled a steak onto Lisa's plate.

"I'm not complaining about my position at home," Lisa called after him as he hurried back into the kitchen. "It's just that, every now and then, you would like for someone else to do it, you know?"

"I guess you can say I'm the reverse of what we deem the standard order in the household. I would cook all the time. My wife very seldom cooked." Jonathan placed the last dish, which was the seasoned potatoes, on the table.

"Why, she didn't know how?"

"Yes, she knew how. It's just that I love to cook." He held her chair for her then went around the table and took his seat across from her.

"I'm impressed. Do you guys have any children?"

"No, no children. And I really haven't thought about having any at this point in my life."

"Why didn't you have any in the course of the ten years you were married?"

"She didn't want to have any children while she was going through school to get her law degree, and when she finally passed the bar, she was well into her thirties. Then we agreed to wait a little longer until she was with a firm or established in her own practice. As the years passed, I decided I didn't want to have any. So, we made a decision not to."

"Wow, sounds like you guys had it all worked out. So what happened? Why did you break up?"

"One day we realized that we were just good friends and not really in love with each other. We discovered that we had nothing in common. She was oil and I was water, she was night and I was day."

"So why did it take ten years to discover that?"

"It didn't take the whole ten years. We knew it wasn't going to work maybe five years ago, but as time passed, it became convenient. We had accrued a lot of bills together that we wanted to get paid off before we separated."

"I see," said Lisa. "She decided not to take the penthouse?"

"Yes, we discussed it and she decided to purchase something closer to her office."

"And then, I assume, her career took off."

"Exactly. I would say she's doing very well for herself."

"What field of business are you in?"

"I'm an architect."

"You design homes?"

"No, I design commercial buildings."

"So you design the big stuff. That's great! Have you designed any here in Austin?"

"Yes, several. If I can keep you here long enough, I'll take you to see a couple of them, private eye Lisa."

"Oh, I'm sorry. Am I asking too many questions?"

Jonathan laughed. "No, you're fine. I'm just kidding with you to loosen you up a little."

"This food is delicious Jonathan, you cooked my steak just right, and you're going to have to give me the recipe on how you made these potatoes. I don't think I've ever tasted them this way before."

"I learned that little secret from a little old woman down in Mississippi, and a few others. We've covered quite a bit of ground on me. You started to tell me a little bit about yourself earlier, but you stopped. Please continue. Tell me a little bit about Lisa. By the way, what was your last name again?"

"Brazile. Lisa Brazile."

"So, Lisa Brazile, please tell me a little more about you."

"Again, I've been married now for five years, some happily and some okay. My husband is Trevor Brazile. Of course, he's in shipping."

"What type of shipping is he in?"

"Well, let me rephrase that. He's in shipping and receiving. He works for a company called Armin Plastics, back home. He's been with them over fifteen years now."

"So in other words, that was his first job, or pretty close too it."

"Yes, just about. He's a good man. A good wholesome man, who hangs out with the fellows on occasion, does not smoke, but drinks in social settings. He's an only child."

Jonathan looked across the table and raised his eyebrows. "Lisa?"

"Yes."

"I said I wanted to hear about *Lisa* Brazile, not *Trevor* Brazile. Are you avoiding the topic?"

Lisa laughed. "No, I was just giving you both of our histories and just happened to start with his first."

"Uh-huh," said Jonathan.

"Okay, me. You want to know about me. Well, I'm in management for Avis. I oversee agent's who work exclusively with CEOs, chairmen, and presidents of companies.

"That has to be interesting. Do you talk with any of them directly?"

"From time to time I have occasion to visit with them directly. Only in some instances, for some reason, they only want to speak with *top* management. I have no children. Not sure if I can even have any."

"Why is that?"

"My husband and I tried for a couple of years. Nothing happened, and I never went back onto the pill. I still haven't been able to become pregnant. We just let it go, and said if it happens, we will love that child to death."

"I see. And what do you do for fun?"

"I love attending the plays that comes to town. Other than that, and hanging out with my girls for an occasional drink, I'm a homebody."

Jonathan smiled from ear to ear. "That's amazing. I pictured you exactly the way you're describing yourself."

"Oh really, Mr. Stalker Man."

Jonathan gestured at her with his wineglass. "I wasn't stalking you. I was looking for light bulbs."

Lisa finished her last sip of wine. "Well, it's getting late, Mr. Baize. I must return to my hotel."

Jonathan looked over his shoulder at the big window. "But, it's still raining out, and I promise I will not bother you if you stayed over. I have an extra room."

"I don't know. I really should try to make it to the hotel. My husband has probably already left several messages."

Jonathan shrugged. "Call the hotel, get your messages, and return his call. Then we can continue talking. I'm having a good time visiting with you and the night is still young."

"I really don't know. I guess I can call him from my cell phone to let him know I'm okay and that I was just out on the town. Where can I get some privacy?

"Anywhere in this penthouse, you want. I'm going to run down to the front desk and let them know you're a guest of mine."

"Why do you need to check in with them?"

"Your car, I don't want them to tow your car."

Lisa's eyes grew wide. "Of course not, I need my car."

Mekyla relaxed her shoulders and closed her eyes to rest them. She was at a good stopping point. What she really needed right now was a nice long bath with candles. She smiled at the thought. After shutting down the computer she went into the bathroom and started the water in the tub. While it was running, she went into the kitchen and made herself a nice tall glass of iced tea. Then she got down a can of Del Monte sliced pineapples from the cabinet. Now she was really in business.

Armed with the iced tea and the pineapples, she made her way to the bathroom for some quiet soaking and soothing before she had to endure another night of gas aroma therapy in bed next to Ian. 'Speaking of my little stink bomb,' she thought as she passed the bed, 'where did he go.'

She found him in the bathroom. "Hey, what are you doing?"

"I heard the bath water running and I thought maybe you'd like to have a little company."

"Well, I only brought enough pineapples for me to eat."

"I don't need to eat on any pineapples. I would prefer to nibble on you."

"You think we should right now, you know, so close to me just getting back from my trip."

"That's all the more reason why we would need to. I missed you very much, Mekyla."

"I know, and I miss you too, Ian. But."

"But, nothing. I need you, Mekyla. Take this robe off," he said as he pulled Mekyla closer to him. The robe slipped to the floor and he began to lay sweet kisses all over her naked body.

As Ian made his way from the top of Mekyla's spine down the curve of her back, she closed her eyes and began to think of him…how she felt whenever he would hold her body close to him and caress it, as if it was the first time each time. Mekyla gave in to Ian's needs and went to bed without eating her pineapples. They sat neatly stacked in her bowl like pancakes.

CHAPTER THIRTY
BREAKFAST COMBO

"Good morning, baby," said Ian as he wandered into the kitchen, still a little bleary-eyed.

Mekyla was putting away the clean dishes. "Good morning Ian. Did you need any breakfast?"

"Yes. What do you have going there?"

"Nothing yet, but I can put something together for you. Just place your order."

Ian smiled. "I'd like to have more of what I had last night."

"I'm sorry," said Mekyla, tilting her head in mock sympathy. "We're all out of that. Can I get you anything else?" She turned away to finish her cleaning. She was wearing her long T-shirt, and nothing else. It had become her habitual way to dress after making love and before taking her shower.

Ian settled heavily into a chair at the kitchen table. "Ever since you got back from your trip, Mekyla, you've seemed different. Did something happen?"

"Different?" she said, glancing over her shoulder. "How do I seem different?"

"I don't quite know."

"I'm not different. Probably still tired, that's all."

"Okay, I'll give it a few more days before I have to whip you in shape."

Mekyla laughed. "Whatever. What's your combination? Eggs, sausage, and toast, or toast, sausage and eggs?"

"Those were the same three choices."

"I know. That's all we have in the way of breakfast choices."

"Well, I guess I would like to have some eggs, toast and sausage, with a little brown sugar."

She smirked and shook her head. "There you go again. Here's a glass of orange juice Mr. Madden. I shall bring the rest to you."

"Thanks, Mekyla. You're so good to me. I can't imagine ever losing you or that good loving you give to me."

"Where is all of this type of talk coming from?"

"I guess I didn't really realize how much a part of my life you've become, until I missed out on you for those couple of weeks you were gone. What's on your schedule today, Mekyla?"

"Well, I'm going to run a few errands after I shower and put some clothes on. And I may be meeting up with Jennifer around lunchtime to finish talking about what we started last night. After that, there's your game and then I'm here at the house."

"How about going out for a movie and dinner tonight?"

"That sounds like fun. It's been a while since we've gone out for dinner and a movie."

"That's what I was just thinking."

Mekyla brought the skillet to the table and loaded up Ian's plate. "Here's your breakfast fit for a king, Mr. Madden."

"Thanks Mekyla. Aren't you joining me?"

"No, I had a piece of sausage with my tea already. Did you need me to refill your juice?"

"Yes, if you don't mind."

"No, not at all," she said, pouring from the pitcher. "And if you need me for anything else, I'll be in the computer room."

"Yeah, okay," Ian said, as he picked up the remote, switched on the TV and began to scan the channels, ending up on one of the sports channels.

CHAPTER THIRTY-ONE
HIS TODAY, MINES TOMORROW

"Jonathan, you startled me," said Lisa, turning around quickly. "Is everything okay?"

"Yes, I spoke with Trevor and he did call, but everything is okay. He just wanted to say goodnight." She put her cell phone back in her purse. "So, where is that spare room of yours?"

"Right this way, Madam." He gestured formally down the hallway. "But would you like to have another glass of wine, before you retire?"

"Yes, that sounds nice, thank you."

"There are even some strawberries in the refrigerator if you'd like."

Lisa followed him into the kitchen. "Did you pick them yourself, Jonathan?"

"I picked them up from an actual fruit stand right outside of Austin, they have the big ones."

"I love strawberries. They are one of my favorite fruits, especially if they are nice and sweet."

"You're not going to be disappointed with these then, because I tasted them before I left the stand. Actually, you are going to see little bites in all of them, because I made sure that each one was as sweet as the next before I paid for them." He opened the refrigerator door and pulled out a bowl of strawberries.

"You are kidding, right?"

"I don't have to be. I can test each one right now to make sure it's sweet."

"Jonathan, I think I can handle a bad one if I came across it." Lisa bit into one of the strawberries. "Mm, these are good. So where is that bed that's going to keep me warm and cuddly tonight?"

He started down the hall and motioned for her to follow. "It will be this room right here," he said, stopping at the door of a large bedroom.

"This is a guestroom? This looks like it could be the master bedroom. You have wonderful taste, Jonathan."

"Thank you very much, Lisa. Can I get you anything else?"

"No, you've been wonderful. Do I need to use the lock on this door?" She giggled the doorknob.

"Only if you're trying to keep out something; you didn't wish to come in."

She laughed. "Have a good night, Jonathan. I'm glad I ran into you in Wally World."

"I'm glad as well, Lisa. I really had a good time tonight. Moreover, I hope this is the beginning of more to come. Goodnight." He started to turn away.

"Jonathan?"

"Yes, Lisa?"

"Can a girl get some kind of sleepwear?"

"I thought maybe you wanted to sleep in your birthday suit." He winked.

"If you don't mind, can I get one of your T-shirts?"

"I think I can rustle up one of those for you."

"If you can make it one of your largest ones, I would appreciate that even more."

"Mekyla," yelled Ian from the living room.

"Yes," Mekyla said, not trying to cover the frustration in her voice, her hands frozen over the keyboard.

"Can I get you to bring me more of that sausage and orange juice?"

"Ian, are you injured?"

"What?"

"Never mind, I'm coming." Mekyla jumped up from her chair, made her way to the kitchen, and began putting Ian's short order together, all the while trying to hold in her mind the scene she was writing. She hurried into the living room with the plate. "Here you go, Ian. Can I get you anything else?"

"No sweetie, this is plenty."

Mekyla turned back toward the computer room, but by that time, all the momentum she'd built up for Lisa and Jonathan was gone. When she realized she'd lost it, she stopped dead in her tracks, turned to face Ian again. "I'm going to go ahead and get in the shower so that I can get started on those errands I told you about."

"Okay, sweetie."

"No sense going back to the computer," she said under her breath. "My groove is gone."

Ian glanced over at her. "Sweetie, are you talking to me?"

"No, Ian, I was talking to myself."

CHAPTER THIRTY-TWO
WHAT'S IN IT FOR ME

"Good morning, Mom," said Jennifer as she hurried into the kitchen, car keys already in her hand. "I'm headed out to run some errands and then go by and see Grandma Bee at the hospital. Did you need anything?"

Ms Holiday, Jennifer's mom. A very bitter woman by choice,

because she felt she'd always gotten the short end of the stick in her family and marriages. And that Junior was the only person she felt truly loved her.

"Wow!" said her mother with a look of genuine surprise on her face. "You must be in a good mood today. You very seldom ask if I need anything."

"I was just trying to be helpful."

"Well, no thank you, but thanks for asking. And I've been meaning to ask you how your grandmother was doing. Is things looking better for her?"

"She's doing as well as could be expected, seeing as how there's nothing more they can do for her." Jennifer checked her purse to make sure she had everything she needed. "Okay, I'm gone. Bye."

"Bye," said her mom.

"Oh, Mom? By the way, Junior wanted to go up to the hospital later with me. When he gets out of the shower would you have him give me a call on my cell? I'll come back by and pick him up."

"Are you sure that's a good idea, for him to see your grandmother?"

"Mom, yes, I do think it's a good idea. It's just that it's sad, but I think it's time, now, for him to visit her."

CHAPTER THIRTY-THREE
GRAZING THE OTHER GRASS

'Okay,' thought Mekyla. 'Mr. Elliott will be here some time in the next thirty minutes. Okay, why am I, of all people, so nervous? Maybe because I haven't quite lost the Krispie Cream donut butt yet, you think? Whatever, whatever. He's just a coach for a college football team. How nervous is that making me, because that's a very important position. And knowing the company he's kept is probably very firm and athletic. Look at my size ten kangaroo pouch I'm carrying that he will never see until after my nervous breakdown from trying to get rid of it. Stop! I'm just going to be hanging out with him. Because I know I have Ian. What am I doing, have I lost my mind? I can do this. Do what? What I wouldn't want Ian to do. Just because I suspect he does this, does that justify me doing it? Now that's a sorry excuse. I'm just pitiful. A pitiful person that's about to tell my alter ego to shut it up. Oh, I hear him pulling up in that loud truck. You would have thought he would have borrowed something a little quieter.'

For a moment, Mekyla barely breathed. Then she heard the knock at her door. "Yes, one moment please," she said softly. She took a moment to compose herself, the opened the door with a smile. "So I see you found it okay?"

"Yes your directions were very clear, thank you."

"Come in."

Mr. Elliot stepped across the threshold and surveyed the interior of the house. "You have a very nice looking home."

"Thank you."

"But for some reason, I thought it might be more feminine looking."

"Oh, yeah, right. My son lives here with me and sometimes he changes things around without my say so. He's trying to make it like a bachelor pad with me still living here."

Mr. Elliot laughed and nodded at the obvious masculine touches here and there. "Are you ready?"

"Yes."

He stood back and looked her over. "Actually Mekyla, I'd like for you to go in and change into some jeans."

"Why? And that's kind of forward of you to insult me in my face. Couldn't you have waited until the day was over and say it on your drive home? Where is your truck?"

"I decided to ride my motorcycle over today. That's why I thought it might be a good idea for you to change into some jeans."

Mekyla furrowed her brow and looked at him askance. "I don't know, a motorcycle."

"I'll be very careful."

"That's what they all say. And then when once they've got you a mile from home, where you are too lazy to walk back and too embarrassed to call a friend, then the story changes."

Mr. Elliot shook his head. "That's when you're dealing with boys. Please go and change into some jeans."

Mekyla threw up her hands in surrender. "Come in and have a seat and give me a minute, Mr. Elliott."

"I believe we're in a setting where you can call me by my first name now."

"I really like calling you Mr. Elliott, if that's all right with you."

He settled into the couch and mumbled to himself. "You can call me anything you like, so long as you're calling."

A couple of minutes later Mekyla emerged in a pair of jeans. "Okay, I'm ready."

In the driveway, Mr. Elliot mounted the bike and kicked over the engine. "Hop on. We're going for a little spin."

"Can we go somewhere that's not so visible?" said Mekyla, swinging her leg over the seat.

"Of course. I remember you're seeing someone, but this is just lunch time." He toed the shifter down into first, eased on the throttle and let out the clutch.

"A lot can happen around this time of the day Mr. Elliott," said Mekyla, raising her voice over the engine.

Mr. Elliot shifted into second, then third. "I actually like the way you say my name."

"I can't hear you back here. What did you say?"

"I said, I love the way you say my name."

"Me too." As Mekyla leaned forward to whisper in his ear she repositioned her hands so that her thumbs where inside his belt loop. "Mr. Elliott, I'm really enjoying myself. I love the way the wind is blowing through my hair."

"I'm glad you're enjoying yourself, Mekyla. We're almost too where I want us to be."

"I guess I forgot how it felt to ride a motorcycle. I must say, it's a really good feeling."

"I glad you decided to trust me on this one."

"I'm glad as well."

In no time they were pulling up at a place that was very familiar to Mekyla. "Have you been here lately?"

"Mohawk Park has a lot of fond memories for me, Mr. Elliott, but no, I haven't been here in maybe a year or so."

"Here, let me help you off, Mekyla."

"Thank you." She gestured to the compartment Mr. Elliot was reaching into. "What do you have there?"

"I've filled this nice little lunch basket filled with goodies."

"What else do you have in your little side pouches?"

"Go ahead and look in there. You'll see a blanket and some wine."

"Oh my, should you be drinking wine and driving this motorcycle?"

Mr. Elliot began leading the way across the grass to a shady spot. "Yes, I'll be just fine after we take a walk and enjoy the scenery."

"If for some reason I forget to tell you later, I want you to know I'm having a wonderful, time thank you."

"You're very welcome, Mekyla. The pleasure of your company is all mines. I knew we would meet again."

"Oh yeah?"

"Yes, anyone who has teeth prettier than mine is going to give up the secret if it has to take us a lifetime."

"A lifetime is a long and presumptuous time. But it's okay, because I do have room for one more friend in my life."

"Mekyla," said Mr. Elliot finally. "Would you mind if I gave you a kiss?"

"Yes actually, I would. I really don't think I should do that."

"I understand. Please forgive me if I'm rushing you into anything."

"You're not. It's just that I'm not sure of what I'm doing and I don't want to confuse the situation by sealing this afternoon with a kiss. Even though the lips you have been blessed with are remarkably perfect. It's getting kind of late. Can we head back now?"

"Of course," he said. They began gathering up the leftovers and folding the blanket.

"Those were some pretty good subs you put together."

"Thank you, compliments of Subway."

"And the wine was a great choice for that type of sandwich. I know that I've already said it but I would like to say it again. You have been really great and this set up was very well thought out"

"Watch the pipe, Mekyla," said Mr. Elliot, as they got back on the bike. "It might still be a little hot."

CHAPTER THIRTY-FOUR
SHE'S MINE ALWAYS

Mekyla came through the front door and went right into the kitchen. "Hello, Termaine," she said with a smile.

"Hey, Mom. Where were you? Your car was out in the drive and I was looking all over for you?"

"Yes, I came by to pick up a few items earlier and then I ran an errand with a friend."

"Mom, what are you getting ready to get into?"

"I'm getting ready to get into my SUV."

"Ah, come on Moms. Let me use vehicle tonight."

"You have lost your mind, son. And besides not being able to drive my vehicle, how is everything else going?"

"I'm cool, other than really missing my daughter."

"I know you do son. Do you think it will help if I called her mom? And until you realize what you're going to have to do, you'll always be singing that same tune. You need to focus on getting yourself together before you can prove yourself to your daughter. Starting with cutting that hair of yours." She grabbed a handful of Termaine's hair.

"No, Mom, the hair stays."

"What are you trying to prove with all that hair on your head? You look as though you're trapped in the seventies?"

"It looks good this way."

"Schonda told me about when you guys were riding in the car and your hair was all in the wind. And she said when the wind settled down you hair didn't. It just stayed in the same position, like the wind was still blowing it. Now that's bad, son."

Termaine put his hands over his face and laughed. "I can't believe she told you that, but that was kinda crazy though."

"Mm hmm," said Mekyla.

"But getting back to what you were saying. Why do I have to prove myself? Here I am, a father that's trying to spend time with his daughter and she blocks it. They want us to be deadbeat dads."

"No, they're just raising the bar, baby. Young women these days are now fed the wrong message from their mothers who had it hard, who never received any help from their children's fathers. Whether it's so or not, they have these phrases pounded into them, like 'deadbeat dads,' or 'take them to court.' Their mother's tell them that that's the only way they're going to get anything out of them. Make them suffer whether they are good fathers or not. They want you to give up, which to me is very silly. If you would just take my advice, and get yourself together, you'll do all right. Keep a job and keep your hair cut, keep your eye on your daughter and don't give up. Then you'll prevail."

Termaine smiled and crossed his arms over his chest. "Thanks, I really needed that talk."

"You're welcome, babe."

"How long are you going to be here?"

"Just for a few more minutes. I'm meeting my girlfriend at Ian's house in just a little bit."

"Oh, okay. Well, I'm going to hit a few corners, and then stop by Grandmas."

"I need to get by there to see Mama myself, but not right now. You pretty much have to take sleeping gear over when going to see Mom."

"She doesn't do me like that."

"I know, because you always have your hand out."

"Love you, and have a nice day."

"I will, son. Love you too."

CHAPTER THIRTY-FIVE
AN UNFINISHED TALK

As Mekyla began to dial Jennifer's cell phone number, she shook her head in amazement at the way that her son had redecorated their house. "Hey, Jennifer, this is Mekyla. Would you like get together in about an hour to finish our conversation?"

"I'm on my way to the hospital for a few minutes and then I'll be right over, okay?"

"Okay, well take your time with that. I'll be at Ian's until his game starts around six. And it's what, twelve-twenty now, so we have plenty of time."

"Well, look for me no later than two o'clock," Jennifer said as she honked her horn at the car in front of her going slow in the passing lane.

"Jennifer, what are you doing? Do we need to get off of your cell phone, before you cause someone to wreck?"

"Yes, let's hang up so I can free this hand to give her the bird."

"Jennifer, some things just never change. I'll see you later, and tell your grandmother I said hello."

"I will. Talk to you later, Mekyla. Bye" 'You really shouldn't be driving Miss Missy.'

CHAPTER THIRTY-SIX
UNTIL CONTROL DO US PART

As soon as Jennifer passed the slow poke in the passing lane, she dialed a number on her cell phone. "Hello, Mom, may I speak with Junior?"

"I took him over to the house of one of his friend's."

"What do you mean? He was supposed to go with me to the hospital. Did he say he didn't want to go? Did you remind him I was coming back for him?"

"No, I didn't, Jennifer. I just don't think it's a good idea right now."

"What do you mean right now? Right now is all we have? Mama, my grandmother is dying, and its bad enough she didn't get to spend more time under different circumstances. But, this is her last opportunity to talk with Junior. I don't have time for this right now Mom. I'll just take him tomorrow. Goodbye."

'I can't believe her,' Jennifer thought as she made her way toward the hospital. 'What am I saying? Yes I can. This is what she does. She runs things. It's definitely time for me to get out of that house, and next week won't be soon enough. Just as soon as I get back from Louisiana I'm going to find me and Junior a place to stay.'

CHAPTER THIRTY-SEVEN
A PROMISE TO FORGET

"Hey Sweetie," said Christy. "I'm going to run to the grocery store to pick up a few items. Did you need anything in particular?"

"Yes," said Trey, relaxing on the couch. "Grab me more Michelob Light, and do we have any pork chops in the freezer? If not, grab some. I'd like to have those for dinner on Sunday."

"Sure darling. I was hoping you hadn't made plans for tomorrow. The kids and I really do miss you. They're taking their naps right now, and I shouldn't be long, okay?"

"And Christ, we'll have that talk I promised you when you get back."

"It can wait. Maybe after your game tonight, okay?"

"Sure, that's fine with me."

CHAPTER THIRTY-EIGHT
MORE HUMBLE PIE

Jennifer walked into her grandmother's hospital room with a smile on her face, trying to be as cheerful as she could. "Grandma Bee, how are you feeling?"

"I'm real tired, Jennifer. What do you have there?"

"It's a camera. I wanted to take some pictures of me and you."

"My hair is a mess, Jennifer not now."

"You look good to me. I'm going to grab one of these nurses to take our picture. I'll be right back."

A moment later, Jennifer was back with a nurse in tow. She handed the camera to the nurse and leaned down to be close to her grandmother. "Okay, smile for me Grandma Bee."

The nursed snapped the picture and handed the camera back to Jennifer.

"Thank you, nurse, for taking this picture for us."

"Happy to do it," said the nurse with a smile.

Jennifer sat in the chair by the bed and looked at Grandma Bee. "I had a surprise for you, but he got out of pocket."

"What was it, Jennifer?"

"Junior was supposed to be here with me right now, but he got hung up with something else. But I will definitely bring him by here tomorrow."

"That would be very nice of you Jennifer."

"Grandma Bee, would you like some ice and some of those fresh and crispy graham crackers?"

"I would love to see you eat some of those graham crackers. They seem to bring the little girl out of you."

Jennifer stood from her chair. "Coming right up, Grandma Bee. I'll be back before you can shake two sticks together."

"I love you Jennifer."

Caught off guard, Jennifer paused and turned slowly and said, "I love you too, Grandma Bee."

Jennifer wandered down the hall to the vending machines, ducked into the nurses' only room and grabbed more of the graham crackers and some ice. She guessed Grandma Bee was right; maybe they did take her back to her childhood. As she made her way back to the room she noticed a flurry of activity by the nurses. They were running down the hall. Jennifer furrowed her brow. It was sad to think that someone in the hospital might be saying their final goodbyes. She just wanted to block those kinds of thoughts out now. She just wanted to sit with Grandma Bee and eat some graham crackers and feel like a little girl again.

But as she proceeded down the hall, she realized all the activity by the medical staff was very close to Grandma Bee's room. She picked up her pace a little, and then broke into a jog. The nurses weren't *close* to Grandma Bee's room. They were *in* her room. Jennifer sprinted the last several yards down the hall.

"Hey, what's going on?" she said.

A nurse blocked the door. "I'm sorry, ma'am, but you are going to have to wait right here."

"But that's my grandmother in there. Is everything all right?"

"No, ma'am, I'm sorry."

"But I was just here. How did this happen?" Jennifer began to cry uncontrollably. "She didn't even get a chance to see Junior. I didn't even get a chance to say goodbye."

"Ma'am," said a nurse, putting a hand on Jennifer's shoulder. "Is there someone I can call for you, someone who can come up here to be with you?"

"Thank you, but I'll call my dad. He should be told." Still in disbelief, Jennifer dialed her father's number. "Hey, Dad, this is Jennifer. I'm here at the hospital and we have just loss Grandma Bee. Why weren't you here? The disconnection is never ending with this family. I'm sorry, Dad, but I need to be alone okay, talk to you later."

CHAPTER THIRTY-NINE
UNFULFILLED CLOSURE

Jennifer placed a couple more calls, and then she dialed Mekyla's number. "Mekyla, this is Jennifer," she said. "My grandmother, she just passed away."

"Oh, I'm sorry to hear that Jennifer. Are you going to be okay?"

"Yes, but I was wondering if it would be all right if I stopped by right now instead of later."

"You know we can do this another time."

"If it's alright with you, I would rather talk now."

"Sure. I'm here at the house. Come on."

"Thanks, Mekyla."

"I'll see you in a few minutes."

"Mekyla?"

"Yes, I'm still here Jennifer."

"I don't quite know how to sort out the feelings that I'm having. I'm confused, because even though she was my grandmother, I never really had the chance to bond with her, you know? Whenever I tried to get to know her intimately, she would put a wall up. And when I tried to understand my feelings for her I became confused. It's funny, but whenever I was around her, we would laugh and joke about anything and everything. She was a person I knew as my grandmother but a stranger at the same time. I often wished that I could become closer to her but I just didn't know how to do that. Not with her. And now it's too late."

"I understand," said Mekyla.

"I guess you could say we were two peas, but in two different pods. Because the more I think about how she was, the more I see our similarities. When I returned to my grandmother's room to discover that she had passed, I can't really explain what I felt. But I know that if we're not careful, we will only think about ourselves and not the other folks that are also being affected by this as well. I called my mom to give her the bad news and she didn't ask what happened. And I didn't quite understand her response to me, so I just sat there in my car and didn't say too much of anything. Then I went on to say that she passed away without any pain just a few minutes after speaking with me. She said to me, 'well, that's sad that she died.' I try not to be so critical of people, but my family is full of the 'what about me?' attitude. I even find myself being the same way. I sometimes notice that I've taken the focus away from the real situation and started to feel sorry for myself. So now I want to stop and think and remind myself that it's not always about me."

"I know how that can happen, I'm even guilty of doing that same act," Said Mekyla.

"And the other sad part is that she didn't get a chance to really know Junior."

"Jennifer would you like for me to come to where you are?"

"No, but thanks Mekyla. I'm going to be all right and I'll be over to your house in a little bit."

CHAPTER FORTY
A CONVENIENT EXCUSE

"Hey, baby, Jennifer is on her way over here. Would you mind if we visited for a while? She just lost her grandmother and she really needs to talk to someone."

"Oh, I'm sorry to hear that," said Ian. "You go ahead and visit with her. That's not a problem. I was going to head over to one of the fellow's houses anyway to watch ESPN. I'm going straight to the basketball game after that. Call my cell phone if you need me, okay?"

"I will, baby, and have a nice day and a good game. Bye."

"You think we have time for a quickie?"

"No, Ian, she's really close by, okay?"

"Mekyla, are we okay?"

"Yes, we're fine. I just need some time, okay? You know the pressure of this book and my friend losing a family member-I'm just overwhelmed right now, Ian, and it has nothing to do with us."

They both heard the car pull up in the driveway. Ian nodded thoughtfully.

"I need this time with Jennifer," said Mekyla. "You go ahead on and I'll see you later, okay?"

"Alright, I understand." As he opened the door, Jennifer was on the verge of knocking. "Hello Jennifer," said Ian. "I'm really sorry to hear about your grandmother."

"Thank you for that, Ian. Are you heading out?"

"Yes, I'm going over to my buddy's house to watch the game."

"Well if I don't get a chance to see you before the game tonight, I wish you guys luck."

"Thanks, Jennifer." He turned to Mekyla. "I'll see you tonight baby, okay?"

"Okay, Ian. Bye."

CHAPTER FORTY-ONE
A CLOSET FULL OF MESS

"Jennifer, come on in and sit down," said Mekyla, leading the way to the living room. "Anything to drink?"

"Do you have any kind of juice?"

"I have some grape juice in there. Would that be okay?"

Jennifer settled into the couch. "That's perfect."

Mekyla poured two glasses of cold grape juice and returned to the living room with the drinks and coasters. "So where were we?" she said, taking the other end of the couch and turning sideways.

"Okay, I believe I finished telling you about the car accident, yes?"

"Yes you did. You were in the process of telling me about the other abortion."

"I told you about the other abortion?"

"You were about to. The last thing you said was that you got pregnant again."

"Oh, that abortion, yes, but let's back up some. I remember telling you that I became pregnant again a few years later. I did consider an abortion, but this time, I hid it so long from my mom that it would have been too dangerous."

"So you had the kid and gave it up for adoption?"

"No, not quite, but yes, I had the kid."

"What do you mean not quite? Where is this kid now, and who is the father?"

Jennifer held up her hands, exasperated. "You're way too excited for me right now. Please let me tell the story."

Mekyla bit her finger. "Sorry. Go ahead."

"My mother found out that I became pregnant again, while in my last year of high school. It was too late to abort, so she sent me away to a boarding school for pregnant young women in Texas. I stayed there until it was time to have the baby and someone did adopt my child."

"So you did give your child up. That's what I said earlier."

"Yes, I know that's what you said earlier. Can I continue?" Jennifer took a deep breath. "When I had my child, a son, my mother came down to finalize all of the paper work, but when she saw her grandchild, she couldn't let go."

"So what happened?"

"She allowed me to keep him."

Mekyla shook her head. "Okay, I'm right here, and I'm still lost. Please either talk slower or talk faster."

"I was allowed to watch my son grow, but unable to tell him who I really was."

Mekyla slumped back, mouth open. “Junior! You’re talking about Junior, aren’t you?”

“My mother adopted my son while we were in Texas and told me that, if I wanted to be a part of his life, I had to understand my place in his life, and that was to be his sister, to save her face. So I have Junior in my life, but as my brother. Even though I had a full academic scholarship that one could be very proud of, which sounds like it can have a happy ending, right? You know, me going college and all. Eight months into school, Mom pulls me out, saying that I had to come home and take care of my own child. I was devastated, not at the fact that I had to keep my son, but at the timing of her request. No stability or guidance in my life. I’m just out there confused.”

“Your mother is mean,” said Mekyla with a scowl. “Dang! That’s why I never go around her. I always knew there was something I didn’t like about her.”

“Well if you think you’re wound up now, wait till you hear the next part.”

“What can possibly be worse than what I’ve heard so far?”

“There were a few more weeks of school left before that semester ended. But before leaving college I got pregnant again, but this time it was by a guy I was dating there in college. He was a football player. I know you're probably thinking to yourself, ‘Wow, three pregnancies before the age of twenty-one.”

“You know, I’m a little speechless right now. I’m still sorta stuck at the stuff about Junior, really, but I’m doing my best to keep up.”

“You know what?” said Jennifer, gazing out across the room. “Until this very moment I don't think I've ever really looked at myself that way. You know, getting pregnant three times before turning twenty-one?”

“Jennifer, you don’t have to continue if you don’t want to. Because I know this is very difficult for you to share. Have you ever thought about seeing a psychiatrist, because, right now you are dealing with a lot of stuff.”

“No. I’m not saying that I don’t have issues that probably warrant the attention of a specialist. It’s that I just can’t afford to have them addressed by someone who has a certificate hanging on the wall that will take my whole check to see.”

“Well, you sure had a lot happen to you in your past. And I know the death of your grandmother is something you’re going to have to deal with. Is there anything else in your present that’s depressing you or stressing you out?”

Jennifer scoffed. “Not at all. Unless you’re referring to my regular monthly stress about bills, or my everyday stress about whatever might be happening at any particular moment, or the weekly stress I put myself through at my job, generally things I wanted to accomplish that week that I couldn’t resolve by Friday afternoon, or stress about my family. And then there's the stress I feel about my living situation.”

“I’m sure a lot of that can be resolved when, and if, you move out of your mom's place, don't you think? All that other stress is just normal stress, to me."

"But, I would like to continue Mekyla. I need to continue."

Mekyla spread her hands. "Sure. I'm here for you."

"I remember me and a couple of college friends going to the college nurse. I don't really remember how I felt about this child growing in me, other than that I knew somehow that if my mom found out, she would want to have it aborted to, if she found out in time. My mother's main goal in life seemed to be making sure we didn't reproduce too early. I guess she didn't want what happened to her to happen to us. I remember her always giving us speeches about how we must have all of our children by the same father.

"I think a lot of girls got those speeches."

"Yeah, but in my case, I'm not sure whether she was trying to protect *my* best interests, or hers. That's something that I'll never know for sure. And, I mean, there's a distinction to be made between the advice you give your children and the requirements you place on them. I don't believe my mother could make that distinction."

"I understand," said Mekyla.

"I was now more than twelve weeks pregnant, and trying to keep it from my mom until it was too late for the procedure. Then she'd have to accept that child. But when she found out and realized it was too late, she made some phone calls and arranged for me to travel to a city in another state that would do the procedure anyway. I remember hearing her talking about it on the phone and saying that she knew there would be a higher risk at this point, but she was still adamant about aborting my child."

Mekyla just shook her head in sympathy.

"As I lay there preparing to have this child suctioned out of me, I was remembering the sound of the same procedure on my first child. I began to cry a stream of tears, because at that point all I could think of was that this was something I would never forgive her for. Not this time. The suctioning was even louder and much more painful that time, and the sound has haunted me ever since. This one hurt me mentally a little more than the other one, only because in my mind I felt it to be more than just an egg. It was my child. Not to say that my first abortion was less important, but this time it was more emotional. I guess I was a little older. And there were other people very much involved who wanted to keep it. I recall the father of the father of this child, begging my mother not to go through with it. He said they would take care of the child themselves. I remember the emphatic sound of my mother's voice when she told them no. There was no compromise in her tone at all. I still keep in touch with the family of the man who was the father. And he understood what I was going through at the time and was always there for me."

There was a pause in the conversation. The room was quiet for a minute. Then Mekyla broke the silence. "Do you still think about 'what-ifs,' Jennifer? As in 'what-if' you were able to have those children?"

"Of course. I've thought about it almost every day of my life all these years. You begin to wonder what the message was that you were supposed to receive from that. You question why God allowed you to get pregnant only to let the child be taken from you. You cry every so often when you began to discover just a little more of what God was trying to teach you. And you feel sad. Believe it or not, after a while, you stop blaming everyone else and look at yourself. But at the time, I blamed everybody *but* me. And I was so confused. When I went home from school around Christmas, it was like I died inside. I felt as though a big piece of happiness that I found in college was taken away from me. And since I couldn't afford to transfer and pay my own schooling, I just got a job and have been at my moms house ever since, because she said that if I wanted to see my son grow, I would have to live with her."

"Wow!" said Mekyla. "So all this upwelling came from your contact with your grandmother?"

Jennifer nodded. When she said, stop the cycle. The thing I was hoping my grandmother would do first was to forgive me, and then give me some advice on how to present this to my son and my mother without causing everyone to be upset with me. But now she's gone."

"What about your father, Jennifer? He never knew the situation with Junior being your son?"

"Yes, I believe he knew. It's just that he didn't want to get involved. He thought, if he did, then he would have to help provide for him, because the father was in Louisiana playing football for Louisiana State. I suppose I'm just grateful she allowed me to keep my son and be a part of his life."

"Do you hear what you are saying?"

"Yes, and I also realize that it's time to make all those wrongs right. But first, I need to go and talk with his father and let him know that he has a son here. Then I need to tell Junior."

"Okay, that's a good plan," said Mekyla. "I want to tell you, Jennifer, that I'm very proud of you for not losing it with your mom. It sounds as though you've maintained a level head about all of this. And a minute ago-when I said there was a reason I didn't like your mom? I didn't mean any disrespect. Please accept my apology."

"Of course. I know you didn't mean anything by what you said. It was just your reaction to what you were hearing for the first time."

Mekyla shook her head. "And with all of that, you now have to bury your grandmother. Do you need any help with those arrangements?"

"I'm sure Dad is going to handle everything, but you just being there would be a big support to me."

"I will be," said Mekyla.

"Thank you, for everything. I'm going to head out. I need to pack for my trip tomorrow."

They both stood. "Okay, girl. You know that my door is always open for you."

"I know, and I appreciate it more than you will probably ever know."

"Jennifer, come give me one of those big bear hugs."

"Love you, girl."

"Love you too, Mekyla."

CHAPTER FORTY-TWO
STRAWBERRY DELIGHT

Exhausted as she was from dealing with Jennifer's emotional outpouring, Mekyla knew she needed to get some writing done if she was going to meet the deadlines she'd set for herself. She looked at her watch and realized she could squeeze in a couple of hours before she had to leave for Ian's game. If there was ever a game she could miss, this wasn't it. There was no telling what Christy might get into if Mekyla wasn't there to keep an eye on her. If she was going to be honest with herself, she had to admit that she was curious about how that whole situation was going to unfold. She hoped her sister was wrong for her sake.

Settled in at the computer, Mekyla cleared her mind of her own life and brought Lisa into focus. Jonathan was bringing her a T-shirt. And then what?

"Thank you Jonathan," said Lisa as her handed her the T-shirt. "Would you mind pulling the door to on your way out, please?"

"Sure," said Jonathan. "Sweet dreams."

'Okay,' thought Lisa. 'Now which one is the bathroom and which one is the closet? Well, there are only two doors, Lisa. Try them both. He's not going to think you're snooping.' She tried the door on the left. 'Here we go. This is a very nice bathroom. I love the color choice. I wonder what his defect really is.' She let her clothes fall to the floor and stepped into the shower. 'Because, a woman doesn't just give up this type of man,' She turned on the water and adjusted the showerhead to pulse. 'Ooh, this feels good; the way the shower is messaging my body.' She thought she heard something outside the bathroom door. "Did I hear the door?" she said out loud. "Jonathan, what are you doing in here?"

"I couldn't stay away, Lisa, I heard you in the shower and I just couldn't stay away. If you want me to leave please just say so. If you would like me to stay, don't say a word. I don't want to do anything, I just want to lay next to you tonight I promise I won't force you to do anything you don't want to do."

Lisa was surprised at her own silence. She began to extend her arm out to Jonathan and pull him into the shower with her. With one hand, Jonathan took the soap sponge and began to wash Lisa's body. With the other he started squeezing and caressing her. As Lisa leaned up against the wall of the shower, she did begin to speak, but only words of consent. Jonathan rinsed the soap from Lisa's skin and picked her up. He carried her to the bedroom, still dripping wet from the shower. He opened the window to let in the scent of the fresh, damp, night air. Nora Jones was playing in the background and two fresh glasses of wine stood on the bedside table next to a bowl of strawberries. Laying Lisa down on the bed, Jonathan began to slowly feed the strawberries by hand. After biting into a strawberry, Lisa sucked the juice from each one of Jonathan's fingers.

"Jonathan, what are we doing?" Lisa said in a soft voice, as she stared into his eyes.

"We're making each other feel good right now. All you have to do is say stop and I will, but please don't."

As Jonathan messaged Lisa body, he reached over and took the bowl of strawberries from the bedside table. In the bottom of the bowl was a thick, sweet juice formed from the natural juices and the sugar Jonathan had added. Jonathan tilted Lisa's head back and poured a little of the juice onto her mouth. He set the bowl aside, bent down and began to lay his soft, careful kisses upon her neck. Slowly, he worked his way down to the center of her body. Then, wrapping one arm around her, he lifted her limp body. With his free hand he poured more juice on her skin. After kissing the strawberry juice off of her, Jonathan began to savor the taste of her body's on juice as he explored the rest of her body with his hands. Lisa's body quivered as if she were a virgin. She began to call out his name in a whisper. And then she made one simple request: "Please don't stop."

Again Jonathan took the bowl from the bedside table. He poured more of the juice very slowly into her belly button, then down her right thigh to her foot. Jonathan began to taste her toes one by one. Raindrops tapped at the window and a cool breeze filled the room with the smell of fresh air that mixed with the sweet scents of Lisa's on body perfume. Lisa's reaction to Jonathan's caresses and kisses became more and more intense. Her body began to twitch and tremble. Jonathan made his way, now, back up her left thigh, then made a pit stop at the center of her body to give Lisa pleasure in every fiber of . . ..

"Mekyla!"

Mekyla jumped at the sound of Ian's voice, booming, so it seemed, out of nowhere.

"Yes," she said in reflex, spinning around.

"Baby, you didn't hear me come in?"

"No. I sure didn't. I guess I was a little preoccupied."

"With what?"

Mekyla shrugged. "I was just daydreaming about strawberries."

"Hmm. Well, I'm going to lie down for a while, wake me around five o'clock, okay?"

"Okay." She watched him leave the room. 'That man must have gone to school on the short bus,' she thought. 'Why can't I get any peace in a house with no children?' She caught her breath and felt her heart begin to calm down. But she wasn't sure whether her pulse had been quickened only by the startling interruption, or by what she'd been writing.

It had been an intense session at the keyboard, to say the least. Mekyla got up from her chair, feeling a sudden need for some iced tea.

'I wonder what Christy is doing,' she thought, making her way to the kitchen. 'I better give her a call to confirm that she's still going to the game.'

"Hello," said the man's voice after Mekyla dialed Christy's number.

"Hello, Trey. I very seldom hear your voice on the phone. Is Christy around?"

"Yes, let me get her for you. But, hey, Mekyla?"

"Yes?"

"Would you tell Ian to bring my bag that I left in his car the other day?"

"Sure, Trey. He's in there sleeping, but I'll tell him when he wakes up."

"Thanks. Hold the line Christy its Mekyla."

"Hey what's going on Mekyla?"

"I was just checking to make sure you were still going to the game tonight."

"I wouldn't miss it for the world."

"Well, okay. Ian's taking a nap, and I think I'm going to go and lay down as well. I'm feeling a little tired myself."

"Okay, well then I'll see you tonight, Mekyla."

"Okay, Christy. Love ya."

"Love you too, Mekyla. Bye."

CHAPTER FORTY-THREE
A MARRIAGE OF ONE

"Trey, darling, what are you doing?" said Christy as she stood in the doorway of the living room.

"Just relaxing before this game tonight." Trey was lying on the couch watching TV.

"It's been a long time since we've made love. The kids are down for their naps and I was wondering if you would come upstairs and make love to me."

"Not right now, Christy. Maybe tonight, okay? I don't want to be tired for the game."

"It's not some kind of professional game, Trey. I'm your wife, and I have needs that you haven't been satisfying for a long time now."

"Don't start with me right now, Christy. If you would listen, I said tonight, okay?"

Christy bit her lower lip and looked out across the living room, as a single tear rolled down her cheek.

"Now, don't start with that crying. Come over here and sit next to me." Trey swung his legs off the couch and sat up. Christy sat beside him. "I love you very much, Christy, and you are the mother of my children. I'm just asking for a little space. I need a little space, that's all. Why don't you find something to do-a hobby or something? You seem as though you just live for me and the kids. Isn't there anything you like to do other than taking care of your family? Let me miss you sometimes."

"Whenever I do go out and do something, you question it."

"Like what, Christy?"

"Like when I went to lunch with Mekyla, you made me feel as though I had abandoned our children to your parents."

"I just would like to know where it is you're going, just in case of whatever, that's all. Like this evening you don't have to come to the game if you don't want to. I know that you don't really like coming to the games, and like I said, I'm going to have a business dinner right after the game."

"No, I would like to be there. I want to be at this game."

"Okay, Christy. Come if you want. But for now, if you don't mind, I'm going to get back off into this game."

"Sure, Trey." Christy said, as she stood up and walked away. She hadn't thought it would be possible to end up lonely in her marriage. She was at her peak and her husband was missing it. 'Go out and get a hobby, huh?' she thought. 'See, this is how affairs of women begin, I'm sure.'

CHAPTER FORTY-FOUR
STRAWBERRY DREAMS

Mekyla reached over to turn off the alarm. She stretched, and then nudged Ian. "Ian, Mr. Gas Man, wake up. It's five o'clock."

"Hey, baby, when did you crawl into bed?"

"I came to bed about halfway into your symphony."

"Why don't you turn over?"

"You were turned over."

"Why don't *you* turn over now?"

"What?"

"I want you to turn over, is what I want you to do, Mekyla."

"What are you doing, Ian?"

"I'm getting ready to make love to my favorite girl. Turn around and back it up to me."

"What about the game, Ian?"

"What about the game. I'm not getting paid to play on this team. They can wait."

Mekyla began to 'back it up,' As Ian said, while she pulled the covers over both of their heads.

"Hey Ian, do you have a bowl of strawberries with some syrupy juice in it?" A whisper from under the covers said.

"What?"

"Never mind. Continue with what you're doing." As the phone rang, Mekyla ripped the covers back down from her face. "Oh no! The phone is ringing, Ian."

"Let it ring, Mekyla. We're in the middle of something good."

"I know sweetie, but you need to get up anyway." She reached for the phone. "Hello."

"Hello, Mekyla, I forgot to ask if I could borrow that one carryon of yours."

"Sure, Jennifer. Ian, stop it."

"What, said the person on the other line.

"I was talking to Ian, Jennifer. When did you want to pick it up?"

"I can swing by this evening or in the morning."

"How about tomorrow morning, okay?"

"Sounds like a plan to me. And I hear something else that sounds like a plan."

"What's that?"

"Sounds like you're getting some toe curling in over there."

"Goodbye, Jennifer." Mekyla hung up the phone and swung her legs out of bed. "Ian I'm going to start you a shower, okay?"

"Mekyla, do you still love me?"

Mekyla looked over her shoulder as she stood up from the bed. "What kind of crazy question is that?"

"A question you're trying to avoid, it sound like."

"Of course I love you, Ian." Mekyla hurried across to the bathroom to start Ian's shower.

"It's just that something's different about you," Ian called after her. "And I can't quit put my finger on it."

"There you go with that 'different' stuff again." Mekyla said, trying to drown the conversation out with the running water for the shower.

"You never did tell me how your trip went," said Ian, raising his voice. "You were gone for a week. Did you meet someone?"

"Of course. It was a convention. I met a lot of people."

"Don't play dumb with me, Mekyla. Did you meet someone who caught your interest in a different way? Now, you know we can talk about anything."

"It was nothing, I went out to dinner a couple of times with this guy, but it was definitely nothing."

"Why would you go out to dinner with another man, when you have me? You were only gone for a week."

Mekyla turned from the shower and stood in the doorway, looking at Ian. "It was just dinner, nothing else. I had been there for four days and wanted to see more of the city. I just ran into him at a nightclub, and we had dinner, that's all."

"I don't know if I like that, Mekyla. I don't want any other men touching what I have. You understand? You belong to me."

"Ian, you're scaring me." Mekyla moved closer to Ian to calm him down. She felt a little scared on one hand, but protected on the other.

"Then you know that I'm serious. And don't think this is some form of insecurity. I'm not insecure, but I'm very serious. Don't confuse the two."

"Come on Ian, let's get in the shower, okay? It was nothing and it won't happen again."

CHAPTER FORTY-FIVE
MY TURF MY RULES

Christy stood at the bottom of the bleachers looking around. It seemed like she was always the first to arrive at the games. She scanned the gym for Mekyla.

"Christy," said a voice behind her.

She turned around. "Hello, Jennifer. I didn't know you were coming to the game." They began to climb the stairs into the bleachers.

Jennifer shrugged. "I always come to the game. Is Mekyla coming? I forgot to ask her."

"Yes, she's going to be here."

"Who were you looking around for just now, Christy? Cashmere isn't here yet, if that's who it was."

"You're a piece of work, Jennifer, do you know that?"

Jennifer smiled as she looked a few steps down. "I have just been saved by Mekyla."

"What are you talking about, Jennifer?" said Mekyla climbing the last couple of steps.

"Christy was just telling me that I was the best piece of art she's seen yet."

"Hey Christy, have you been here long?"

"No, I just got here."

"Have you seen her?"

"Oh, so you were looking for Ms. Cashmere."

"No, our Girl Scout here says she hasn't seen her, and if she hasn't seen her, she's not here. Trey is supposed to meet a couple of clients here tonight."

"His clients are coming to the game?"

"Yes, that's what he said, Mekyla."

"What are you guys going to do after the game?"

"No, not me, remember. He's taking them out for a business dinner afterwards and said that I would just be bored if I came along."

"Oh, yeah, I remember us talking about that."

"Is this a female he's taking out to dinner?" Jennifer asked, hanging on every word Mekyla and Christy spoke.

"Now why do you need to know that, Jennifer?" Christy said, furrowing her brow.

"I was just wondering, that's all."

"I told Ian about my date in Austin," said Mekyla.

Both Christy and Jennifer snapped to attention.

"Get out of here, girl, no you didn't," said Christy.

"Yep, I told him."

"Well, what did he say or not say, do or not do?" said Jennifer. She looked at Christy, who was laughing. "Hey, I wanted to cover everything in one question."

"Well he semi-blew up at me. I think the blow was kinda softened a little, because we had sort of just finished making out. So it kinda turned me on, seeing that forceful side of him."

"You are a sick individual, Mekyla," said Christy. "Don't play with fire. You just might get burned."

"What are you saying?"

"What you told *me,* Mekyla. That I was to be careful what I asked for, because I just might get it. You were trying your hand with Ian, and he probably bit a little. But the next time he's going to give you back some of whatever fire you're playing with."

"You do listen to me, huh Christy? I do have to admit that I was scared a little."

"I guess I'm missing something," said Jennifer. "Did you sleep with this guy in Austin, Mekyla?"

"Oh look, Christy!" said Mekyla, pointing discreetly with her chin. "There's Ms. Cashmere with her pink one on today. But she has somebody with her, a tall, chocolate, baldheaded treat. So Christy, I guess we can lay Jennifer's flight of imagination to rest."

"Hey, that was something that I actually heard," said Jennifer, ruffling at the challenge to her skill as a gossip. Then her eyes got wide. "Okay, who is she waving at? And who just waved back with the biggest smile a man could ever have on his face? Mr. Trey Love. I rest my case."

Christy frowned. "Are you sure they were waving at each other?"

"Girl, you can still see Trey's hand print in the air." Jennifer said, with a half smirk on her face.

"Christy, there has to be an explanation," said Mekyla. "Let's not start jumping to conclusions."

Jennifer scoffed. "Mekyla, come on now. You just saw him waving at her."

"Christy, let's just go."

"Why would I do that, Mekyla? I'm the wife, remember? You don't screw with the person that has papers on the man. I'm going to go down and say hello to her, that's all." Christy stood up with a fake smile plastered on her face.

"I don't think you should do that, Christy," Mekyla said. She grabbed her sister's wrist and pulled her back down to her seat.

"Let her go down there and have a little talk with her. What's it going to hurt?"

"Jennifer, now you know that's not a good idea. You're a troublemaker. Why are you trying to start something?" Mekyla began to gather her stuff, knowing it was time to leave and take Christy with her.

"I'm just saying, she's a big girl, and she's curious."

"I'm going," Christy said, standing up again.

Mekyla slung her purse over her shoulder and shot to her feet, barley managing to grab her sister by the sleeve. "Wait up, Christy. Don't go walking up on the lady like you're bad. Remember, you could be wrong on this one."

Christy looked over her shoulder. "But I could be right also, Mekyla."

"Do you want to be right, Christy?"

"No, of course not, but I need to know. I need to know."

"Okay Christy, we're going to go up to this lady and introduce ourselves and let whatever else happens, happen, okay?"

"Okay."

"Christy, don't forget to ask her if she's screwing Trey," Jennifer said in a loud whisper.

Mekyla, still holding onto Christy's sleeve, turned back to Jennifer. "If you don't mind. I can't play referee with you to as well. I don't get it anyway." She turned to Christy. "Why do you guys pick at each other?"

"I couldn't tell you, Mekyla. I think it started a few years ago when Jennifer and I had some type of disagreement. Over what, I can't remember. All I can recall is that me, her and Trey were standing there talking about something. I don't know. Who knows? But, I'm willing to put it to rest, if she is."

"Sure, Christy," said Jennifer. "It's sleeping."

"Sleeping? You mean it's been put to rest?"

"Okay, how ever you would like to word it."

Christy opened her mouth to say something else, but Mekyla cut her off. "Okay, Christy, what will you say first?"

"I'm just going to introduce myself as Mrs. Trey Love."

"Huh!" Jennifer said, with a sneer on her face.

"What was that for, Jennifer?"

"Nothing, I didn't say a word," said Jennifer.

CHAPTER FORTY-SIX
LET'S NOT MEET AGAIN TOO SOON

As she approached Ms. Cashmere, Christy managed to form a smile that wouldn't seem entirely fake. "Hello," she said. "My name is Christy Love. I've seen you here once before. Are you from here?"

The woman stood and smiled. "No, I'm from Louisiana. My name is Boa, Boa Elliott, and this is Dallas Rangel, my partner."

"Boa. That's an interesting name. Is that short for something else?"

"No, that's my given name."

"This is my sister, Mekyla Williams, and our friend, Jennifer Holiday."

"Well, it's nice to meet you all."

"Do you have family that plays for either one of these teams?"

"No, I'm here on business. So, Christy Love. Trey Love wouldn't happen to be your husband, now would he?"

"Yes, he is actually." With a look of surprise, Christy stated, "You must be the clients."

"I would be curious too, Christy. You have a very handsome husband."

"No, it's not like that, it's just that . . .."

"Hey, Christy," said Mekyla, nervous about what more might come out of Christy's mouth. "Let's go back to our seats. The guys are getting ready to play."

"Sure. Mekyla. Boa, enjoy the game and it was a pleasure to have met you."

"Excuse me, Boa," said Jennifer.

"Yes, was it, Jennifer?"

"The cashmere sweater is beautiful with a very unique feminine cut. May I feel it?

"Sure."

"Who's the designer?" she said, taking a bit of fabric between her thumb and forefinger.

"It's my line. I design them myself. If you're ever in New Orleans, look me up. My shop is under Boa."

"I will, thank you. As a matter of fact, I'm traveling to Louisiana tomorrow."

"What a coincidence. Well again, ladies, it was nice to meet you all."

"Boa," said Christy. "If you are ever in my town again, my husband and I would love to have you over to our house for dinner. Goodbye."

CHAPTER FORTY-SEVEN
THE UNSTOPPABLE FORCE

"Christy, I cannot believe you," said Mekyla as they returned to their seats. "It was like you were a dog peeing on her territory. I just hope this is not going to affect their business meeting with Trey tonight."

Christy put her hands over her face for a moment, shot her sister a frustrated look. "Why didn't you stop me, Mekyla? Trey will kill me if I messed this deal up for him. Why did I go on and on with my silly little antics?"

"You were unstoppable, Christy. Just unstoppable. When you set your mind to something, there's no way to steer you into another course. It's our family curse. Let's just watch the game and pretend we're having a good time. This is probably the last game we get to come to. Seriously, we're three grown women. Well, for sure two grown women." She shot Jennifer a glance. "And we get kicked out of the basketball game for being trouble makers."

"Hmm!" said Jennifer. "Me, myself, I think that was mild compared to what Christy really should have done, because the girl is clearly doing Trey."

"Jennifer, shut that pothole of yours and let's just watch the game. I truly don't know why we come anyway, if we're not complaining, we're starting something. I'm not coming to any more games. You girls are just too much for me."

"Mekyla's right, Jennifer. I'm a little fed up with myself as well. And why are you encouraging me? I know that we're not the best of friends, but why or let me say, what's in it for you?"

"Nothing, I was just a participator, that's all."

"No wonder we hang out. Nobody else would put up with any of us. I'm cheating on a man that's basically perfect for me. Jennifer, you have some serious issues going on in your life, and Christy, you're throwing little temper tantrums as if you were some high school girl. Put a fork in me, I'm done. No, actually I'm burnt up. Do we even listen to the advice we give each other? Because if we did, I do believe we would be changed women."

"Mekyla, calm down, you're going to raise your blood pressure," said Christy.

"I probably need to go to the house. I need a change of scenery. Heck I need to hang out with different people. I'm sure you guys are not healthy for me. I think I'm going to start hanging with my other sisters."

"Whatever, Mekyla. I'll talk with you tomorrow, okay?" said Christy.

"Did you hear anything that I just said?"

"Yep, but you're my sister. You can't get rid of me that easy, but now Jennifer, on the other hand . . ..."

"Don't start, Christy. Mekyla would never sever our friendship."

"I'm leaving. Bye guys."

"Love you, Mekyla. Just get you some rest. I'll need to call you tomorrow to let you know what happened with me and Trey, okay."

Mekyla shook her head. "Sure, Christy. Jennifer, did you need me to stand by the phone as well, even though I just ended my love for you guys."

"I'll update you on what happened in Louisiana when I get back, but you get you some rest for now, okay?"

CHAPTER FORTY-EIGHT
LISA'S TOUR GUIDE

"Lisa," said the man's voice on the phone. "This is Jonathan. What happened? When did you leave?

"I guess it was somewhere between five and six this morning."

"Is everything all right? I wanted to fix you breakfast this morning."

"Yes, everything was wonderful. That's why I felt I should leave."

"Are we still open to letting me show you the town?"

"Of course. I would love that, Jonathan."

"Then I'll pick you up around noon. That way we can have some lunch and see some of my creations along with Austin's older landmarks, and maybe even take a drive down to San Antonio."

"That sounds wonderful. I'll see you at noon. You do know where this hotel is, right?"

"Yes, I have you on lock."

About two minutes after twelve, Lisa stepped off the elevator and walked across the lobby. As she neared the front desk, she saw Jonathan speaking with the clerk.

"Yes, can you ring Lisa Brazile's room, please?" he said.

"Jonathan," said Lisa. "I'm right here."

Jonathan gave her a big smile, and then turned to the front desk clerk again. "Never mind," he said. "Thank you." He turned to Lisa again and scooped her up in a big bear hug. "Lisa, you look wonderful."

"Well thank you, Jonathan. I felt pretty, today. So where do we start first?"

"Do you like exotic foods?" Jonathan said, as he opened the car door for Lisa.

She gave him a skeptical look as they began walking toward the door. "Such as?"

"Such as alligator, frog legs, and maybe some oysters."

"Never tried any of it. Do they have burgers?"

Jonathan laughed as he held the door for her. "No, not today, Lisa. First, we're going to Razoos to have some lunch and then we're off to some sites. Would that be okay with you?"

"I'm all yours."

"Well, that's a relief."

"A relief?"

"Well, yes. When I woke up and didn't see you there, I didn't know what to think. I decided to just call you and hope I didn't offend you last night."

"No, it's just that I wound up being overwhelmed by confusion, guilt and happiness at the same time."

Jonathan nodded. "I understand. I apologize for any situations I may have put you in that were uncomfortable."

"No, you were very gentle with me. I went along with what happened, because I wanted it to happen as well."

After a brief drive, they walked through the doors of Razoos. "Here we are, Lisa. And I wasn't entirely serious about the exotic foods. I want you to order whatever you want to eat. They have other things besides alligator and frog legs."

The hostess escorted them to a table and Jonathan held Lisa's chair for her.

"This is a very quaint place," she said, sitting down. "I love all the memorabilia they have hanging with the fish net."

"This is one of my favorite places to eat. I have another favorite spot called Pappadeaux. Have you ever eaten there?"

"No, and I believe we have one back home."

"Could I convince you to have dinner with me there tonight?"

"Hmm, let me check my schedule. Minus the strawberries."

"What, you didn't like the strawberries?"

"That's the problem. I loved the strawberries."

The waitress brought their orders and Lisa did a double take on Jonathan's plate.

"Oh my! You're going to eat those oysters slimy like that?"

"Yes, with a gallon of hot sauce."

"You're killing me, Jonathan. Killing me softly."

"Here. At least try a piece of the alligator." Jonathan stabbed something fried with his fork and raised it to Lisa's mouth.

"Mm, that tastes good. Kinda like chicken."

"Nevertheless, it's definitely gator. Chicken? I can't believe you are one of those 'everything tastes like chicken' people."

As they finished their lunch, Lisa started squirming in her seat. "Okay, I'm getting excited. Let's wrap this up and see the sights."

"Yes, ma'am." Jonathan paid the check and escorted Lisa back to the car. "We have a full tank of gas, you have your seat belt on, and we are ready to ride." He started the car. "First, I wanted to take you out to Lake Travis and Lakeway Marina."

As they approached Lake Travis, Jonathan explained that it was the largest and longest lake in the Highland Lakes chain. "It's popular with boating and fishing enthusiasts. Excluding me. I've never been one for the water."

"Oh this is beautiful," said Lisa, taking in the panorama of the area. "I love the way those homes sit up on the hills. They must cost a fortune."

"Fortune is right. This area is for the millionaire clubbers. Me, myself, I'm just a thousandaire."

Lisa laughed. "I'm sure that's not a word, Jonathan."

"The big attraction down closer to my home downtown, is the Congress Avenue Bats."

"The bats have their own home here in Texas?"

"Yep, we have what you call "Bats Entertainment." It's home to 1.5 million Mexican free-tail bats that migrate here every year. The Congress Avenue Bridge is a great place to witness the dramatic night flight that occurs every evening."

"You have all this stored away in your head, huh? I don't think I could be that descriptive of my home city, and I have lived there all of my life. I'm impressed."

"And then, downtown on Sixth Street, at the intersection of East Sixth Street and Congress to I-35, we have what we call a truly Dr. Jekyll and Mr. Hyde experience. Because by day, it's bustling with the office workers going about their normal routine and tourists attracted by the many landmarks and historical buildings in the area. However, by night the area transforms, becoming a glittering strip of bars and live music clubs. I'm going to have to take you to experience it one evening before you leave. And let us not forget the drag on Guadeloupe Street and MLK to Twenty-ninth. You have the funky shops that the Drag is know for, the joys of street vendors at Twenty-third Street, beads and baubles at Nomadic Notions, and other funky finds. Then you have some sights in Fredericksburg, a town outside of Austin, which is also a quaint German colony town that seems almost like a fairy tale. There are antique shops that you would probably just love and then there are the historic buildings and boutiques, and German restaurants."

"You're amazing, Jonathan. If I haven't said it enough, thank you for showing me Austin. But, I do know that Oklahoma University kicks University of Texas' butt every year."

"Yes, that game there in Dallas was bad this year. I believe OU whooped our butts like we were in high school. However, I'm sure 2004-2005 will be our year here in Texas. I can just feel it."

"I'm having the time of my life. I feel like a person inside of me has been set free to explore and not worry what other people may think of me."

"That's the good thing about going someplace where no one knows your name. You can become the person that you always knew you were. Would you like to take a drive down to San Marcos?"

"Is that far?"

"No, it'll probably only take us another thirty minutes or so from where we are."

"Okay, now you are going to give me detailed information on San Marcos, is that it?"

"Actually, I do have a little information stored in my brain about San Marcos." Jonathan thought for a moment. "Actually, the only thing that comes to mind about that area at the moment is the Tanger Outlet Center, which, I'm sure, has close to every name brand store there is. Then, a little further south, you have San Antonio, about another thirty-minute drive. That, of course, is the home of the San Antonio Spurs, but it also has the River Walk, which is a whole other world. It's a canal system built below the city streets along the San Antonio River. There are hundreds of shops and restaurants to choose from in the downtown area. Then there are the large cypress trees hanging over the water's edge, and impressive stonework."

"The way you describe the cities and their sites in such detail, I feel as though I've already seen them. No wonder the people in Texas love their state. It's a wonderful place to visit, and I guess, to live."

Mekyla pushed herself back from the computer and blinked several times. She suddenly realized how tired she was. She checked the clock on the wall. Nine o'clock. Ian would be getting home any time now. She saved her document, shut down the computer, and went into the kitchen to see what she could fix for dinner.

They had just had spaghetti the other night, so that wasn't going to work. She tried to think of what else she could cook well. 'Ian is pretty much like Mikey,' she thought. 'He'll eat anything presented well.'

CHAPTER FORTY-NINE
SLEEPLESS IN TULSA

Christy sat on the stairwell waiting on Trey to get home from his dinner meeting. When she heard the truck pull into the garage, she quickly ran up the stairs and hopped into bed. Christy lay very still as she pretended she was asleep.

Trey turned on the bedroom light. "Christy," he called out.

Christy just lay there.

"Christy, wake up."

Christy figured she couldn't ignore him any longer. She opened her eyes. "What? What's wrong, Trey?"

Trey crossed his arms over his chest. "If I have to say, it's only going to make me that much angrier."

Christy sprung up from her horizontal position and immediately began talking. "Trey, if you would have been listening to the conversations me, Mekyla, and Jennifer were having, you would understand the concern that I had."

Trey raised one eyebrow.

As soon as Christy saw that, she began to rework her story. "Well, maybe 'concern' is not the word that I'm looking for. Maybe the word is curious."

"Christy, I'm not a child that you have to watch over. If you have so little trust in me, then maybe we should seek other options, because nothing can last if there's no trust."

"Wait a minute, Trey. You're overreacting to this whole thing. I merely went up to the woman and introduced myself, that's all. I didn't accuse her of anything."

"She said that you were in her face with your posse, and you guys pretty much drilled her."

"Now that's not true about us being a posse. I don't want to lose us, Trey. I'm very sorry for what I did. It will never happen again."

"You better hope it never happen again, because if it does I will leave."

"Please apologize to Boa for me, Trey."

"Everything is all right. We're closing the deal on Monday."

"Great! I'm very happy for you," Christy said, with a look of confusion on her face, not knowing how she became the only villain in this argument.

Trey pulled off his shirt and shook his head, exasperated. He started into the bathroom. "Christy, would you go down and grab me a Michelob while I take a quick shower?"

"Sure, Trey," she said.

Trey closed the bathroom door and immediately Christy heard the shower running. She started down the stairs for the beer, but stopped when she heard his cell phone ringing.

'Now who could this be calling Trey at this hour?' she thought. She picked up the phone off the dresser and looked at the caller ID. "Private," was all it said. She frowned at the phone. Why would the caller need the call to be private? She was already in enough trouble with Trey. She figured answering the phone would only throw her from the frying pan into the fire. 'Just think happy thoughts,' she said to herself as she put the phone down and headed for the kitchen. 'Get this out of your head. It could be any number of people. Trey does work in advertising. He meets lots of potential clients. Just get your husband's beer before he gets out of the shower. When does this marriage stuff get better? I thought if you made it past the five-year mark, you were to be one of the lucky couples. Luck sure has a funny way of presenting itself.'

In the kitchen, Christy popped a couple of Advil's for her future headache before grabbing a beer out of the refrigerator.

CHAPTER FIFTY
BROTHER JUNIOR

Jennifer hovered in the doorway of Junior's bedroom. "Hey, Junior, can I come in?"

"Sure sis, what's up?" Junior said, as he continued to pack his clothes for school.

"Oh, I see you're starting your packing early, college man to be. That's part of the reason I'm here, actually. I wanted to tell you that I'm very proud of you and your accomplishments. I know I never expressed those things to you before, but all that's going to change."

"Thanks, sis. And, hey, cover for me tonight. I met this cutie and will probably be at her house most of night. If Moms asks where I am, tell her that I'm at one of my boys' houses, okay?"

"Junior, just remember to use protection. Always use protection," Jennifer said, with a newfound look of concern on her face. "When I get back from my trip, I'm going to have something very important to talk with you about, okay?"

"Okay, Jennifer. What's with the serious face?"

"We'll talk on Monday when I return."

Hey, I'm sorry to hear about your grandmother Jennifer."

"Thanks, Junior. I'll see ya."

"Pull the door closed for me, Jennifer."

"Sure, no problem," Jennifer said, but she took a long looking at him in a way she'd never done before. She wondered how he would react when he learned that he was her son.

Jennifer dialed the number and listened to the phone ring several times. 'I hope I don't get his damn voice mail again,' She thought. 'I know he told me not to call his phone this late at night, but this can't keep until Monday.' The voicemail picked up and Jennifer rolled her eyes as she waited for the beep. "Hey, it's me. Call me back tonight. I really need to talk to you about something, okay? Please call me back."

She set the phone down on her bedside table and went into the bathroom to finish packing. She was putting things into her vanity bag when the phone rang. Startled, she dropped the bag and ran to the phone.

"Hey, you," she said.

"You are ruthless, aren't you? Meet me in thirty minutes at our spot."

"I'll be there," Jennifer said, grinning from ear to ear. She felt a rush of excitement. She ran to the closet and picked out her sexiest dress, then to the dresser for a negligee to put on under it. 'He loves when I wear something sexy. Something I'm sure he's not getting at home anymore, which is good for me. I know I'm getting me some tonight.' She stopped suddenly and took a deep breath, telling herself to slow down and stay calm. But she really couldn't stay calm. She began to hurry even faster as she got ready for her night out.

After her shower, she dressed and wiped the steam off the mirror to check her look. She glanced at her wristwatch as she began to put it on. Only ten minutes had passed since the phone call. Now all she needed to do was get to the hotel safely and, hopefully, after him. She dashed to her GMC Denali and raced to meet her lover. As she approached the hotel she reminded herself once again to calm down. 'I don't want to appear anxious,' she thought. 'Heck! Who am I fooling? That desperate message on his voice mail was enough to make him think I'm psycho.' Scanning the garage of the hotel, no truck. 'I can't believe I beat him here, he better not stand me up.'

"May I help you?" said the desk clerk.

"Yes sir, I would like 833, is it available?"

"Yes, Ms. Love, you're already checked in."

She took the key card from the desk clerk. "Thank you very much. Have a nice evening."

In the hall outside of 833, she inserted the key card in the slot and pushed the door open. "Hello, love," she said with a smile.

"Hello, Jennifer. And before you start with that mouth of yours, I'm not here to explain or be lectured. I would just like to have sex. Are we clear?"

"Clear as a bell, Daddy. But do we have to call it sex? Why don't you ever use the word 'love?' 'Make love?'"

"That's not what we do, Jennifer. Take off this dress and let me see what you have on under there for me."

Jennifer began to take off her dress that he never complimented her on. "Can we just pretend tonight that you love me? Just tonight?"

"I can't do that Jennifer, but I will make you feel satisfied, very satisfied. I love this little outfit right here, wrapped around this nice little frame of yours." He grabbed her and began to kiss her.

"Ooh, I love it when you do that to me. Don't stop," Jennifer said, as they both disappeared up under the covers.

Suddenly, he pulled the covers down and swung his legs out of the bed.

"What are you doing?" Jennifer asked.

"I hear my phone vibrating. Hold on a minute. Don't you say a word?" He grabbed his phone. "Hello," he said. "No, I'm not in the house. I'm on my way back. I couldn't sleep and I was low on Michelob, so I went to the store to grab more. I'll be there in a little bit. Go back to bed." He hung up the phone.

"So you're leaving?" Jennifer said, with a look of anger and sadness.

"If you focus more on the time that I'm still here, we can get this done."

Jennifer didn't want him to leave without giving her the attention she so desperately needed, but she also didn't want to be carelessly treated as just a piece of meat. "I think you should leave now," She said. "No, don't leave. I want you to stay."

"Make up your mind, woman. You're about to mess my mood up."

"Please stay. Just stay as long as you can." Jennifer's eyes began to water.

CHAPTER FIFTY-ONE
MY BIG BABY

Ian wandered into the kitchen yawning.

"Good morning, Ian," said Mekyla. "Are you going to church with me this morning?"

"Yes, but let's take separate cars. I'm going to stop by a buddy's house to watch some ESPN for a while."

"Did you want me to fix you breakfast, or would you like to stop off and get those croissant breakfast sandwiches you love so much?"

His eyes lit up. "Yeah, let's just do that. If you don't mind, I would like to go with a nice shirt and Dockers this morning, instead of the whole jacket and tie ensemble. While I hop in the shower, would you put it together for me?"

"How did you manage before I moved in with you? I'm going to start assigning little things for you to do for me."

"I love it when you take care of me. And you know I would go to the moon for you. All you have to do is ask."

"We really need to talk, Ian."

"What do you want to talk about?"

"Maybe, this can wait until after church."

"Are you sure? Because we can ride in the same car if that's the problem."

"No, that's not it. It can wait. I'm sorry, go ahead and get in the shower before we start to run late."

CHAPTER FIFTY-TWO
A NEW BRIEF PROSPECTIVE

As the church service let out, Mekyla and Schonda walked slowly down the steps together.

"Schonda, I need to start coming to church more than once every other week. I guess I never realized how much it helps my week, my day, and my life."

"Mekyla, this is basically the only time I get to see you these days. Let's hang out more."

"I would love that. I was just telling Christy and Jennifer that same thing. How are my niece and nephew doing?"

"They're growing up. They asked about spending the night with their aunt Mekyla."

"One weekend very soon. You know that sermon was right on point this morning. Boy, was he talking to me!"

"I know. I felt it also. Let's go have lunch. No, actually Tere is cooking today. Why don't you and Ian come over and have dinner with all of us?"

"I'd love that, Schonda. Just let me give Ian a call to see if he would like to swing by. He got out of here pretty quick because of those sports channels. He hasn't really had a decent meal-well a variety of meals-since I moved in. We use to eat out a lot before."

"It must be love."

"I keep hearing that 'love' word."

"What do you mean, that 'love' word, Mekyla? Are you not in love with Ian?"

"I don't know if I know what it feels like to be in love, to be honest with you."

"Mekyla, I believe you know there's something you need to get out of your system. Get it out and then focus on what you have before it's too late."

"You've been talking to Christy?"

"Yeah, but that doesn't mean anything. I'm your sister just like she is. I know what's going on with you whether we talk every day or not. You've always been this big flirt, and unfortunately it's going to take you being hurt in your heart before you realize what you have in front of you."

"Don't say that, Schonda. I don't want that to happen."

"What are you doing to prevent it? I think you like putting them to the test, but it's going to get old. Remember, you're dealing with men now, and not boys."

"Well, I'm going to get going, Schonda. I'll meet you at Tere's house in a little bit, okay? Call her and let her know we're coming."

"All right, I'll see you and Ian there."

"Yes, it will be Ian. I'm not going to bring any other man. I haven't become that bad, Schonda."

CHAPTER FIFTY-THREE
A MOMENT OF TRUTH BRINGS A LIFETIME OF CONFESSIONS

Mekyla answered the phone and immediately heard Jennifer's voice.

"Hey girl, it's me. I'm glad I caught you at home. There's one more bag I need to borrow of yours."

"Come on over, Jennifer, I'm here for maybe another hour and a half or so. We're going to Tere's house for an early dinner."

"I'm close by. I'll be there in about ten minutes."

"Okay, see you when you get here."

Mekyla dialed another number. "Hey, Christy, it's me," she said. "We're going to Tere's house for dinner. Are you and the kids coming over?"

"Yes, we're going. Tere called me a little while ago."

"I'm going to drag Ian over there with me. Why don't you ask Trey to come as well?"

"Actually, Trey wanted to have pork chops for dinner, but I did want us to have a family day today, so yes, I'll ask him to come along. We've been at each other's throats. Well, *I've* been on *his* case here lately. A change would be good for us."

"Well, then if not Trey, I will definitely see you and the kids there," She said. "Oh, hey, I hear the doorbell. Jennifer was coming over to borrow another one of my bags for her trip. I gotta go."

"Okay Mekyla. Say hello for me. Love ya. See you later."

"Sure, and I'll say it like you mean it too. Bye. Love you."

Just as she hung up the phone, Mekyla heard a knock at the door.

"I'm coming, Jennifer," she said, as she sprinted to the door. She opened the door to find Jennifer standing there with a smile on her face. "So you're all packed and ready to go and find your baby's daddy, huh? What part of Louisiana are you going to, anyway?"

"New Orleans. I'm going to New Orleans."

"You're not going to be driving in the dark too long, are you?"

"No. Well, maybe a couple of hours or so. I was supposed to be out of here way earlier than now."

"You know, I've been thinking a lot about what you shared with me, and I just wanted to share something with you. I'll be quick."

"Sure, Mekyla. What's on your mind?"

"I believe I'm in love and I believe I should express that to him in words."

"So you're finally going to tell Ian that you're in love him?"

"Nope. I'm not talking about Ian."

"What do you mean, you're not talking about Ian?"

"No, Jennifer, it's not Ian. But don't get me wrong. I do have strong feelings for him, but I don't believe I'm in love with him."

"Then why did you agree to move in with him?"

"Loneliness and not listening to my own heart, I suppose. I don't know. I still could be wrong."

"So, who is this second person?"

"I'm not going to say right now. I need to give him a call, because I haven't actually shared it with him yet."

"So, do you even know if he loves you as well?"

"I don't know. This time I don't care if he's in the same place as me. I'm just going to follow my heart on this one. I've been like a light bulb in a dark room. Like the desert waiting for the rain. I've just been sitting here waiting for him. Because I believe he's the only one who can bring hope and complete happiness into my life again."

"Mekyla, I've never heard you talk like that about a man before."

"I'm remembering the story you shared with me about your loss, and it made me remember the sadness that came from the first love of my life."

"Okay, who is this mystery person, if it's not your son's father, whom I thought you fell in love with twice? Something I was wrong about, apparently."

"It only seems that way because we were together so long. But the man I'm referring to is Jonathan. The guy I met in Austin."

"But you've only known him basically a weekend. Hold your thought, I need to pee." said Jennifer.

"I'm going to continue talking because, you need to get on the road."

"But while I'm in bathroom?"

"You can still hear me talking through the door. Heck, it's just us."

"Something happened in those few days I was with him that I have never experienced in my adult life. He gave me that intimacy that I longed for, not just the making love part, but the walks, the communication, and our same interests."

Jennifer shook her head. "No. Hold on, Mekyla. I need to see facial expressions." She closed the bathroom door and Mekyla strolled back to the living room.

A minute later, Jennifer rejoined her. "Okay, I'm ready. Go on."

"During a small window of time, I was the happiest girl on earth."

"Well, Mekyla, you know I will stand behind you one hundred percent on whatever you decide to do. And I need for you to repeat all of that you said before, I need to see this look you have, the in love look."

"Anyway, so, I said all of that as a way of explaining that I'm calling him. I'm going to do it."

"Okay, I'm right here with you. I'm sure I can give my best friend another ten minutes or so of my support."

"Thanks, Jennifer. Here I go."

Mekyla picked up the phone and dialed the number Jonathan had given her when they first met. "May I speak to Jonathan?" she said into the phone.

"This is Jonathan."

"Jonathan, good afternoon, this is Mekyla. Before you say anything, just hear me out, okay? I'm remembering when you first introduced me to Nora Jones. I play it every time I began to write now. It relaxes my mind and allows me to recreate that one moment in time where I felt completely warm and very safe in your arms. For me it was a connection at first sight and embrace. Before you respond to what I'm saying to you, Jonathan, let me read you this poem I wrote for you. And I want you to know also that there are no, and will never be any, regrets, if for some reason you're not in the same place as me."

MY SPECIAL SOMEONE

I'm remembering the first time I heard your voice. That faint whisper of hello that could have made any girl moist. I'm remembering our first evening. The mozzarella cheese, I shouldn't have eaten. The structure of your body, the dip in your back, the grip of control. I'm remembering, I was no longer so cold. I'm remembering how I tried to push away, and very thankful you knew how to convince me to stay. I'm remembering our first goodbye. That first soft kiss on the lips, then on my thigh. I'm remembering my sexy chocolate treat. My special someone so true. Selfishness aside.
I'm remembering only you.

"That was beautiful," said Jonathan.

"Jonathan, I know I have someone in my life right now, but I miss you so much. And I just needed to say that to you, because it's something that has been on my mind for a while now."

"Mekyla, is there a number I can call you back on, my wife if here."

"Oh, I'm sorry, I didn't know. Please accept my apology. Goodbye Jonathan." Mekyla hung up the phone and covered her face with her hands.

"What, Mekyla?" said Jennifer? "What happened?"

"His wife was there. I can't believe I just made a fool of myself." Mekyla said, her voice wavering.

"I'm sorry, Mekyla. Are you going to be okay? You didn't mention the fact that he's married. That's really unlike you to fool around with a married man."

"He told me he was married, separated, and in the process of a divorce."

"You know, Ian is going to be here in a little bit. Do you want to ride around for a little while?"

"No, Jennifer, but thanks for asking. I'm going to need to be alone for a little while, if you don't mind."

"Sure. I understand. Just call me if you need me, okay?" Jennifer stood up and began walking toward, the door, but stopped. "Mekyla, should I cancel my trip?"

"Of course you shouldn't cancel your trip. Don't even think about canceling this trip, Jennifer."

"Well, if you're sure, then I'm going to head out to inform Junior's father."

"Yes, of course. Good luck with that, and call me when you get there."

"I will. And you know something? After that whole thing with my grandmother and my talk with you, I knew it was time to end all the lies that were overshadowing my life. Losing my grandmother was the first time I've cried in a very long time. I've been in a place, as you so eloquently stated, somewhere beyond my tears. I thank you for that, and for the friendship and patience you've extended to me."

"You're very welcome, Jennifer. And I want you to know that, because of our talks and small confessions, I can now see my life in a different light. With that said, as messed up as my life is as far as commitment, I still would not change one thing. Not one thing. I wish you luck, and happiness with what you have to do, Jennifer."

"Thank you. And you call me if you need me."

"I will. Thanks. Love you girl."

"I love you too, Mekyla, but I've got to scoot. I need to be on the road like right now basically, in order to beat the night at this point."

"Okay girl. Be careful and take your time.

"Yep," said Jennifer. "I'm off to Louisiana."

"That's interesting."

"What's that, Mekyla?"

"I just remembered this guy I just insured came in from Louisiana."

Jennifer nodded. "Those Louisiana men are carriers of some pretty good genes."

"Well that's something I'll never find out about," said Mekyla as she sat in her recliner, twirling a CD on her finger. "See you later, and again, drive carefully.

CHAPTER FIFTY-FIVE
WORLDS APART

Christy found Trey on the couch reading the sports section. "Okay, Trey. It seems like you've been trying to avoid me all day. I'm not going to ask you about that late night run. We're all meeting at Tere's house for lunch/dinner. Would you like to come?"

Trey tossed the paper aside. "Maybe for a couple of hours, then when we return home, I would like to have those pork chops I asked you to buy the other night."

"I remembered. They're in the sink thawing out."

"Are the kids ready?"

"Yes, we're all ready."

"Okay, let's load up then," Trey said. He went to his truck to make sure it was cleared out for the kids.

Christy followed him out and the kids began to climb into the truck. "Trey, you know I have another doctor's appointment, so I'm either going to take the kids to your mother's house or to my mom's, which do you prefer?"

"It doesn't make any difference to me, whichever you decide. Have you told your mom about this yet?"

"No, I'm not ready to involve the rest of my family."

"Try not to put it off too long, I'm sure they would like to know and offer the support you need."

CHAPTER FIFTY-SIX
A FAMILY DINNER

"Hello guys," said Mekyla as she walked through the door of Tere's house. "I smelled this food a block away. And I guess Ian could too, because he almost ran me off the road trying to beat me here when we met up at the corner."

How does one describe Tere, the sister with impeccable taste, the one who's the little entertainer of guess all the time? Lives as if they have money to burn and loves to eat out. But also loves her husband Ashton very much.

As Tere gave her a hug, she noticed a painting on the wall of the foyer. "Is this new, Tere?"

"No. Probably to you, since you don't stop by and visit often."

Ian came through the door behind Mekyla.

"Hello, Ian," said Tere.

"Hey, Tere. Where would you like me to put all this Michelob beer?"

"There's a big cooler in the kitchen. If you'd just stick them in there, I would appreciate it."

"Hey," said Mekyla, swatting Tere on the shoulder. "I haven't seen your little footprints around my house either." She nodded at the painting. "You've always had great taste."

"Let's have a night out like we use to do. Just the girls. Someday soon, okay?"

"That sounds great, Tere. I do need to catch up on the family drama."

"Yeah, you can tell us about your latest situation."

"Yes, of course. My stuff. Speaking of which, has the little informer, Christy, made it yet?"

"No, I haven't seen her, but Schonda's out back."

"How's that husband of yours, with his fine self."

"Taking care of me," said Tere. "And very well, I might add."

"You look very happy, and I'm proud of you."

"Thank you. That's very nice, coming from my big sis. How's the book coming alone?"

"I'm heading into my last one hundred pages."

"Now that sounds like a lot to me, but I'm sure it's something you're going to knock out real soon."

"I'm looking at maybe another couple to three weeks, if I stay on my schedule."

"Am I in your book?"

"There are no kids in this book, sweetie."

"Forget you, Mekyla. I'm going in to check on the food. You wanna come?"

"No, I'm going to try and find Christy, but I'll be in after a little bit, okay?"

"Don't sneak out of here. You're good at disappearing," Tere said, as she shook a finger at Mekyla.

Mekyla found Christy in the back yard and walked up behind her. "Christy, I need to talk to you," she said in a low voice. "Meet me somewhere."

Christy spun around. "Mekyla, what's wrong? Why do we need to meet? I'm right here."

"Damn it, Christy, I would like to be away from everyone. Can you just say where? I can't think, and I really need for you to say where, okay? You come to Tere's house more often than I do."

"Okay, Mekyla, there's no need to bite my head off. Meet me at – uh – uh – in our truck. Let's go to the truck, and if we have to we'll drive around, or we can find a room in this mausoleum of Tere's. Whatever you want to do."

"Okay. Let's go to the truck first. I'll be out there waiting on you."

"Mekyla, you're scaring me. I've never seen you so desperate like this."

"I'm just a little anxious, that's all. I'll see you outside."

"Okay. Just give me a few minutes to make sure the kids have their plates and I'm on my way out."

Christy walked through the back door and nearly ran into Ian. "Hello, Ian. It's refreshing to see you outside of that basketball uniform."

"Stop by the house anytime, Christy. You know you're welcome."

"I know. I'll start stopping by more often. Have you seen my husband?"

"He's up stairs with Deon and Ashton watching sports."

"Okay, thanks. Hey kids, are you getting enough to eat? Be sure and thank your Aunt Tere for the food. If you need me I'll be outside talking with your Aunt Mekyla."

"Christy," said Schonda. "When you go outside, would you check the meat on the grill?"

Christy paused. "Well, I was going out front to talk with Mekyla."

"Oh, okay, I'll get it. Don't worry about it."

"Are you sure?"

"Yeah."

"The exercise would be good for you anyway. It will bring the baby here on schedule or maybe even earlier."

"I heard you say outside and I just assumed you meant out back. Is everything okay?"

"Yeah, everything's fine," said Christy, heading toward the front door. "I'm just going to show Mekyla something, that's all."

Christy had her hand on the front door knob, but was still talking to Schonda when the door opened. "Mama, you startled me," she said.

"Do people always startle you when they come in through the front door, Christy?"

"No, I was just – never mind. How are you? You're looking good, Ms. Lady."

"Thank you. I guess I have to wait on family gatherings to see you and my grandchildren, huh?"

"Mom, you just saw the kids at the baby shower."

"Christy, you're looking peaked. Are you eating right okay?"

"Yes, I just had a long night, that's all. Mekyla is waiting on me outside. I'll be right back."

"I didn't see Mekyla out there."

"She may have been in the truck."

"Why would she be sitting in the truck?"

"Mama, I'll be right back, okay?"

"You kids are so strange and secretive. She is coming in, right?"

"Yes," Christy said, as she closed the front door.

"I see Mama caught you at the door." said Mekyla.

"Yes. How did you manage to escape her?"

"I saw her coming down the street and I jumped in your truck pretty fast."

"Okay, what's up with you, Mekyla?"

"I'm going to tell Ian about my friend in Austin."

"No you're not."

"Yeah, I am."

"No you're not, Mekyla. What's come over you? Have you gone crazy? You barely know this man. And you want to risk everything you have on a possibility?"

"I can't stop thinking about him, and I did something that would be deemed stupid, from the way it turned out."

"Go on."

"I called his house, right? And spilled my guts, basically, about how I felt about him, and he didn't have time to talk."

"Meaning, he was in a business meeting? What?"

"No, his wife was there."

Christy closed her eyes for a moment and shook her head. "You know what? I don't want to hear anymore, because you have lost your mind and I'm going to help you put your life back in perspective. I'm a wife, remember? I won't be able to understand whatever it is you're getting ready to go through."

"I don't know, Christy. I know you're probably right, but these feelings I have, here I go–I believe to be love."

"But this is a sticky situation. Just be sure. Somehow I thought those words would be spoken about Ian, but love can be a tricky thing. You know I'll be here for whatever. Just be the smart woman that I know will be."

"Thank you for that, Christy."

"Now let's go in before Mama sends a search party out for us."

"Christy, it looks like you're losing weight. You need to stop worrying so much about what Trey is doing and start taking care of yourself. Tere suggested we have one of our girls'-night-out things. I thought it would be nice, and long overdue."

"I would love that," Christy said, pushing open the door to the house.

"Can we get a game of spades going, or what?" Mekyla blurted out.

"Mekyla, come over here and give your mom a kiss. We missed you at the baby shower. Schonda received lots of gifts. Has she shown you any of them yet?"

"No, Mom, I haven't been over to her house yet. So, Mama, did you bring your cards, or what?"

"You know I brought my cards. You know Tere will never have them available here in her house. This house only entertains guests who sip on wine and champagne and make small talk. Tere's probably somewhere having little heart attacks, dealing with all of her nieces and nephews at one time, with all these little collectors' items lying around."

"Well, there is a gang of kids in here."

"Where is my grandson?"

"He called me when I was on my way over here. He should be here anytime now."

"Will he be bringing Cheyenne?"

"I'm not sure. He and Cheyenne's mom are going through something right now. So, let's get the game started. Who's up for spades?"

"Tere, fix a couple of platters for me and the fellas," Ashton said as he reached into the cooler and grabbed more bottles of beer for him and the guys. "Make on a variety of meats and the other, maybe just the corn on the cob. And bring it upstairs, please?"

"Ashton, don't you and the guys want to come down stairs to eat?" Tere said, in a very low voice.

"I'm not going to ask these grown men to come down and eat at the table. We're going to eat in the entertainment room. So please bring the platters up, okay?"

The doorbell rang and Tere threw up her hands. "Will someone get the door for me, and can I get some help with this food?" She blurted as she began to fix the platters for the guys.

"I'll get the door," Schonda said, as she tugged one of her daughters along, dragging her on one of her legs. She opened the door to find Termaine and a young lady standing on the porch. "Hello, Nephew. Give your auntie a kiss on the cheek."

"That will be my pleasure. Aunt Schonda, I don't know if you ever met my friend Shandalyn?"

"No, I've never met this one. I'm Schonda, Termaine's aunt."

"It's very nice to meet you," said Shandalyn.

"Did you get your car running?" said Schonda.

"Yes, I fixed the one problem. Now I'm just sitting back waiting on something else to go wrong."

"Boy, you and those cars. Well go on in. Your mom and your grandmother are in the den."

"Is Deon here, Auntie Schonda?"

"Yes, he and all of your uncles and future uncles are upstairs."

"Okay, thanks." Termaine started toward the den leading Shandalyn by the hand. "Hey, Grandma, what's going on with ya?"

"There's my grandson. And who is this you have with you? That's not my great granddaughter's mother."

"No, Grandma. This is Shandalyn, everybody. Hey, Mom."

"Hello, sweetie, and hello Shandalyn. It's very nice to meet you."

"Thank you Mrs. Williams."

"Please have a seat, Shandalyn. And there's food in the kitchen and out back."

"Thanks, Mom," said Termaine. "I'm going to go up and see what the fellas are up to."

"So Mama," said Mekyla, shuffling the cards. "Are you ready for me to whoop up on you again in another hand of spades."

"You didn't beat me the first time, Mekyla. I know you cheated somehow. That's all you and your cousins do, is cheat."

"Now that you have given the losers speech, are you ready to play another hand of spades?"

"This time I'm dealing," said Mekyla's mom, holding out her hands for the cards. "How is your friend Jennifer holding up after the loss of her grandmother?"

Mekyla placed the deck in her mother's hand. "She's doing fine, thank you. She's on her way to Louisiana, actually. I'm glad you mentioned her because I need to give her a call. I haven't heard from her since she left. In fact, go ahead and deal. I'm going to make this quick phone call."

Mekyla dialed Jennifer's cell number. "Hello, Ms. Knucklehead," she said when Jennifer answered. "Why haven't you called me?"

"Hey, what's up? You said to call you when I made it to New Orleans."

"How are you holding up?"

"Just a little tired, but I don't have long to go."

"Well, still call me when you make it in, okay?"

"I will. What's all that noise?"

"We're all at Tere's house, remember, nosey."

"Why do you wait until I left to have a big gathering?"

"It was a last minute kind of thing."

"Did Ian come along with you?

"Yes, I pulled him away from his basketball game with his friend, but I'm sure he's watching it upstairs."

"Is Christy there?"

"Yeah, she's here."

"So, Trey isn't there?"

"No, Trey's here as well. Why do you ask?"

"Well, I thought that there might still be some tension between them from the other night."

"No, they're fine. Okay, well just call me when you get there, and drive safe."

"All right, Mekyla. Talk with you soon."

"Who was that asking about Trey?" said Christy.

"Oh, that was Jennifer. Just asking who all was here."

"And Trey was the only name I heard you say."

"Yeah, but okay, let's get back to the card game," Mekyla said, giving Christy the brush off. "How are those fellas doing upstairs anyway?"

"I took a couple of trays up a few minutes ago. They must be doing okay. Ashton hasn't come back down since."

"Schonda, how are you doing over there? You look like you're about ready to pop?"

"Just taking it easy, just taking it easy. Hey, Christy, did you cut your hair." Schonda asked, as she wrestled with her very active daughter.

"That's what's different about you. You cut your hair," Tere yelled as she pointed the fork with a cob of corn on the end of it.

"Yes, I kinda trimmed it a little."

"It makes your face look thinner. Heck you whole body is thinner."

"Running after these kids and caring for my husband. I guess is starting to catch up with me."

Mekyla's mom tossed her cards on the table. "I guess the game sort of faded on us."

"Oh, no," said Mekyla. "We'll play more in a minute, Mama."

"Christy, now I told you if you need any help with those children just let me know."

"I know Mama, it's just that Trey feels they're my job and that's why I'm not working."

"I'm not going to get in your business, but regular working people take a little time off for themselves."

"I know, Mama, but I'm fine, okay? It's getting late, Trey wanted pork chops for dinner. I'm gonna go up and see if he's ready to head out."

"Baby, I didn't mean to run you off. You sit down and enjoy your sisters."

"Well, he had mentioned to come and find him after a couple of hours, because he wanted to rest before work tomorrow," Christy said, as she headed for the stairs to call for Trey.

"Okay, Tere, where am I most needed on the cleanup crew?" said Mekyla as she stood up.

"Loading the dishwasher would help out tremendously."

"I'm on it. Tere, this was great. So you cook every Sunday after church, because a girl can get used to this good cooking. I forgot how well you could cook. You did a good job."

Mekyla loaded the dishwasher and wiped down the counters. "I'm getting a little tired myself," she said. "I'm sorry if it seems like we're eating and running, but you gotta know when you feed people like this, that next step is sleep."

"Mekyla, did you even eat yet?"

"No, I thought I would just take a plate home, if that's okay."

"Did you want me to put you something together?"

"No, you know how picky I am. I'll do it." She walked back into the den and started talking before she'd even entered the room. "Hey Mama, did you get those cards ready?"

"I'm not studding you girl. Those cards been ready and put away. I'm in here trying to get myself some sleep."

Mekyla laughed and turned to her little sister. "Schonda, can I get you anything?"

"No thanks, Mekyla. I'm fine. But thanks for asking."

"Shandalyn, are you okay?"

"Yes, Ms. Williams. But can you go up and get Termaine for me?"

"Sure, I need to go up to get Ian as well," Mekyla said, as she headed for the stairs.

Christy followed her out of the den. "Hey," she said in a half whisper.

"Hey, Christy. So you guys about ready to head out?"

"Yes. But tell me why she asked about Trey."

"Oh yeah, well we were talking, like I said, and she asked about Ian first, and then you while she said, 'Well, then I guess Trey is at home.' Then I said, 'No, Trey is here.' That's the Trey you heard me say."

"I still don't understand why she would suggest that about Trey."

"Well she did say your name first."

"You know what I'm trying to say. Don't be trying to protect your friend."

"I'm not. What else did you want me to say? Oh, because I did ask her why the inquiries about Trey, and she mentioned our night out at the basketball game, and I guess she wanted to make sure you guys were straight."

"I'm leaving it alone for now, Mekyla," Christy said, as she noticed Trey coming down the stairs.

"Oh, hey Trey," said Mekyla. "Would you call Ian, to come down please. Oh, and Termaine too. Thank you."

She turned to her sister and lowered her voice. "Christy, we'll talk about it later, okay?"

"That one you can place a bet on."

"There you go, getting ready to probe me like I'm the psychic woman or something."

"Kids, let's go," Christy said as she gathered up her crew. "Mama is over there sleeping like a baby. Tere, it's been great. Please give me more notice next time, so I can come over and help you with some of this."

"I will. Thanks, Christy. You know I like to entertain guests, so it wasn't a problem."

"Where's my sister with the keg belly? Schonda, baby, come and let me try and hug you."

"No one could wrap their hands around your butt, during your last pregnancy?"

"Ooh, yeah, I was big during that one. Goodnight everybody. Love ya."

"Have a good evening," said Trey as he placed a hand on Christy's shoulder and steered her toward the door. "And give my mother-in-law a kiss for me when she stops snoring. I can hear her way over here."

"Ian," said Mekyla. "Are you ready, sweetie, and did you get enough to eat?"

"I'm stuffed. Tere you put your foot in this one. Thanks for having us over. I had a great time."

"You're welcome anytime, Ian."

"Termaine," said Mekyla. "Come over here and plant one on the cheek." She kissed her son on the cheek as well. "Love you, son. Again, it was nice meeting you Shandalyn."

"It was nice meeting you as well, Ms. Williams."

"Schonda, love ya," Mekyla said as she gave her sister a big bear hug. "If I don't see you this week I'll see you at church, okay?"

"Okay, love you too. Bye."

Waiting in the truck, Trey reached over to open the door for Christy, put the truck in gear and drove off.

"So Trey," said Christy. "Did you get enough to eat, or would you still like for me to cook you some pork chops when we get home?"

"I'm full now, but I'll probably get a little hungry later, so yes, go ahead and cook them."

"I didn't see you the whole afternoon. Did you have a good time?"

"Christy, I'm not a child. Me and the guys watched some sports, played a little pool, and ate the barbecue." He glanced over at his wife. "Why are you holding your head? You're getting another one of those headaches?"

"It's just tension. It'll go away in a minute."

"Your problem is you try and read too much into things. You try too hard. Just relax and enjoy life, because all that stressing is not going to help your situation."

"Somehow your words just don't comfort me at all, Trey."

"Maybe when we get to the house, I'll do something special for you," he said in a low voice. Then he reached to turn up the radio so the kids wouldn't hear what they were saying.

Christy sat quietly for a moment, not knowing whether to be grateful or suspicious. Then she looked at Trey. "So you're going to reward me tonight?"

"That's what you've been nagging me about for the last few weeks, right?"

"There you go accusing me of nagging you again. It's been months since you've held me."

"Do you want to or not?"

"Yes, of course I want to. It's not like I have other options waiting in the wings, other than my tools at home."

"You need to get rid of that stuff."

"I will when you decide to make love to me on a regular basis."

"Will you lower your voice? I can only turn this music up so loud. We'll finish talking about this when we get home." He turned the music back down.

CHAPTER FIFTY-SEVEN
BACK TO THE PENTHOUSE

"Mekyla, I have always enjoyed your family's company. They are really down home regular people."

"Thank you, Ian. I'm sure your family is the same way. But what's strange about it is that me and most of my family are in the same city, but very seldom see each other. I never really hear you talk about your family, and I would love to meet your parents. Here we've dated now going on three years and I've never met your folks in person."

"I've always offered to drive down to Georgia for you to meet them, but our schedules never really allowed it. But let's definitely make some time real soon, Mekyla," Ian said, as they stood in the garage of their home.

"I think I'm going to get a little writing in, and then I'm turning in early," said Mekyla.

"I'm gonna hit the shower and lay it down myself. Mekyla, it's been a while since we watched a movie together, so just this once, maybe you'll only type for about an hour and then come lay next to me."

"Sure, I think I can manage that." Mekyla said, as she headed for the study room.

"Ian?"

"Yes?"

"It was a good thing you going out late last night to get more Michelob, because it came in handy at Christy's get together."

"Oh, yeah, I couldn't sleep for some reason and I walked around outside for a little bit and then went to the store." Ian said, scratching his head as he recalled what all happened that night.

"Okay, well I'll see you in a little bit."

Mekyla settled in at the computer and cleared her head. 'So okay, Jonathan was showing Lisa the sights and what happens next?' she asked herself, while she popped in Aaliya's, O*ne in a Million* CD instead of Nora Jones.

"Well, what do we have here?" said Lisa. "This looks like a familiar place."

"I thought maybe we'd come back to my place and have an early dinner."

"You did, huh? I don't know if we should do that, Jonathan."

"Why not? I'm not going to do anything you wouldn't allow me to do."

"Your famous quote, huh? Where was the door attendant when I needed him the last time?"

"I think the little fart called up or sent some kind of signal for you to leave early this morning."

"No, that was my conscience, and a little too late I might add. I'll stay as long as there aren't any strawberries involved."

"Oh, there definitely won't be any strawberries, I bought some peaches this time."

"Jonathan!"

"I'm just kidding, Lisa. I thought you had a good time."

"I had a real good time. So much so that for a moment I forgot I was married. I love the way your home smells. It has a combination of many pretty scents that I can't describe."

"Would you like more wine?"

"No thank you. That's what got me in a little trouble the last time. Can I help you cook this time?"

"Sure. Come on in and grab one of the aprons hanging in the pantry."

"So what's on the menu tonight?"

"I thought we would have some salmon with white saffron rice, fresh asparagus with hollandaise sauce and some fresh sour dough bread. Start out with a nice salad. What d'ya think?"

"That sounds wonderful. But in order for it to taste as good as it sounds, you probably want to get somebody else to help you."

"Oh, come on! You'll do just fine. Tell you what. All of the ingredients for the salad are in the refrigerator. Why don't you start with that?"

"Now *that* I'm sure I can handle. You're not watching any sports today?"

"Those sports can wait. This is your time," Jonathan said, as he gave Lisa a kiss on the back of her neck.

"So, would you like me to pour you a glass of wine?" Lisa said, as she moved away in slow motion.

"Yes please. Do you eat just the tips of the asparagus or the whole spears?"

"To be honest, I've never eaten asparagus, tips or spears.

"Okay, you're trying something new tonight. I would absolutely have fun with you, just in experimenting alone. When I was touching and caressing you the other night, I could tell you were conservative, and – now don't take this the wrong way – inexperienced. That was a complete turn on to me. A man should know it's definitely okay to experiment with his wife, explore possibilities of new pleasures for you." Jonathan said casually, as he seasoned the salmon. "Lisa, I believe that's enough salad for an army."

"Yes, of course," Lisa said. She took the hem of the apron and brushed it across her forehead to wipe away the moisture.

"Would you mind lighting the fireplace and a few of the candles on the dining room table?"

"Now you're asking me to multi task. You see, I over did the salad. You sure you want to trust me with fire?"

"Why don't you put a CD in? One, of your choice."

"You really have a nice CD collection. How about some Al Green? *Let's Stay Together*."

"That's one of my favorites. That's a nice choice," Jonathan said, as he approached Lisa.

"Okay, what are you doing? I know that look," Lisa said as she looked into Jonathan's eyes.

"I've wanted to do this all day," Jonathan said. He grabbed hold of Lisa's head, pulled her to him, and gave her a long, soft kiss on the lips.

"We shouldn't be doing this, Jonathan," Lisa said, as she grabbed a hold of Jonathan's hands in an unsuccessful attempt to pull them away from her face."

"The only woman I've had feelings for in the last ten years has been my wife. What I'm feeling for you is not lust. It's a genuine affection. I'm truly attracted to you the person, and I want to know more about you. I don't want to stop. I know you're married, and I know this is going to be an unfair request. But please, consider me. Choose me, Lisa. Choose to stay with me. Don't answer now, because I know that's a very tall request, but those are my feelings."

"Jonathan?"

"Yes?"

"I smell your sour dough bread."

"Yes, of course. But please think about what I just asked of you."

'Okay I'm stopping here,' thought Mekyla. 'Remembering that fire she made really made her sleepy and all tingly inside.' Mekyla closed down her computer and headed for the bedroom.

"Hey sweetie, so what did you come up with as far as a movie to watch?"

"I thought we would watch *Man on Fire*. It's playing on Pay per View."

"That sounds good to me. Let me get in the shower and I'll be right out. So what time is it scheduled to start?" Mekyla asked, from the bathroom.

"It will start in another fifteen-minutes, or so. I've already selected it so we wouldn't miss the window of opportunity," Ian said, as he approached the bathroom.

"Okay. Ooh, you scared me. Didn't you already take your shower?"

"Yes. It's just that I've been feeling some strange vibes, and just want to know if we're okay."

"We're fine, Ian. I just had some things on my mind and I'm dealing with it."

"Is it something I can help you get through?"

"No, not this time. I need to do this one on my own."

"I love you Mekyla."

"I know Ian. Okay, let me get in the shower and I will be right out," Mekyla said as she continued to undress to get into the shower.

"Mekyla, I know I don't want anyone else but you. You are that one true thing in my life."

"Uh-huh, okay," Mekyla said in a very low voice of shameful confusion.

"Would you like some popcorn?"

"That sounds good." 'And why don't you lace mine with cyanide?'

"What was that, Mekyla?"

"Nothing, I didn't say anything."

"That was good timing. The movie is about the start. Are you comfortable?"

"I'm fine. Did you get everything you need? Can I get you something to drink, Ian?"

"I knew I was forgetting something. Yes, please."

"I'll be right back. I'm going to grab me some of this barbeque from Tere's house. Did you want any?"

"I didn't know you brought home a doggy bag. I think I have room for another piece of one of those ribs, if you have enough."

"Yes, I grabbed two of each. I knew you would probably get hungry again. We're going to break the no eating in the bed rule this one time."

"When was that rule made?"

"When I said it out loud is when it became a rule. No paper required on house adult rules."

"Well there were a lot of things I said out loud. Are they house rules as well?"

"I'm sure they're not."

"Lopsided now, and will always be, I'm sure," Ian said, as he made himself and Mekyla comfortable for the movie.

CHAPTER FIFTY-EIGHT
BREAKING NEWS

"Okay, I've put the kids down for bed. What are they saying on the news? Please turn it up?"

"Sounds like there was a bad accident on 75," Trey said, as he turned the television up.

"Breaking news," said the announcer. "There has been a terrible car accident on Highway 75, just south of McAlester, Oklahoma. I'm told there were at least four cars involved, and so far, at least two people have been airlifted by EMS helicopter to the nearest hospital in Dallas, Texas. We will have more on this story as it becomes available to us. We now return you to your regularly scheduled program, but please stay tuned to News Channel eight for further developments on this story, as they become available."

"I hope no one died in that accident," said Christy as she went back to preparing her bath. "I wonder how it happened."

"Christy, I know I haven't given you the attention you deserve. I've been under a lot of stress, trying to seal this deal with Boa Elliott and Dallas Rangel, in spite of what may have happened at the game."

"I've apologized to you for that."

"I didn't say that to try to get you to apologize," said Trey. I'm saying *I* would like to apologize. That's all."

"Apology accepted," Christy said. She leaned over and gave her husband a kiss on the cheek. "So, do you want to join me in the tub, or are you going to stand there and watch me?"

"I'm going to do both," Trey replied, as he grabbed Christy from behind and held her naked body close to him.

CHAPTER FIFTY-NINE
TRUE CONFESSIONS

"That was a pretty good movie," Mekyla said, as she wiped the tears from her face. "I have to admit, that probably was one of the best movies I've seen Denzel in yet."

"Hell, *I* almost cried," Ian said. He gathered the plates full of bones from the barbecue and the popcorn bowl with the un-popped seeds rolling around in the bottom.

"Thanks for clearing this for me."

"No problem. We're a team."

"Now, we're a team. Okay, teammate, grab me a glass of water please. No, actually, I can get it myself. My adrenaline is flowing. I think I'm going to write again, just for a few minutes."

"I'll be glad when you finish the book, so I can have you all to myself again."

"Hey, Mr. Selfish Man, you dropped something," Mekyla said, as she grabbed a small afghan to wrap around herself. She walked down the hall wearing nothing but her tank top and panties and the afghan. Mekyla removed the disc from her locked desk drawer. As she thought about the conversation she'd had with Jonathan earlier in the day, tears began to roll down her face.

"Mekyla, are you okay?" Ian asked, hearing her sniffles as he passed to go back into the bedroom.

"Yes, I'm fine."

"You're crying."

"I was just thinking about him."

"Him, who?" Ian said, with a hint of anger in his voice.

"Um, I was still thinking about the movie, that's all."

"I wouldn't have thought a movie would affect you that way. You don't usually get that emotional over movies. It was only the one scene, really. Are you sure there's nothing else on your mind, because, if you're thinking about when I left for a little while to get some air and the beer, that's all it was."

"What are you rambling on about? Is there something you would like to share with me?" Mekyla asked, with a look of curiosity.

"That's what I've been saying this whole time. That there's nothing you should be worrying about. I'm totally in love with you and only you."

"You're being weird."

"Don't stay up too late Mekyla. You know how I love to feel your body next to mine."

"Sure," Mekyla said, as she put her hands on her head to fight the massive tension headache that was preparing to break over her.

'Who am I fooling?' she thought. 'I'm not going to get any writing done tonight. But I'm not ready to go in there and face Ian either. He's being too weird right now, and I really don't know how to gage it because of the crap I have on my mind.' She reclined in her chair, propped her feet up on her desk, and folded her hands across her forehead in an attempt to pull herself together. She forgot how old and tired the chair was. After a moment, it gave way and she fell backwards onto the floor.

"Ouch," Mekyla said, as she lay there on the floor laughing in disbelief. She spent a moment checking her elbow and shoulder for injuries. 'Forget it,' she thought. 'I'm just going to stay right here on the floor for a while. Because I know Mr. Blow My Back Out is down for the count. He can hear me sniffle, but he couldn't hear me fall to my death.'

CHAPTER SIXTY
AFTERGLOW

"Trey, that was absolutely wonderful."

"I'm glad you enjoyed it baby. Now let's get some sleep, I have a long day ahead of me tomorrow."

"Good night, darling." Christy said, as she turned to her side thinking about how foolish she had been the past few days.

CHAPTER SIXTY-ONE
VOICE MALE

"Morning, Ian. How are you feeling?"

"Believe it or not, I'm still full from yesterday. I think I'm going to skip breakfast this morning."

"You know I start my vacation this week. I was going to wait until the end of this week, but I think I'm going to start it a little earlier, maybe tomorrow."

"So what did you decide to do? Would you like to go away somewhere?"

"If we did, I would only want to write most of the time, so we probably shouldn't. I thought I would really get some writing done, since I'm nearing the end."

"So give me the update on Jonathan, Trevor, and that tramp, Lisa." Ian said, as he finished dressing for work.

"Okay, you're too deep for me. I think you should wait on the book to be complete."

"Well, she is. Okay, I'm getting out of here, call me later and I love you, Mekyla."

"Okay, have a nice day, Ian."

Mekyla got herself together and into her vehicle for the drive to work. "Hello, Marie. Sorry, I'm running a little late. I needed to make a quick stop by the pharmacy to pick me up some Tums. My stomach has been feeling upset lately. It could be that late night eating we did last night. Marie, can I get the papers on Mr. Elliott?"

"You should be able to find everything you need on the computer."

"I know, but I hand wrote a number on his papers and I need it now."

"So, what's going on with that?"

"That meaning Mr. Elliott, I really enjoyed his company and just wish to maybe have a soda with him one afternoon, nothing more than that," Mekyla said, as she tried to get the conversation from yesterday off her mind.

"Soda, afternoon, okay I'll get the papers out of the filing cabinet for you."

"Thank you, Marie. How's your son doing?"

"He's having a birthday coming up in a few months. My baby will be eighteen before I know it."

"But he's only three now, right?"

"Yes, Mekyla, but you know what I mean."

"What I know is that you should take lots of pictures and be very involved in your son's life, so you won't feel like he grew up over night."

"I'm going to really miss you while you're on your extended vacation Mekyla."

"I'm only going to be gone for a week, maybe two. You'll do just fine. I'll e-mail you a list of all my pending items, in case you need to deal with them for some reason. I've spoken to most of my clients and they're aware that I'll be out of the office for the next week or two, so you really shouldn't get many calls for me that I know of."

"Oh, and Marie, don't forget."

"I know, Mekyla, water the plants on Friday." Marie replied.

"Yes. Thank you for that. Well, okay. Looks like you have everything under control here. I wonder what Christy is doing for lunch today."

"Is that the drama one, or the married one?"

"That's not nice Marie, but it's the married one and her name is Christy. My sister's name is Christy. You're not writing all of this down, are you? I mean, I'm not going to see it in some book some day, am I?"

"Of course I wouldn't publish anything without your permission first. I'm just kidding I don't have anything written down about you or your family."

"And why do you call the other one, whose name is Jennifer by the way, the drama one?"

Marie shrugged. "It's just that whenever I see her, she always has some type of gossip going on. Always."

"Isn't it fair to say we all gossip?"

"Yes, but she just rubs me the wrong way. She seems sneaky."

"Rubs you, huh? Maybe she wants to see if you swing the other way."

"Stop it Mekyla. You know what I mean."

"Okay, I hanging up now, I've decided to stop there first. I should be there in a couple of minutes."

"Okay, see ya."

"Mekyla, I forgot to tell you, there was this guy on the answering machine saying he loves you also, and that he'll be here in Tulsa by the time you get to work this morning. First, I thought it was a wrong number, but then I thought about your name, which is not a common name, so I saved the message for you to hear."

"What are you talking about?"

"I left it on the machine."

"I'll be there." Mekyla said, as she waited on the light to turn green as she look at her office building, 'I wonder what in the world has Marie so worked up about.' Pulling into her parking space, Mekyla approached her office door. "Okay, go ahead and play answering machine again, please. I can hear it while I put my stuff away."

"You have one saved message," said the machine.

"Hit the button to start it, Marie."

"Okay, Mekyla. Calm down. I've never seen you this excited before."

"Hello, Mekyla," said the voice on the machine. "This is Jonathan. You hung up the phone before I had a chance to say that I had misplaced your card. I told myself I was putting it in a place I wouldn't forget, but failed to realize that it would take someone with a brain to remember that special place. I ransacked my house to locate this card. And now I find that the only number on it is your place of business. The papers to our divorce were delivered to my now ex-wife, because she finally decided to sign them. The reason why she was here was that she wanted to bring them to me personally and get the remainder of her things. To ensure this message reaches you. I'm on my way to Tulsa, Oklahoma to claim the true love of my life. Because now that I have heard from you and know that we're on the same page, I'm not going to lose you again. The drive should only be about six and a half, to seven hours, so I'll be getting in late. I'm going to check into a hotel and I'll see you in the morning. Love always, Jonathan."

"Marie, did you hear that? The love of my life is on his way to see me."

"I thought Ian was the love of your life. Who is this Jonathan person?"

"Don't ask, Marie. I'll explain everything later. He should be here any minute now."

"Mekyla, which route, would he have taken?"

"Coming into Oklahoma? Highway 75. Why?"

"Well, did you see the news last night about that car pile, up on Highway 75?"

"No, I didn't, what happened, and around what time?"

"Well it was on the ten o'clock news, but they did a news break during my favorite show, which was on around, say eight PM."

"That would have probably put Jonathan on the road around the same time. Marie what if – what if Jonathan was in that accident? I have no way of contacting him other than his home number."

"Go in there and call him, Mekyla."

"I'm scared, Marie, because if he doesn't answer, it's just going to make it worse. I'll just sit here and wait for a while." As Mekyla sat in her office filled with heightened emotions and waterfalls in her eyes, she began to reflect on their moments in time. How he held her in his arms and the way he complimented her.

"Mekyla! Mekyla!"

Startled by the sound of Marie's voice, Mekyla quickly answered.

"Yes, Marie."

"Christy's on the phone."

"Marie, why are you yelling?"

"I really don't know, but phone."

Mekyla picked up the phone and immediately started talking. "Christy, he was on his way here and now I don't know where to find him to make sure he's okay."

"Who are you talking about?"

"Jonathan."

"Jonathan who? Oh yeah, Jonathan. Now what are you talking about, and what do you mean you don't know how to find him? Does he not live in Texas anymore?"

"There was an accident on Highway 75. Marie said it happened last night."

"Yes, there was."

"Did you see the news, Christy? Are you going to make me ask you every question here?"

"Yes I did, but . . .."

"Well, what did they say?"

"Okay Mekyla, you're making me nervous. Just hold on and I'll tell you what I know. As Trey and I were settling in from the trip from Tere's house, there was a news break that said there were at least four cars involved and two people taken by air to the nearest hospital, which was in Dallas."

"Christy, he had to come through Dallas and down Highway 75 to get here. He said he would be traveling last night, and was going to be here at my office this morning. Do you think he was in that accident?"

"Mekyla, sweetie, I really don't know. Can't you call him on his cell phone or something?"

"No, I only have his home number and I'm scared to call it."

"Do you want me to come down there to be with you?"

"I'm going to give it another hour to hear from him, and then I'm headed to Austin."

"Call me before you decide to do anything, okay? And what about Ian? Did you forget you have a whole relationship with him?"

"All I know is that I need to see him again so I'll know what to do. I'll call you. Christy, Christy!"

"Yes, I'm here Mekyla."

"Sorry, I was trying to catch you before you hung up the phone, what was it you called for anyway?"

"Oh, it will keep. Just call me as soon as you hear something."

"Okay, I will. Goodbye Christy. Christy."

"Yes. Mekyla."

"Don't tell the others. I don't want them to know right now, okay?"

"Sure, of course. Know for sure this is what you want. Ian, he's a good guy to lose. Even though he's not totally where you want him to be, there's potential. You're not totally where you should be either."

"I know, Christy. Thank you for that."

CHAPTER SIXTY-TWO
GIVE ME A SIGN PLEASE

"Marie, did I get a call from Jennifer?"

"No, she wasn't on the answering machine."

"She was also traveling yesterday on Highway 75. I probably should give her a call. Please cancel all my appointments for today that you can't handle yourself. And only patch through my family, Ian and my friend coming in from out of town," Mekyla said, as she grabbed her cell phone where she had Jennifer on speed dial.

"Sure, Mekyla. I don't know what's going on, but I'm sure not going out for lunch today," Marie said, as she began to clear her desk of any distractions.

"Crap, I'm getting her answering machine. Hey, Jennifer, it's me. I haven't heard from you this morning. Please give me a call back to let me know you made it okay. Bye."

"Marie, I'm in my office undisturbed please. Unless it's the group

I mentioned before."

Preparing for her vacation, Mekyla placed a call to an old friend.

"Thank you for calling City Farm," said the receptionist. "How may I help you?"

"Mrs. Taylor Ellis, please."

"May I tell her whose calling?"

"Yes, tell her it's her good friend Mekyla."

"Sure, hold on Mekyla."

"Are you ready for me to take over your agency, and do a better job than you?"

"Of course, that's why I asked the best. I have a huge favor to ask of you. I'm probably going to leave sooner than Friday, maybe as early as tomorrow."

"Hey, count me there."

"You know you only have to peek in every now and then. You don't have to stay all day. Marie is a very competent worker. I trust she'll do fine."

"Not a problem. So where are you and Ian going?"

"What I thought about doing was hibernating in the house to get this book finished."

"Why don't you go somewhere? Check into a hotel. You'd probably get even more done that way."

"No, I better not. I got myself into some trouble the last time I went away."

"You're going to have to tell me all about that when you get back. But consider your office taken care of."

"Thank you, Taylor, very much. I owe you."

"Have a good week, Mekyla. Bye."

CHAPTER SIXTY-THREE
YOUR SECRET IS SAFE WITH ME

"Good morning, darling. Last night was absolutely wonderful. Actually the whole day was great."

"Good morning, Christy. What's for breakfast?"

"I've cooked you some bacon, eggs, grits and toast."

"Can I get some orange juice with that, please?"

"It's coming right up."

"Who was that you were on the phone with?"

"Oh, that was Mekyla."

"Is everything alright?"

"I'm not sure. She just received what would appear to be disturbing news."

"Like what?"

"Well, I don't think it's appropriate to share this with you."

"Why not? I'm your husband."

"Well, when she was away at the convention a couple of weeks back, she met this guy there. And I guess you would say that there was an attraction."

"Oh really? So I take it Ian doesn't know about this."

"Of course he doesn't know. She isn't sure herself. Well, maybe she is sure. I don't know. Your breakfast is getting cold darling."

"So let me make sure I'm hearing you right. Mekyla goes off to a convention for one weekend . . .."

"No, it was a week."

"A week, weekend, whatever, she was gone for a short period of time. And she meets this guy, and ends up having an affair with him?"

"We were just talking about what constitutes an affair. Technically it wouldn't be an affair, because she and Ian aren't married."

"Christy, don't ramble. I hate it when you ramble. She cheated on the man. It's the quiet ones you have to watch."

"Mekyla's really a good person; she's just not sure right now."

"If you think that stuff is okay, then maybe I should be watching you a little closer. Grab me more orange juice."

"Here you go, have a good day at work. I'll be in the laundry room if you need me."

"Actually sweetie, I'm gone. Kiss those kids for me."

As soon as Trey was out the door, Christy called Mekyla.

"Thank you for calling City Farm Insurance. This is Marie."

"Hello, Marie. May I speak to Mekyla, please?"

"Who's calling please?"

"This is her sister, Christy."

"I'm sorry, Christy. I had to make sure it was a family member."

"I understand, but may I speak with her please?"

"Mekyla, Christy on line one," Marie said.

Mekyla picked up the phone. "Hey, what's up?"

"I would have called you back sooner, but Trey just now left for work. Have you heard anything?"

"Nope, and I've made arrangements to take off earlier than I had planned. I'm going to Austin."

"Somehow I knew you were going to say that. Another thing, now this was sort of an accident, for the record, I told Trey about your friend."

"I'm not even going to ask how that was an accident. It doesn't matter. It's now going into the afternoon hour and he's still not here and no phone call."

"How are you going to explain your little trip to Ian?"

"Well, I do have this vacation time on my side, but I think I'm going to be completely honest for once in my life. What's the worst that can happen, him leaving me? I don't know what I'm doing, Christy. I just don't know."

"Well, like I said Mekyla, I'm right here for you."

"Thank you. But, you know what? Actually, I do want to know. How did it slip out, you telling Trey about my situation?"

"Well, I was still excited from last night. We did it."

"You did it? What do you mean, you did it?"

"You know. We made love."

"You haven't been making love?"

"No, we hadn't made love for a few months."

"Months! What man goes for months without making love to his wife? I'll tell ya who. A man that's getting it somewhere else, that's who. So that's why it bothered you so much when Jennifer started all this mess with the cashmere sweater lady. Mrs. Boa Elliot, was it? Who was very pretty, I might add. Heck, if I was a man, I would cheat with her."

"Mekyla, stop it. Before you leave I really would like to talk to you about something."

"Sure. Would you like to talk today?"

"No, today is really no good. I have to take the kids to their sporting events and then come home to prepare dinner. Maybe tomorrow you can stop by the house when I put the kids down for their naps."

"Just give me a call, and we'll go from there, okay?"

"All right, Mekyla. But still call me before you make a final decision on what you're going to do."

"I will. Love ya. Bye."

"I love you too."

As soon as she hung up the office phone, Mekyla picked up her cell phone and hit the speed dial button for Jennifer. All she got was voice mail again and she ended the call. Determined not to let the situation drive her crazy, she decided to find something constructive to do. "Marie, do you have one o'clock out there as well?"

"Yes, it's one o'clock."

"Why don't you go ahead and take you lunch? I know you haven't."

"I thought I would just sit around here in case you needed me for something."

"No, I'll be fine. Oh, by the way, I'll be starting my vacation as of tomorrow instead of the end of this week. The agent, Taylor Ellis, will be looking in on you from time to time. Everyone who needs to get a hold of me will know how to get a hold of me. For all others, I'll return in a week or two. Okay?"

"Sure, Mekyla. I won't give out your number to anyone. I brought my lunch; I'll just eat it here. You go head."

"Thanks, I'm no good here anyway, besides I need to take care of some other business before heading home."

"Have a nice vacation Mekyla."

"See ya, Marie."

'I think I'll surprise Ian, since it's still lunch time,' Mekyla thought, as she got into her vehicle.

"Hello, may I speak to Ian, please?"

"I'm sorry, he's not available at this time. Is there a message?"

"No, no message. I'll just try him later. Thank you."

'Well, so much for having a spontaneous lunch date with Ian,' She thought. 'I guess I'll grab some shrimp fried rice with some garlic chicken from Ming Palace Chinese Restaurant. Yeah. That sounds good.'

CHAPTER SIXTY-FOUR
A BAD CONNECTION

"Thank you for calling City Farm, this is Marie, how may I help you today?"

"Hello, may I . . .?"

"Hello. I'm sorry but I can barely hear you."

"May I . . .?"

"I'm sorry, we must have a bad connection. Please try calling back, thank you." Marie hung up the phone. 'Well, that was weird,' she thought.

CHAPTER SIXTY-FIVE
MY TRUTH AS I SEE IT

"Hello, Termaine."

"Hey, Mom."

"What's going on with you?"

"Mom, I need to know what I can do to see my daughter on a regular basis."

"Well, Termaine, there are a lot of things out there in your favor, but you have to meet the qualifications. As I said before, you need to focus on getting yourself together for whatever. Stay on your job for another few months and we'll see about getting you some type of joint custody. You must have a good, stable record in order to even have a chance."

"Mom, I really miss my daughter."

"I know you do, son. It hurts me more seeing you like this. I know you have a good heart and good intentions, but just continue to stay focused, and it will happen. What are you doing today?"

"I'm done for the day."

"Would you like to meet for a late lunch? I was going to stop at the Chinese restaurant, but I've changed my mind on that."

"Yeah, that sounds good, Mom. Where would you like to meet?"

"Let's meet at our favorite spot, Zios."

"I'll see you there in say ten to fifteen minutes."

"Okay, I'll be there," Mekyla said pulling into the left turn lane to make her way toward the restaurant. 'Let me try Jennifer one more time. I can't believe she's not returning my calls. She better return home safely, that's all I know. There's a good parking space. What do I want to do with this vacation time?' Mekyla asked herself, as she walked into the restaurant.

The hostess asked as she approached the entrance to the restaurant. "How many would be dining this afternoon?"

"There will be two of us, thank you."

"Would that be smoking or nonsmoking?"

"Nonsmoking section please."

"Please follow me," the hostess said, as she escorted Mekyla to a table.

"Your waiter would be with you in a moment. Can I get you any water?"

"Yes, please. Can you also bring one for my son? He'll be here momentarily."

"Termaine," Mekyla said quietly, as she waved her hand in the air. "You look nice."

"Thanks, Mom. So have you ordered yet?"

"No, the waiter hasn't made it over yet. So, are we having our usual, or are we going to try something new?"

"No, I would rather have the usual. You know how you have a favorite at each place you go out and eat at."

"Yes, I understand, because I don't want to try anything different either."

"Hi, my name is Peyton. I'll be your waiter this afternoon. Would you like to start out with an appetizer?"

"No thank you, Peyton. We would like to have two, chicken parmesan's over fettuccini, with white sauce."

"Would you like to have anything to drink?"

I would like to have some iced tea, and my son would like to have…What would you like to drink?"

"I'll have a Michelob Light in the bottle please."

"Your order will be out in about ten minutes."

"Thank you, sir."

"Michelob, huh? What are they, the hottest seller of beers? Ian always has those in the refrigerator. The last time we were here you ordered Dr. Pepper."

"I mean no disrespect, should I order that Dr. Pepper, Mom?"

"No, you're fine. It's just that you're all grown up. So, tell me about Shandalyn."

"Like what? She's just a friend."

"But somehow they think they're more than just friends, when it comes to an end."

"I can't help it if they're more attracted to me, than I am to them. I'm just having fun right now. My main focus is on my own family."

"And that's okay, because you're still young. There is no big rush to be engaged or married right now."

"What about you Mom? Have you and Ian thought about getting married?"

"It has crossed my mind a few times. Actually, I believe females start to think about that stuff way before its even time. Then life happens, then storms happen, then maybe real love happens."

"So is Ian your real love?"

"I don't know yet, Termaine. I don't know."

"Mom, when does one know that its real love?"

"For me, it was with your dad. I didn't know I was in love with your father until he was gone. The feeling I remember having is that I would think of him ever day as if he was still there. I became more aware of him not being there then when he was there. I guess you could say I took advantage of our time. Meaning I believed it to be his job and not a privilege to have someone by my side every day. You know it when you're going about your day-to-day activities and then, without any warning, tears just start to run down your face. You know it when you're with that person, and you feel secure and protected. You know it when you can laugh and cry with that person. You know it when you can go into the rest room and do something other than pee, while they are close by. You know it when you're spiritually, financially, and physically satisfied with that person. Finally, I feel you know it when you would do almost anything to change some of the words you said to make them go away."

"I know you said you didn't know until it was too late with my dad. Going back to my question before, what about Ian? How do you feel about Ian?"

"I truly don't know the extent of my feelings for Ian. I'm one of those people who look the part, have the part, but don't really feel the part. You could say I'm just there with someone whom everybody else strongly admires. Thank you. Can I get more water please?"

"This looks good."

"I know and it smells good as well. The bread is always so fresh. I'm getting full just looking at it. How's your security job coming along, is something you're looking to make a career out of, law enforcement?

"I probably wouldn't pivot to a police officer, but I was thinking about becoming a PI."

"Okay, that sounds exciting, digging into other folks business and private lives."

"Hey, Mom, are you going to eat your second piece of chicken, if not, put it in a to go box, I'll eat it later."

"You know I never do."

"Hold on. My cell phone is vibrating. Hello." 'Mekyla, did you call earlier?' said a voice on the other line.

"Hey Ian, I wanted to see if you were free for lunch, but I've just finish eating with Termaine." The voice said, 'I was in a meeting. That's too bad I missed you, having lunch with you is well overdue. Well, since you'll be off for the next few days, maybe when can have lunch together one day soon. Mekyla, I've got to run. I'll see you later tonight.' "Okay, Ian, bye."

"Hey, Mom, go ahead and put your extra chicken in this box so that I can have it for later."

"This was nice, we're going to have to start back doing this more often. I miss our lunches we use to have."

"Me too. You know I'm always free for a free lunch."

"I know you are. I just know you are," Mekyla said, as she sent her credit card with the waiter. "I've started my vacation early, so you're going to have to reach me either on my cell or at the house."

"What are you going to do for your vacation?"

"I don't know yet. I may drive down to Austin again. There's something I need to take care of there."

"Do you want some company?"

"No, not this time. But maybe when I get back we can go somewhere, just the two of us. Thank you, Peyton. So, are you ready to head out, Termaine?"

"Ready when you are. Thanks for the lunch, Mom. Who loves ya?"

"My mom," Mekyla said as she gave Termaine a kiss on the cheek. love you too. Next time you see my granddaughter, give her a big sloppy kiss for me."

"I will."

CHAPTER SIXTY-SIX
TOUCHING BASE

"Hello."

"Mekyla, where are you?"

"Hey, Christy, I'm just leaving the restaurant. I had lunch with Termaine."

"I called your office and Marie said you were gone for the week. I thought to myself, 'I know this girl hasn't taken her butt to Texas without telling me.'"

"Nope, I'm still here for now, but that's not to say that I'm not going to take off in the morning," Mekyla said, as she got into her vehicle.

"I would ride with you, but you know I have children."

"Thanks, but no thanks. I need to do this one on my own."

"So are you going to drive out or take a flight."

"I'm going to fly out this time and rent a car."

"You sound a lot more calm."

"I am. But I still haven't heard from Jennifer."

"Since Tere's house?"

"Yeah. I don't know what to think of that, Christy."

"She'll call. She's probably just busy doing whatever it is she does."

"She's in real estate, but that's not the reason she went there. Okay, can we finish this conversation when I get to the house, because I'm sure it's not safe to be talking and driving at the same time?"

"Yes, of course. Just call me when you get ready to take off, or did you need a ride to the airport?"

"I guess I didn't think about that. Yes, I need a ride."

"Okay. Well, just call me at least a couple of hours ahead of time."

"Sure. Okay, Christy. Kiss those kids for me."

As Christy hung up the phone she began to think about Trey and the new feelings developing between them. 'Okay, what are we having for dinner tonight? Maybe I should cook all of Trey's favorites tonight. Since we're sorta like on a newfound love for each other.'

CHAPTER SIXTY-SEVEN
A MISSED OPPORTUNITY

"Thank you for calling City Farm. This is Marie. How may I help you?"

"Mekyla . . .."

"I'm sorry. We must have a bad connection. I can barely hear you."

"May I speak to Mekyla?"

"Mekyla will be on vacation for the next two weeks. Is there a message?"

"No, thank you."

'Wow, that person sounded terrible,' Marie thought to herself, as she began to close out her files for today.

CHAPTER SIXTY-EIGHT
DINNER AND A MOVIE

"Hey, Ian, what are you doing home so early?"

"I thought I would surprise you."

"I'm surprised."

"So, I thought we would catch an early movie and then come back home and make love all night."

"Okay, well, what did you want to go see?"

"Whatever you want to see."

"I don't know what's playing. Actually let's go to Blockbuster's and rent a couple of movies and stay in tonight."

"Whatever you'd like to do. It's your vacation. So, I'll go and find a thriller and the chick flick for you. Did you want to order out tonight?"

"Maybe we'll just order a pizza."

"Are you okay? You look tired."

"Yes, I had a lot of stuff on my mind. And this book is draining me mentally."

"Why don't you take a nap, and I'll wake you after a couple of hours."

"That sounds like a plan. I'll see you when you get back, Ian," Mekyla said, as she flopped onto the recliner. 'Okay how am I going to tell him about the trip to Austin? I'll just say there's some unfinished business I have there that needs my attention. Oh, he's not going to buy that. He already knows about the dinner I had with the guy. Maybe I won't tell him, not until I arrive in Austin. Yeah, that's what I'll do. That's such a trifaling and cowardly way, but it works for me.'

"I'm not even in the mood to write anything tonight. Maybe I'll get some work done on my laptop while I'm on the flight. Okay, a bath would be nice right about now. I probably have another thirty minutes before Ian returns. Maybe with some aromatheropy candles. A nice CD. I guess I'll listen to me some Ray Charles as a salute to him. I know I'm not in Georgia, but that song was to meant to be translated to whatever city and state we the listeners love and desire. Oh yeah, this feels good,' Mekyla thought, as she lowered her body into the bathtub. 'What's my plan going to be when I get to Austin? I can't just show up like the Lone Ranger coming to get my man.'

"Mekyla."

"Yeah."

"Who are you talking to?"

"I was just thinking out loud. That was pretty quick."

"There's one right down the street. I would love to get in there with you."

"No, I'm on my way out," Mekyla said, as she sat up straight in the water.

"So, you decided not to take a nap. Instead you took a nice bath."

"Yep. I figured I had plenty of time to sleep tonight."

"Maybe not. That's why I wanted you to take a nap. I thought maybe we could have some serious bonding time. Before, during, and after the movie."

"Oh, really?" Mekyla said, as she began to put on her tee shirt and granny panties, hoping they would turn him off.

"What's with those panties?"

"It's getting close to my cycle."

"Right now?"

"Pretty close."

"So we can probably still . . .."

"No, I don't think so Ian."

"Ah, man! Are you ready for me to start up the movies?"

"Sure, whenever you're ready. So what did you get for me?"

"I rented *Terminal* for you and *Trapped* for me."

"*Trapped*? Isn't that an old movie?"

"Yes, but I didn't get a chance to see it."

"But I did hear it was a pretty good movie."

"Let's watch yours first, because I know you're going to fall asleep on the second one. Did you still want to order pizza?"

"I'm not hungry, but order a small for yourself."

"You know, I'll probably just make me one of those nice ham and cheese sandwiches you make for me so well."

"Is that a hint?"

"Only if you're not tired, please."

"That'll work for me as far as the movie choice first. Ian, can you turn the sun down some?"

"I can do the next best thing. I can close the blinds and turn the lights out."

"Don't get in my warm spot. I'll be right back with your sandwich."

CHAPTER SIXTY-NINE
MY SHRED OF HOPE

"How was your day, darling?"

"I have to admit, I thought I would be very tired from yesterday's activities, but actually all in all it was okay."

"That's good. Were you ready to eat, or did you want to wait awhile?"

"Give me about thirty minutes to shower. Hand me one of those Michelobs out of the refrigerator, please."

"You're already low, I thought you went out the other night to get beer."

"I did. Okay, I'm headed up stairs. If you don't mind, bring my food upstairs when I get out of the shower, okay?"

"Sure, Trey. I'll bring it right up." 'Actually, I'll be right up,' Christy said to herself as she headed for the stairs.

"Christy, is that you?" said Trey from inside the shower.

"Yes."

"We're out of soap in here. Would you hand me another bar. Baby, what are you doing?"

"I'm getting in the shower with my husband."

"Christy, not now, baby."

"Yes, right now, Trey. I still need you and I need you right now," Christy said, as she began to soap Trey up from head to toe.

"What's come over you."

"I'm not going to wait on something that belongs to me anymore. As long as you're my husband and we live under the same roof, I'll have you whenever I need you."

"Where is this aggression coming from?"

"There's no one else in my life but you, Trey, and I have needs. I want my husband to fulfill me the way that I know you can."

As Trey pulled Christy close to him, he stared into her eyes and began to kiss her in a way that was as passionate as the first day he met her. "Christy, I will always love you, even though I may not show it all the time. You are the mother of my children and my wife forever."

"Thank you for that, Trey," Christy said, as her tears were washed away by the shower.

"I promise we can continue this once I get some food in my stomach. So, let me finish this shower and you go down and fix my plate and then the evening is all yours, okay?"

"Okay, Trey," Christy said, as she removed herself from the shower with a smile of satifaction on her face.

'I think I'm getting my husband back,' she thought as she put her robe on. 'I don't know what happened, but I'm getting him back. And this was before he knew I cooked all of his favorites. Oh, my. He's going to get a nice little bonus treat tonight.' Making her way back up the stairs with his food, she called out. "Trey, where are you?"

"I'm in here with the kids."

"Oh, okay. I'll just set your food here in the bedroom. I see you're about finished with the first beer, did you want me to bring you up another Michelob?"

"Yes, if you don't mind."

"No, not at all.

"My kids are growing up before my eyes."

"Yes, they are. Maybe you can come and watch them play at some of their games."

"Yes, I've been meaning to make time for them, but I guess I'm going to need to try a little harder."

"Thank you for that."

"For what, Christy?"

"I don't know how to explain what's happening, but it's making me very happy. Is everything okay, did you need me to get you anything else?"

"Yes, actually, stay close by, because I'm going to want you to refill my plate. This is very good. You must have put your foot in this one, Christy."

"Thanks, Trey. I even made dessert."

"Maybe much later on the dessert. After my next plate, I'm sure I'll be stuffed."

"Your cell phone is ringing, Trey. Do you want me to get it for you?"

"No, I'll check it later, thanks."

"If you need me, I'll be downstairs putting the dishes away," Christy said, as she headed for the stairs. 'I wonder why his phone rings late in the evening. It couldn't be business. We're in a good place right now. I'm not going to start assuming anything.'

CHAPTER SEVENTY
NEWS BRIEF

"Good morning, Ian."

"Good morning, bright eyes. You're up early for a person that's on vacation."

"I needed to talk to you before you left for work."

"Okay. Is that breakfast I smell?"

"Yes, I made you some bacon, eggs and toast. You know, the usual."

"So what's up?"

"I wanted to let you know I'll be flying out of town today for a couple of days."

"Oh? Where are you going?"

"There is some unfinished business I would like to take care of in Austin."

"Austin? What's unfinished in Austin?"

"It has to do with my book."

"And you have to fly all the way to Austin to take care of that?"

"Yes."

"Well, what if I said I didn't want you to go?"

"I would still go. I have to do this, Ian."

"Do what? I thought it was business with the book, but your tone of voice makes it sound more personal."

"It is. Well, what I mean is that I need to know what these feelings are that I have for this person."

"You're going to Austin to chase some man. And what do you expect for me to do? Sit here and wonder if you're going to return?"

"He was actually on his way here to see me, and I believe the reason why he didn't make it is because he was a part of the accident that took place on Highway 75 last night. I'll understand if you want me to move my things out."

"Why did you wait until this morning to bring me this mess? Now, I'm going to have this on my mind all day. I thought we had something. What am I supposed to do with this request? I don't know what to do, Mekyla. I love you. I don't want to lose you. You're having conversations with another man. The two of you are making plans to see each other. Don't make me beg, Mekyla," Ian said as he attempted to hold back the tears forming in his eyes.

"I know this may sound selfish, but I believe I know that I don't won't to lose you either, but this is something I have to deal with, otherwise I will always wonder."

"Mekyla, can we deal with this when I get off of work?"

"I've already scheduled my flight."

"Before we even talked about this? I need to go into work for at least a few hours. Can you delay it for a few hours for me please?"

"Ian, the sooner I do this, the sooner I can return. I'm really not trying to be hurtful, but just please let me do this."

"Two days? Two days is all you're asking for?"

"I need at least two days."

"I can't believe this. I've got to put my foot down Mekyla. If you're not back in a couple of days, then I want you gone from here. I can't take this kind of mess. I thought we had something."

"We do, Ian, and I understand," Mekyla said, as she stood in front of the dining room chair with tears rolling down her face.

"How are you getting to the airport?"

"Christy offered to take me."

"So, Christy knows everything?"

"No, not quite."

"Well, it sounds like you two have it all worked out. I'm going to work," Ian said as he turned away and headed for the door.

"Ian?"

"Yeah?"

"It's not you. You're great. You are everything a woman could ever ask for in a man. It's just that sometimes things present themselves, and in order not to have all the what-ifs over my head, I need to have closure."

"Do what you have to do Mekyla. Goodbye."

'What am I doing?' Mekyla thought as she began to dial Christy's phone number. "Christy, hey it's me."

"Hey, Mekyla. I was hoping I wouldn't get this call this morning. So you're going to do it huh?"

"Yeah, I have to."

"Okay. What time do you want me to pick you up?"

"Come in about a couple of hours. That will give me plenty of time to prepare to board the flight."

"Okay, I'll be there."

"Okay, see ya," Mekyla said. She began to pack the rest of her things for the trip with teardrops falling on her hands as she folded her clothes. 'Okay, now for a quick shower, and I'll be ready to go. Now this could be none other than my son calling me,' thought Mekyla as she scrambled for her cell phone. "Hello."

"Mekyla."

"Jennifer."

"What's up girl?"

"What's up? Where have you been, why haven't you returned my calls?"

"For some reason I was out of range, down in the swamps, you know."

"I've been worried sick about you."

"Worry no more my, sister. Boy, do I have some stuff to tell you."

"I'm just glad it wasn't you in the car accident on Highway 75."

"Oh yeah, I saw that accident. Terrible accident."

"What do you mean, you saw the accident?"

"I was a few cars behind the people that were involved going south."

"Okay, so the only cars that were involved were headed south on 75?"

"No, the people who were headed south on 75 fell asleep at the wheel, or something, I guess. They veered over into the oncoming northbound traffic, collided head-on with the first car, which caused a chain reaction involving several other cars behind that one. But none of the others were as badly crushed as the two that hit head-on."

"Okay Jennifer, I need for you to think. Do you remember a silver Jaguar involved?"

"Why am I trying to remember what cars where in this accident, Mekyla?"

"Please just try and remember and I will explain in a minute."

"Well it wasn't one of the two main cars that were in the accident, but hold on. There was a silver car that appeared to be a nice one, but again it was smashed in the front and the rear. So I don't really know what type it was. There were several onlookers and I guess one of them called for help, because an EMS helicopter was right there within about twenty minutes. Traffic was going slow and I saw the helicopter fly overhead as we were moving along. So what's the deal?"

"Jonathan may have been in that accident."

"Austin Jonathan?"

"Yes."

"Oh my. Well, I wish I could tell you more, but it was getting to be dusk and I didn't stick around to really get a close look at everything. A lot of the time, you feel like you're getting in the way more than helping."

"Jennifer, I'm going to get in the shower. I was on my way to Austin to see Jonathan."

"But I thought you were going to let that alone, since his wife was there."

"It turns out she was there to give him the divorce papers and he left a message on the answering machine at the office saying that he would be in town that evening and that he will stop by my office the next morning, but he never did. So I'm now praying it wasn't him in that accident."

"Wow. So you're going after your man?"

"Well, he's not my man, but yes, I need to know."

"One quick thing before we hang up, Mekyla. When I was in Louisiana, I stopped by Ms. Cashmere's shop."

"But what about Junior's father, how did that go?"
"It's all tied together."
"What do you mean?"
"We're going to need more than a few minutes. When are you returning?"
"I'll be gone at least a couple of days."
"We'll talk when you get back. Have a safe trip, and good luck."
"Thanks, Jennifer. See ya," Mekyla said as she looked at the clock on the nightstand. 'Oh, I really need to take my shower and finish the small details. First I need to find out what hospital he's in, if any. "Yes, operator, I'm not sure which hospital I need to ask you for in Dallas, Texas, so can you give me a number for each one of the major hospitals in Dallas, please."
"Ma'am, I have several listings. Would you like them all?"
"Yes, please," Mekyla said. She wrote each number down as it was given to her. "Thank you very much, operator." 'Okay, now that I have the numbers. Let me take that shower and try to call all of them before Christy gets here.'

CHAPTER SEVENTY-ONE
WEDDING HELP

"Hello."
"Christy, this is Schonda."
"Hey, Schonda."
"I'm about a month away from having this baby and I need to finish the planning for the wedding. Can I get you to come over and help me with some stuff?"
"I thought you would never ask. But first, I have to take Mekyla to the airport."
"Where is she going?"
"Oh, uh, she has some business with that book again out there."
"Oh, okay. Then maybe you can stop by afterwards."
"Give me a couple of hours and I'll be there."
"Okay, thanks Christy."
"You're welcome."
"Kids, are you ready? We need to go pick up auntie Mekyla," Christy said, gathering her keys and purse.

CHAPTER SEVENTY-TWO
IN SEARCH OF LOVE

"Josey Lane Hospital. How may I direct your call?"

"I need information on a possible patient, please."

"How can I help you?"

"Do you have a, Jonathan Baize – I mean Omari – as a patient there?"

"No, I'm sorry, but I don't find anyone by that name."

"Thank you."

'They have so many hospitals there, but I must not give up. Cross my fingers.'

"Southlake Emergency Care Center. How may I help you?"

"I'm calling to get information on a patient, please."

"What is the name?"

"Jonathan Omari."

"How do you spell the last name?"

"O M A R I."

"Mr. Omari is in room 1082, ma'am. Would you like for me to connect you?"

"No thank you," Mekyla said, as she slowly put the phone down.
"Yeah, who is it?" Mekyla said, startled by the doorbell. "I'm coming."

"Hey, are you ready? You look spooked, are you okay?"

"I was just calling around to all the hospitals and emergency centers in the surrounding Dallas area. I found him. He's at Southlake Emergency Center."

"Are you going to be okay?"

"Yes, I just need to get there."

"Okay, well, where's all your stuff?"

"It's in the bedroom. Just grab that one carryon, I'll get the rest. I need to grab my lap top. Okay, Christy that should be everything. Ian."

"I just wanted to see you one last time before you left. I guess I was really hoping you decided not to go."

"He was a part of the wreck that happened on Highway 75. He's still in the hospital."

"Christy, you can go ahead and leave, I'll take Mekyla to the airport."

"Well. Mekyla, is that okay with you?"

"Ian, Christy's kinda already here."

"And it's not a bother," Christy blurted out.

"Mekyla, it's me, Ian. I'm not going to hurt you."

"Christy, it's okay. I'll ride with Ian."

"Call me when you get ready to take off, okay."

"Okay, thank you for coming over to drive me. Bye kids."

"See ya, Ian," Christy said, with a look of hesitation.

"Okay, well, I'm ready, Ian."

"Are these the only two bags?"

"Yes. I'll get the door," said Mekyla. 'Don't let this man go loony on me,' she thought as she closed the door. "So, did you get what you needed to get done at the office?"

"Not really. But I did get a chance to delegate some of the work."

"So, you're not going back to the office?"

"I will go in a little later, probably when everyone has left for the day. What time is your flight?"

"In another forty five-minutes. We're okay on time. We should be there in about another five minutes or so."

"Mekyla, did you and this guy have sex?"

"No. No we didn't, Ian."

"So what's the deal? What is it you feel he can give you that I can't?"

"It's hard to explain. I don't know if I know how to explain it to you without hurting us. I know if the situation were reversed I would be just as confused or upset as you are. But I can't stop these feelings that I have, and I don't know if I want to. And at the same time, I don't want to lose you or you to lose me. Because I know what it feels like to have you, and if it's the opposite to not have you, I know I don't want to have that feeling."

"Which airline are you taking?" Ian said as he approached the departure section of the airport.

"I'm flying Southwest Airlines."

"Did you want to check any one of these two bags, or do you want to take them both on board with you?"

"I think it would be okay to take them both with me, probably easier."

"Do you already have your ticket?"

"Yes, I printed it off the computer."

"I can only walk you to the security check. Are you going to be okay with these bags?"

"Yes, I'll be fine."

"I love you, Mekyla," said Ian. He pulled Mekyla close to him and gave her a long kiss on the lips.

"I'll call you when I get there, Ian. Bye."

CHAPTER SEVENTY-THREE
YOU'RE MY BABIES DADDY

"Yes, where can I find Brent, the football coach?"

"He's out on the field with the players. He'll be finishing up in another three to four hours. They're going to have a meeting after practice today."

"How do I leave a message for him?"

"He has voice mail. Let me dial it for you."

"Thank you. Brent, hi, this is Jennifer Holiday. Long time no talk. Give me a call on my cell phone. I have something that I need to talk to you about. The number is 918-481-1234. You still sound the same. Give me a call. Bye. Thank you for doing that."

CHAPTER SEVENTY-FOUR
THE FINAL MEAL

'Okay, I need to relax my mind. Maybe I can get in a couple of chapters before I land in Dallas. Lisa and Jonathan were about to have dinner.'

"Jonathan, this looks absolutely wonderful. You're absolutely wonderful."

"Thank you, Lisa. I would love to do this for you every night if you would only let me."

"That's something I can't answer right now. You know I'm married and you're in the process of a divorce."

"Taste the asparagus and tell me what you think."

"Remember this is my first time eating this, so don't get offended if I don't like it."

"I won't."

"Okay, this is workable. It wouldn't be the first vegetable I would go out to buy, but it has potential to make it on the dinner table on special occasions. Now for this Salmon, it's absolutely to die for. It has a butter lemon taste to it. You're going to have to show me how you did this the next time I'm in town."

"I would love to teach you everything I know."

"You always have the right thing to say. You are so charming and fun."

"Lisa, I don't want you to leave tonight, the way you did the other night. I don't want to scare you away, but sometimes you just know when it's right."

"I know, and that's the part that's scaring me so much. I know I love my husband, and I know he loves me. But I'm having these feelings with you."

"Sometimes, Lisa, love is just not enough to fulfill all of those cravings."

"I don't want to hurt my husband."

"But it's hurting you to stay with him. Just take some time and think about it. You have all the time in the world to make up your mind. I won't put any pressure on you if I just know that I'm a possibility."

"Thank you, Jonathan. You are so wonderful."

CHAPTER SEVENTY-FIVE
GIVE ME A BREAK

As Mekyla, made her way to the Avis rent-a-car counter, she began to look for her confirmation. "Hello. I'm not sure where I put my confirmation. Can you look me up by name?"

"Yes, ma'am. And your last name please?"

"Williams. Mekyla Williams."

"Yes, Ms. Williams, we have you in an intermediate. Something like a Toyota Camry?"

"That would be fine."

"I just need to have your signature on this line please. I see you waived the insurance coverage."

"No, I won't need any additional coverage. I'm an insurance agent. Trust me, I'm insurance poor."

"Ms. Williams, you can just go right through those doors and you'll find an Avis attendant waiting to assist you in locating your vehicle."

"Thank you very much. You have a nice day." Out in the parking area, Mekyla was directed to her rental car by the attendant. She started to walk towards the car he'd pointed out, and then stopped. "Excuse me," she said. "Can you give me directions to Southlake Emergency Care Center?"

"Certainly," said the man.

Mekyla wrote the directions down. "Thank you very much," she said.

The Camry was nice, but going from an SUV to a regular sedan felt weird. 'I wish the airline could have just dropped me off at the hospital,' she thought. 'Dallas traffic freaks me way out. They drive as if they're in a rush to get everywhere.'

She saw her exit coming up and realized she needed to get over into the right lane. For some reason, she felt powerless in the mid-sized sedan. In her SUV she felt in control, looking down on the other drivers, big and in charge. "Thank you," she said out loud as a courteous driver allowed her to change lanes. As she tried to drive and look at the directions to the hospital at the same time, she missed her turn. 'Oh, well,' she thought. 'I'll just loop around and take the scenic route.' The scenic route turned out to be a busy highway, and by the time she got back to where she needed to be, she heaved a sigh of relief. 'These highways are going to be the death of me,' she thought as she parked the car. 'What was that room number again? Ten twenty-two, ten eighty-two, it was ten something. I'll just ask when I get to the tenth floor. Or is it the thousandth floor? Everything's bigger in Texas."

Stepping off the elevator, she approached the nurse's station. "Excuse me," she said to the woman behind the counter. "Can you give me Jonathan Baize's room number?"

The woman checked the computer. "We don't have Jonathan Baize listed on this floor."

"Are you sure? Was he here? I just called a few hours ago and they said he was on the tenth floor."

"The only Jonathan we have on this floor is a Jonathan Omari."

"Yes, that's him."

"His room is 1022." She pointed. "Right over there."

"Thank you. 'Okay, move, Mekyla, he's right there.' As Mekyla opened the door slowly, through the crack of the door she saw a woman sitting in a chair. Startled and confused, Mekyla began to slowly close the door.

"Hello, can I help you?" The lady said in a soft whisper.

Mekyla slowly opened the door again. "I'm sorry, I must have the wrong room."

"What is the patient's name that you're looking for?"

"His name is Jonathan Baize," Mekyla said, as she glanced over at Jonathan lying peaceful in the hospital bed.

"Yes, then I'm sorry, you're in Jonathan Omari's room."

"I'm sorry. I meant to say Jonathan Omari. I keep thinking of a character in this book."

"Well, this is my husband's room, and he's asleep right now. Are you a colleague of his?"

"No, I'm just a friend. Please excuse me."

"Is there a message for him?"

"No, no message." Mekyla said as she slowly backed out of the room and closed the door.

"Excuse me, nurse, can you tell me when Mr. Omari will be released?"

"Are you family?"

"I'm a friend. I'm just a concerned friend of Mr. Omari's."

"He's scheduled to leave tomorrow."

"So his injuries weren't that severe?"

"No, we just want to watch him for at least forty-eight hours."

"Thank you very much. Can you tell me which way to the visitor's parking lot?"

"Just follow this yellow line to the elevators and go to the first level and the parking garage would be to your left."

"Thank you again," Mekyla said, still fighting back her tears.

In the hospital bed, Jonathan opened his eyes. "Who was that, the person who was just here?"

"It was some lady claiming to be a friend of yours, but she kept mixing your name up she says, with a character in a book. She's probably a patient here in the hospital."

"I appreciate you handling the business with my car, but you don't have to stay here. I'll be getting out tomorrow."

"I know we're divorced now, but you'll always have a friend in me."

"I know, and I thank you for that. But I don't want to take up any more of your time. I know you have a practice to oversee. I'll call you when I get back to Austin."

"Did you want me to call a dealership to get you a loaner to get back to Austin?"

"Yes, call one of the Jaguar dealers and see if they would deliver it to the hospital."

"I'll set everything up with them and ask that they give you a call on your cell phone. I'm going by the penthouse to pick up those last few items and I'll just leave the key on the mantel over the fireplace."

"Again, thanks for everything that you're doing for me."

"Hey, we had a wonderful relationship. It's just that the marriage part didn't work out. You'll always have that special place in my heart," she said as she leaned over to give Jonathan a kiss on the cheek.

"And you in mine. Be sure to lock it up when you're done."

"Goodbye, Jonathan."

CHAPTER SEVENTY-SIX
A SISTER'S ADVICE

Hello."

"Hey, baby, this your Aunt Mekyla, may I speak to your mom."

"Mom, get the telephone. It's Aunt Mekyla."

"Mekyla."

"Christy, I was just in his room."

"So, how did it go?"

"Terrible. His wife was there."

"I thought you said they were divorced."

"Well, that's what he said. I don't know what to think right now."

"Just come on home."

"I can't, Christy. Not just yet. I'm just going to hang out for a bit. I'll keep in touch. Everyone knows how to get a hold of me if they need me."

"What about Ian?"

"Oh, yeah. I'll give him a call here in a little bit. I doubt if he would even want to hear from me."

"Girl, that man loves you, but everybody has their limits. Don't burn that bridge. You just might want to cross back over it one day."

"Thanks for the advice, little sis, I'll call him when I get settled into the hotel. Bye."

"Love ya, Mekyla, and be careful."

'Austin should only be like a two-hour drive from here. It's still kinda early. I can make it there before dark. Okay, I'm doing it,' Mekyla thought as she turned the car around to connect to Highway 35E.

CHAPTER SEVENTY-SEVEN
JENNIFER MAKES CONTACT

'I don't recognize this number. Now who could this be?' "Hello, this is Jennifer."

"Well hello stranger."

"Who is this?"

"This is Brent. Brent Elliott."

"Brent. That was fast. They said you would probably be held up for some hours."

"We got out a couple of hours early. So to what do I owe the pleasure of your personal appearance?"

"Can we meet later? It's something that's going to require a face to face talk."

"That sounds serious. Is everything okay?"

"Yes, everything is fine. Well, I just lost my grandmother. But that's not why I needed to see you."

"I'm sorry to hear about your grandmother. Would tomorrow be okay? I have some other business to take care of when I leave here today?"

"Sure. Then let's say seven o'clock tomorrow."

"Seven is fine. I'll call you around six, to find out where."

"Thank you for calling me. It's been a long time."

"Until tomorrow, Jennifer, have a good evening."

"Thanks, you too." As Jennifer sat with her hands folded to her chin at her desk, she glanced over to see her colleagues staring through the window of her office again. "What? I swear I work with a bunch of people that road in on the short bus." She picked up the phone again to find out about the funeral arrangements. "Hello, Dad, this is Jennifer. How is everything coming along as far as the funeral arrangements?"

"Hello, baby. Mother had good insurance coverage, which should take care of all of her expenses and then some. The funeral is scheduled for Wednesday at one PM at the Church of Christ on Peoria."

"I believe that's the church Mekyla attends."

"Mother didn't really belong to any one church, as far as I know, and they were the most reasonable and kindest group out of all the congregations I spoke with."

"Dad, let me know if you need any help with anything."

"Baby, I will. What I would like most is for us to spend more time together."

"We'll see, Dad. You have my cell phone number. Just give me a call if you need me to do anything. So, I'll talk to you later."

"Bye, baby."

Jennifer looked out her office door. "Nicole, can I get the file on the Swanson's property?" she said as she dialed up Mekyla's cell phone.

"Hello."

"Mekyla, this is Jennifer."

"Hey, what's up?"

"Where are you, and when are you headed back home?"

"I'm on my way to Austin."

"So everything must be going well. Good, good. Don't you attend the Church of Christ on North Peoria?"

"Yes, me and most of my family attend there. Why?"

"Well, that's where my grandmother's services will be held."

"Oh, okay. When is the service?"

"It will be on Wednesday at one. You'll be there, right?"

"To be honest with you, Jennifer, and this may sound insensitive, but I totally forgot. Would you please excuse me, I'm headed for Austin in a car. And to be even more honest, I'm not ready to come back home to face

Ian right now."

"I understand, Mekyla."

"But she'll definitely be in my prayers."

"Take care of what you need to do, Mekyla. Thank you, and could you also bring me the Johnson's file."

"What?"

"Sorry, I was talking to Nicole. Okay, Mekyla I'm going to get off of here. I'm playing catch up. Oh, and remind me to tell you about Brent Elliott."

"Who? You're breaking up."

"Mekyla, are you there?" 'I guess the connection was lost. I'll call her back later.

"Jennifer?" said Mekyla. 'I lost our connection. It sounded like she said Brent something. Who knows? I'll just talk with her about it when I return. Waco, Texas. This seems like a nice little town to raise kids in, for someone other than myself. Okay, there's the sign for Austin, eighty-four more miles. That's what? Another hour or so. This is a really nice radio station. One-oh-seven dot seven. They play a lot of nice oldies. I really like this one,' thought Mekyla as she listened to Mariah Carey's *Whenever You Call.*

'Wow, this one is going to sure enough make me cry.' "Love wondered inside, stronger than you, stronger than I. And now, that it has begun, we cannot turn back, we can only turn into one. I will never be too, far away to feel you, and I won't hesitate at all, whenever you call. And I'll always remember the part of you so tender I'll be the one to catch your fall, whenever you call. And I truly inspire, finding my soul, there in your eyes. And you have opened my heart and lifted me inside, by showing me yourself undisguised. And I won't ever be too far away to feel you. And I won't hesitate at all, whenever you call. And I'll always remember, that part of you so tender, I'll be the one to catch your fall, whenever you call . . .. something, something, I can never remember that last verse," Mekyla said, as she began to hum the rest of the song.

'Okay here we go.' Prompted by the radio, the words came back to her. "I won't ever be too far away to feel you, and I won't hesitate at all, whenever you call. And I'll always remember, that par of you so tender, I'll be the one to catch your fall, whenever you call." 'Yeah, that was a good song. Oh, okay, what is this Mariah Carey night? I like this one too.' "I'm thinking of you, in my sleepless solitude tonight, if it's wrong to love you, then my heart just won't let me be right. Cause, I've drowned in you and I won't pull through, without you by my side. I'd give my all to have, just one more night with you. I'd risk my life to feel your body next to mine, cause, I can't go on living in the memory of our song, I'd give my all for your love tonight." 'Oh, this is just too much for me right now, I need to change this station,' Mekyla thought, as she scanned the channels only to find a lot of talk radio.

'What are they talking about? Oh, that wasn't nice to say that the only kid that two ugly people would make is either a cat-dog baby or a cartoon. But it was kind of funny, but definitely wrong. What else is out there…well that song should be off by now, so let me get back to one-oh-five dot seven.'

'Okay, some Barry White.' Mekyla began to hum his song.

CHAPTER SEVENTY-EIGHT
JENNIFER INSISTS

"Here you go Nicole, if you would get a copy of each one of these files to the closing companies, I would appreciate it. Also, I will be leaving for the rest of the day; I'm burying my grandmother tomorrow."

"I didn't know I'm sorry to hear that she passed."

"Thank you Nicole. So I won't be in. I'll just see you on Thursday."

"Is there anything I can do for you, Jennifer?"

"Sounds like my father has a handle on everything, but thanks for offering. Nicole, could you pull my door closed please, thank you." Jennifer said, as she began to dial a number.

"Well, hello, my tall caramels treat."

"Jennifer, so have you made it back to town?"

"Yes, I made it back very early this morning. Did you miss me?"

"You were only gone for what, a couple of days?"

"Where are you?"

"I'm in my car, headed home."

"Make a detour and meet me at our spot."

"I can't do that."

"Why not?"

"That's a wrong question. Maybe some other day Jennifer, I'm really not in the mood, okay?"

"I got gypped the other night. We were interrupted by your phone the last time. Come on, I'll only have you detained for about an hour."

"You don't give up do you? Have everything arranged and I'll be there in thirty."

"You got it. Bye."

CHAPTER SEVENTY-NINE
DOUBLETREE DEJAVU

"Oh, I got the answering machine. Ian, it's me. I just wanted to let you know where I was, and that I will be giving you a call when I arrive to the hotel, okay?" 'Oh, I remember this entrance. I'm not far away from the hotel now. I need to just stay on this highway and I'll run right into it. Well, maybe not right into it, you have to do all these loops around here in Austin. Okay, here we go.'

"Hello, here are my keys and here you go, now don't spend that in too many places." Mekyla said, as she handed the bellman a tip.

"Yes, you should have a room for Mekyla Williams."

"Nice to have you back again, Ms. Williams."

"Thank you."

"Would you like to have the same room?"

"I don't see why not I didn't have any problems with it before. Actually, if you can radio the bellman to bring my car back around and have my luggage just delivered to my room, I would appreciate it. I'm going to run a couple of errands before I get settled in."

"Sure, that wouldn't be a problem. We'll take care of everything."

"Thank you very much."

CHAPTER EIGHTY
IS THIS LOVE?

"Hey, sweetie, you're late getting in today."

"I stopped off at the gym to workout for a little bit."

"When is your next game?"

"We're going to be out for the next three weeks, and then start back up."

"Are you hungry?"

"No, not yet. I'ma head up and take a quick shower. So give me about thirty minutes before you prepare my dinner, okay? Have you eaten yet?"

"No, I thought I would wait on you tonight."

"Good, I would like to look at your beautiful face across the table tonight."

"That was sweet, Trey. Did you want a Michelob?"

"Yes, let me have one. Thank you baby. I'll be down in a bit."

'Am I the bomb or what? My husband loves me, my husband loves me,' thought Christy as she folded the laundry.

CHAPTER EIGHTY-ONE
MY DEAREST JONATHAN

"Hello, Mr. Doorman, sir. I don't know if you remember me or not, but about a couple of weeks ago, I was a guest of Mr. Baize's. I mean Mr. Omari's."

"Yes, I remember you. It was kind of late."

"Well, the first time, but the second time I returned it was early. I was wondering if you would turn the key on the elevators, so it would allow me to slide this letter under Jonathan's door."

"It would be my pleasure, ma'am."

"Thank you very much, Mr. Doorman," Mekyla said as she entered the elevator.

'This is such a wonderful building. Okay, here I go. I don't know why I'm all nervous. He's not even here," Mekyla thought. She stepped out of the elevator and oriented herself.

'Okay, it was to my left. Uh, what, what is she doing here? And she still has a key to his place. I can't believe this,' Mekyla said to herself, standing with one foot in the elevator and the other in the hall.

The elevator doors dinged and she jumped back into the elevator and rode it back down to the lobby. 'I can't believe this. I can't believe I was so gullible as to think that this man was the one. Christy was right, but for some reason it still doesn't feel like she was.'

"Did you find everything okay?" said the doorman.

"Yes. Thank you again for allowing me to go up. Have a nice evening."

"You do the same, ma'am."

'I guess this just wasn't meant to be. Let me try Ian again. Still no answer, I guess he's still out. It's probably best we don't talk right now, because I still don't know what I might say.'

CHAPTER EIGHTY-TWO
NOW THAT'S A GOOD ENDING

"There's no sense in wasting a perfectly good hotel room that's paid through tomorrow. I'll just see Junior and Mom after work tomorrow. I'm going to visit with my son's father in exactly twenty-four hours. This week is going to be all right with me," Jennifer said, as she stretched across the hotel bed.

CHAPTER EIGHTY-THREE
WORN OUT

"Did you want me to wash your back for you, Trey?"

"No, baby, I'm fine."

"Dinner will be on the table in five minutes, is that okay?" Christy said, as she gathered Trey's clothes from the bathroom floor.

"I'll be down in four minutes."

'No wonder he hopped in the shower. These boxers have a musty-sweaty odor to them. He should start taking showers at the gym before coming home.'

CHAPTER EIGHTY-FOUR
PLAYING GAMES WITH JONATHAN

'Oh yeah! This Grilled Chicken Caesar Salad is the bomb. Bennigan's never lets me down. Okay, where was I? Lisa was debating whether she should stay or not.'

"We only have a few more days before I leave for Tulsa."

"Lisa, I want you to know those few days that we had were some of the best days of my life," Jonathan said as he pulled Lisa close to him and stared in her eyes.

"Jonathan, I – I . . .."

"Yes, Lisa?"

"Would you like for me to refill you glass?" Lisa said as she leaned down to grab her wineglass.

"Lisa, that's not what you were going to say. Please say what's on your mind. Don't let this become a missed opportunity."

"It will keep, Jonathan. So, what kind of games do you have?"

"What?"

"You know, scrabble? Or maybe you'd like me to kick your butt in a game of spades."

"I believe I have some cards around here. But if you're going to cry when I whoop up on you, then we probably shouldn't play."

"Bring it on, mister," Lisa said as she made herself comfortable on the floor in front of the fireplace.

"Here you go."

"Oh no. Not the bowl of strawberries. What happened to the cards?"

"There right here. The deal is, whenever I win a hand of spades you have to eat one of these strawberries."

"That's not so bad."

"The thing is, they're filled with an alcoholic beverage."

"Oh yeah? Well that's okay, because I don't plan on losing."

"I won this hand. You have to eat one of the strawberries."

"Hold on. I thought you meant after each game."

"No, I said each hand won."

"Fine. I'll eat your little drunken strawberry."

"Are you cheating? How do you keep winning these hands?" Lisa said, while trying to contain her laughter.

"You're feeling the liquor, huh?"

"You're trying to get me glossy eyed."

"Yep."

"Why? You don't have to get me glossy eyed for whatever it is your trying to attain, because I felt that way before the first strawberry."

"Come here," Jonathan said as he reached for Lisa's hand. "I don't know what it is you're doing to me, but I know that I don't ever want this feeling to end."

"I know exactly how you feel Jonathan," Lisa said as she leaned over and pressed her lips up against Jonathan's right cheekbone and then his left. "I'm still not ready for what you need, Jonathan."

"It's okay, Lisa. I just want to pleasure you. I want you to feel good." The glow of the fireplace illuminated Lisa's body as Jonathan began to remove her clothes.

"Turn over," he said. Then he began to message Lisa's body starting with her neck.

"Ooh, that feels good, Jonathan. I love the way your hands feel on my skin. They're so masculine."

Jonathan worked his way down to the crease of Lisa's back, then down the side of each one of her thighs. He poured the juice from the strawberry into the crease between her thighs and calves. Then he kissed her thigh and sucked the juices from the strawberries.

The ringing of the phone broke Mekyla's concentration. Exasperated, she reached for it. "Hello."

"Mekyla, this is Ian."

"Hello, Ian. I tried calling you a couple of times, but you were still out."

"I'm glad you made it okay. Are you checked into a hotel?"

"Yes, I'm here now. I was just writing and eating a Caesar salad."

"Did you see him?"

"Yes and no."

"What do you mean?"

"Well, I went by the hospital and he was there, but his wife was also there."

"Are you okay?"

"Yes, I'm fine. How are you?"

"I'm doing okay. I miss you Mekyla. I can't shake it, and I don't know if I want to."

"I'm staying here for another week or so, just to get some writing done."

"You're going to wait for him?"

"No, I'm not going to pursue that anymore. But I still need to get my thoughts together. It's not fair to you for me to be there right now. I respect you too much to continue to put you through the confusion I'm going through."

"But that's what couples do," said Ian. "They go through it together."

Mekyla bowed her head. "I'm not sure if I want the together part right now, Ian. Please give me this time, and we'll talk when I return."

"If you're not returning to me completely, then I'm not sure if I would want you to return to me at all."

"I understand your position, and I completely respect it. Ian, I want you to know that I completely understand the man that I had in you. At first I didn't really know it. But when I left this morning, right then I knew what I had and lost at the same time. I'm sure, down the road, there's a lesson in all of this, but right now I don't know what it is. I just know that this is where I am now, and that, for some reason this is where I'm supposed to be."

There was a pause, and then Ian said, "Mekyla, call me if you need anything."

"I will, Ian. Goodnight."

"Goodnight, Mekyla."

"Ian?"

"Yes?"

"I haven't been feeling very well."

"What, are coming down with a cold? Sometimes a climate change will mess with your immune system."

"The pain is more in my stomach area."

"Well, what did you eat?"

"Not too much. I really don't feel like eating."

"Mekyla, could you possibly be pregnant?"

"I don't know, Ian. I don't know."

"If you were, would it be mine?"

Mekyla closed her eyes and threw her head back. "I'm not going to have this conversation right now. Let's just talk about it some other time."

"Don't back-burner this, Mekyla. I don't know how you could be pregnant anyway. We've been very safe and really haven't been that active lately."

"Goodnight, Ian." Mekyla hung up the phone with a look of concern on her face.

CHAPTER EIGHTY-FIVE
PROMISES OF LOVE

Christy looked up from the kitchen table as her husband strolled into the room. "Good morning Trey. You must have been really tired last night. As soon as you laid your head down, you were out like the light."

"I guess I didn't realize how tired I was. I know I haven't been giving you the attention you need, Christy. But things are getting ready to change. With the basketball league being on break for a few weeks, we'll have a lot more time to spend together as a family. I know the kids think I've lost my senses. You're a good woman, Christy, and if I haven't said it lately, I love you for everything you've done for me and our children."

Christy smiled. "There aren't too many couples get a chance to fall in love for the second time. I love you Trey."

"I love you also, Christy." Trey wrapped his arms around his wife and snuggled up against her.

"Did you want breakfast, Trey?"

"Sounds good to me, but not too heavy, just something light."

CHAPTER EIGHTY-SIX
THE FACE IN THE PHOTO

Jennifer stood up as soon as he came through the door. "Well, Mr. Elliott. I would know that smile from a mile away."

"Hello, Jennifer. You look absolutely stunning."

"Well, thank you. Let's get a table. Did you find it okay?"

"I lived at TGI Friday's, when I lived here. How did you know I was in town?"

"I didn't know, actually," said Jennifer as the hostess showed them to their table. "I just made it back in town from Louisiana when I stopped by your office."

"Is that right? Were you there on business or pleasure?"

"I went down there specifically looking for you."

"So, after all these years, you decided to pay me a visit. How sweet is that? Here I am thinking our mutual classmate told you I was in town and remembered that we dated a few times."

"Who are you talking about?"

"Trey, Trey Love."

"No, Trey didn't tell me. I didn't remember that you guys knew each other."

"We played high school and college ball together."

"Oh, okay. So, did you guys talk about me?"

"We did some reminiscing, but your name never came up."

"Hmm, okay. But anyway, the reason I was tracking you down was to share some information with you that is almost eighteen years old."

"Is this some news that's going to require a drink?"

"Well, Brent, it just might." She reached across the table and took both of Brent's hands in hers. "We have a son."

Brent stared at her and blinked.

"Did you hear me, Brent?"

"Yes, but I'm still trying to process it. And also, find the words to say that that's impossible."

"What do you mean impossible? We were together back when I became pregnant."

"Yes, apparently you became pregnant, but not by me. I'm not saying this to hurt you, but I used protection each and every time I had sex with a female."

"Did we? Well, okay, yeah maybe you did, but I guess it broke."

"No, I would always check that as well."

"You're not that thorough. Besides, we have a son that exists."

"I'm afraid we're going to have to get some proof on that. And besides, I wasn't the only one you were intimate with back then."

"There were no others. Uh, well, maybe one other. But, I'm sure he's yours," Jennifer said with a look of uncertainty.

"Does he have my features?"

"I was so sure he was yours, that I didn't even explore the other possibility. Would you like to see a picture of him? He's getting ready for college on a football scholarship." Jennifer took a snapshot of Junior out of her purse and handed it to Brent.

"He's a very handsome young man. What's his name?"

"Junior."

"Junior. Meaning J R period?"

"Yes. His full name is Brent Elliott, Jr."

Brent sat back in his chair. "Jennifer, how could you do this without speaking with me or even telling me about this kid?"

"My mother wouldn't let me discuss it with anyone."

"Well, at some point you became an adult. Why would you make this kid miss out on a whole life with his father? Why do women do that?"

"Sometimes there are reasons out of our control."

"So, do you know where this other guy is, because, clearly, he's not my son? You can just look at him and see that he has none of my features."

"Actually, the other man I have in mind is someone I would have loved to have a child with. Not trying to be mean or anything, but this guy happens to be the love of my life."

"May I ask you a question?"

"Yes, of course."

"Why now? Why would you reveal this now?"

"I've always wanted you – well the father – now him, to know about Junior. It's just that I couldn't, I truly couldn't, without breaking a promise to my mother. But now that he's becoming an adult and through talks with my now late grandmother, I realized it was time. Not only to free my soul of all the lies. But, also allow Junior the opportunity to choose for himself."

"So, are we okay with this, or do we need to do something further?"

"No, I can clearly see that he's not your son. You have to understand. I went through a lot back then, and I was just stuck somewhere in time. And your face was the one that stuck with me."

"I think I'll have that drink now. Okay, when you got to Louisiana, who told you, I was here?"

"Long story made short. I met your sister here in Tulsa at a basketball game. She gave me the name of her shop in Louisiana. Coincidentally, I was headed to Louisiana anyway. So I stopped by her shop before heading to where I knew we have mutual friends from college. So in your sister Boa's cashmere shop, I see this picture of you there and put two and two together."

"So you met my wife."

"Boa's your wife?"

"Yes."

"But, didn't you have a little sister?"

"Yes again. But Boa's not my sister."

"Wow, this is getting weird. This is truly a small world. I love the sweaters by the way."

"My wife is a great designer."

"And her partner, Dallas Rangel?"

"He's her brother."

"Oh." Jennifer smiled and shook her head. "It's really good to see you again."

"I guess you're going to have to figure out how to explain the name situation?"

"Well he's had it for almost eighteen years now. No sense in taking that away."

CHAPTER EIGHTY-SEVEN
A TEXAS BREATHE AWAY

Taylor Ellis looked up from her temporary desk when she heard the door open. "Hello," she said, greeting the customer.

"I'm looking for a Mekyla Williams," said the man.

"I'm sorry, she'll be out for another week on vacation. But if there's anything I can help you with, I'd be happy to do so. Would you care to have a seat?" She pointed to the chair in front of her desk.

"Another week, huh? Okay, may I leave my card with you? And could you make sure Mekyla receives it as soon as she returns?"

"Yes, that's not a problem," said Taylor, reaching for the card. "Jonathan Omari. You're out of Austin?"

"Yes, I am."

"And you're an architect. Are you scouting a place to start construction on something?"

"No, this is something personal."

"Gotcha. I will be sure she gets this message."

"I would appreciate that. You have a nice day."

"You do the same," Taylor said as she watched him walk out of Mekyla's office.

Taylor set the card in a prominent place so that she wouldn't forget about it. Marie was still at lunch, but the office was quiet. Now was the perfect time to call her office and check up on how things were going over there. She picked up the phone and was about to dial when Mr. Omari reappeared in the doorway.

"Excuse me again," he said. "Do you know if she left town or stayed in town for her vacation?"

"I believe she did leave."

"Okay, thanks again."

"Goodbye, Mr. Omari.

CHAPTER EIGHTY-EIGHT
TIL DEATH DO US PART

With her heart pounding, Schonda held the phone and waited for her mom to answer it. "Mama, this is Schonda," She blurted out as soon as she heard her mother's voice. "I need you to meet me at the hospital."

"Why, what's wrong?" Mrs. Brinkley asked. Immediately she grabbed her baseball cap with which to cover her hair, and scanned the room for two shoes that matched. "Where in the hell are my shoes? I've got shoes and more shoes, but I can't find two that match?"

"Mama, slow down before you give yourself a heart attack. St. John's Hospital admitted Christy about thirty minutes ago."

"What's happened?"

"Mama, I'll explain everything when you get here."

"Schonda," Tere called from the end of the hospital hallway."

"Tere, I'm over here," Schonda said over her shoulder. "Mama, I need to go. Tere is screaming my name. I'll see you when you get here. I don't know what floor or room number they are going to take her to, but she's in emergency surgery right now. I'll see you when you get here."

Tere came hurrying down the hall. "Hey Schonda, have you heard anything yet?"

"No, not yet. Where's Kimberly?"

"She's on her way up. She had to park the car."

Kimberly's the sister that very seldom makes appearances to the family gatherings. Even though she has no children, she's always overwhelmed just with work and school.

"How did you know she was here?"

"One of the kids called me and told me their mommy was taken to the hospital by ambulance. How sad is that – to see your mother lying unconscious like that?"

"How are they doing, could you tell?"

"They're fine. I took them to Trey's parents' house, because I guess he is missing in action."

They heard quick footsteps and turned to see their sister hurrying down the hall.

"Hey, Kimberly," said Schonda.

"Is Christy okay?"

"Don't know yet."

"What happened?"

"Don't know that either."

"Okay, does anybody need coffee?" said Tere. "I can sure use a couple of cups, right now myself."

"Yes, Tere, if you would grab me a cup, thanks," said Schonda.

The sisters heard a familiar voice interrogating the nurses. "Where's my baby?" said the voice.

"Oh lord, do you hear Mama coming?"

"Yes, I just tried to tune it out."

"Tere, please," said Kimberly. "You know no one can tune that woman's voice out.

"You're probably right, Kimberly, but I attempt to do it every time. I'm convinced that one day, I'll succeed."

"How did she get here so fast anyway? It felt like I was just talking with her right before you started screaming."

Tere bowed her head and lowered her voice as their mother approached. "Mama probably has a siren hidden somewhere and she breaks it out for emergencies."

"Have you all seen my baby? How is she? Is she all right?"

"We don't know anything yet, Mom."

"What reason would my baby need to be in the hospital? Does anyone know anything yet about why she would have a need to be here in an emergency fashion?"

'Okay, she's not going to stop repeating herself.' thought Tere as she looked for somewhere to sit.

"No, but when they brought her in she was unconscious," said Schonda.

"Mama, don't start worrying yourself. She's going to be all right," said Tere. She then stood and started pacing the floor, having decided against sitting down. "I've prayed over my sister, because I still have questions to ask her about life."

"Tere, this is not about you."

"I know that Schonda."

"Anyhow, why would you say that?"

"Shush it, Tere."

"Shush *your* fat mouth."

"Here comes the doctor," said Schonda.

"He may be coming to see another family that's waiting," said Tere.

The doctor approached, looking serious. "Are you Christy Love's family?" he said.

"Yes sir, we are."

"Doctor, how is Christy doing?" Schonda asked with a hesitant tremble in her voice.

"She's doing fine. We've pumped her stomach, but we're going to keep her for a few days to run more tests. We just want to make sure it didn't damage anything and then later I'll have another doctor visit with her."

"What happened? Pump her stomach of what?" Tere asked with a hint of frustration.

The doctor turned to the older lady. "Are you Christy's mom?"

"Yes doctor, I am."

"Well, Mrs. Love . . .."

"No, that's Mrs. Brinkley."

"Oh, pardon me. Mrs. Brinkley."

"Yes, that daughter and this daughter, Tere, are both married. These two are just shacking, and I have another one who is also apart of the just shacking group."

"Mama, please. He didn't ask you all of that." Kimberly turned and took a few steps away. "I can't believe she just said that to this man," Kimberly muttered under her breath. She turned and looked at her sister. "Tere, where did you get this coffee? I can see it's going to be a long afternoon."

The doctor shuffled through his paper work and spoke without looking up. "Mrs. Brinkley, it seems as though she took a large quantity of pills at once."

The sister's all looked at the doctor in shock.

"She has never done anything like this before," said Mrs. Brinkley. "How soon will we know if there is any serious damage?"

"We'll start the tests today, but we won't have any definitive results before tomorrow, possibly two days."

"You mentioned another doctor," said Schonda. "What would be the reason for the second doctor?"

"I'm going to have a psychiatrist visit with her before she can be released."

"Psychiatrist?" said Tere. "What's the reason for the psychiatrist?"

"We need to know why she took so many pills at one time."

"Well, didn't she tell you? Because I'm sure it was for a headache, she does have several little ones at home."

"I'll visit with Christy maybe later today or tomorrow." He held up his hands to calm the women. "Believe me, that's just my standard recommendation. In the case of an overdose, I always have my patients speak with a staff psychiatrist before releasing them." He glanced down at the chart again. "And it didn't help her existing situation any."

"What existing situation?"

He looked up, surprised. "Oh, is that something she hasn't shared with you yet? If so, that's something you'll have to speak with her about."

"Can we see her now?"

"Yes, you may, but her throat is going to be very sore making it hard for her to talk. So, you probably want to limit the questions until maybe tomorrow."

"Thanks for everything, doctor."

"You're welcome and I'll see you tomorrow."

"I knew they were going to keep her," Kimberly said as she flopped down into the chair.

"Okay, since you know so much, Kimberly, what kinds of questions will the psychiatrist ask, and what is this other thing she has?"

"Schonda, he or she is going to ask intelligent questions," said Kimberly. "Nothing like the one you just asked me. Everybody feels they know any and everything about whatever. And maybe she wasn't ready to tell us about every little detail of her life. This is why I'm so distant. Let's just let her tell us in her own way, and not interrogate her right now."

"She did take more pills than what's considered normal to fight – what was the ailment we were using – headache? However, before they will release her with no doubts of her doing it again, they would like to know why."

"Just because you're a phlebotomist, you think you have doctor's knowledge of how things work, huh Tere?"

"Do we really know why she did it? Does anyone have a clue?" Schonda blurted out to break up the little spat that Kimberly and Tere were having. "Why is it that we don't know what's going on so serious in our sister's life?"

"I was wondering when that was going to be said. I'm sure it has something to do with Trey," Kimberly said sounding very certain of herself.

"Well, he does keep her all cooped up in the house with those kids and she doesn't really have a life anymore," said Schonda.

"She chose to have that life and I believe she's happy in it, Schonda."

"Happy? She sure has a strange way of showing it." Kimberly said.

"Let's just go see how she's doing. Gaah-ly! Boy, I tell you this family can't come together even in a crisis." Tere said, as she headed down the hall.

"Pipe down, Tere, before the whole hospital hears our business," said Schonda.

"I don't care. Let them hear me. I'm upset. My sister is lying in there probably about to die and you're worried about who might hear us."

"There is just no talking to you, is there?" Schonda said, I she held her stomach and rolled her eyes.

"Just go on, Schonda, before I kick you in the knee."

"You're so silly, always talking about kicking somebody in their knee and haven't done it yet." Besides, I'm pregnant, you crazy lunatic."

As the family began to enter the room, Christy opened her eyes. She had recognized the voices of her family echoing throughout the hospital. Christy looked over at the door and gave her mom a big warm smile, a smile that said that it was good to see familiar faces reassuring her she was still on the time side of life.

"Hello, baby," said her mom. We're not going to stay long. We just wanted you to know we were here for you. The doctor said all was well, but that you would need to speak with a psychiatrist before you can leave this place. They must think you're crazy or something."

Schonda frowned deeply. "Why does she need to see a psychiatrist, and why are we telling her this right now?"

"A psychiatrist, huh?" said Tere. "I guess that's apart of your prescription. Basically if you don't swallow the pill correctly, then no go home for you."

Kimberly looked up at the ceiling, exasperated. "You always have some smart remark about everything."

"Lighten up, Kimberly. I was just kidding. You gotta do what you gotta do to get some free therapy. You think she's not going to take advantage. Every one of us probably needs to sit on somebody's couch," said Tere between sips of free hospital coffee and small bites of the graham crackers she'd discovered when she was snooping around one of the hospital's entrances that said, "staff only".

"Yes, I'm sure each and every one of us probably needs some type of therapy. In Christy's case, it's not such a mystery anymore."

"Tere," said Schonda. "Do you think you could be a little more sensitive to Christy's feelings? We're sitting up discussing her at a time when she doesn't have an opportunity to defend herself."

"You know this is something that's been brewing for a long time. You people are just being phony and it is about to drive me insane. I wish Mekyla were here."

"We're going to let you get some rest Christy," said Mrs. Brinkley. "We'll just see you tomorrow. Apparently, everybody is caught up in their own little world right now, and I don't want this type of talk to upset you." She looked down at her socks noticing that the texture was different.

"Before we leave, has anyone called Trey?" said Schonda.

"Yes, I tried, but no answer," said Kimberly, shrugging. "So I just left a voice message for him to come to hospital."

"I can't believe I put on two different socks," Mrs. Brinkley said, still staring down at her feet.

"Socks?" said Tere. "Is that the only thing you've noticed? Your shoes aren't in the same family either."

"Mama, I think Christy is trying to say something," Schonda said.

Everyone moved closer to Christy's bed to hear what she was trying to say.

"What Christy? I can't hardly hear you, baby," said Mrs. Brinkley, concentrating on her daughter's mouth as if she could read her lips.

"Tere, don't tell Mekyla I'm in the hospital," said Christy in a very raspy voice. "She'll just cancel her plans and head back this way."

"Christy, you know we can't keep this from Mekyla," said Tere.

"Besides we already called her and I can't take it back because her flight should be leaving in a little bit."

"Tere, what is it with this 'we' stuff?" said Schonda. "You went in a corner and called her all on your own."

Tere shook her head. "You know we made a pact a long time ago that whatever happened to one of us happened to all of us."

Schonda sighed and nodded. "As much as it's going to hurt me to say it, you're right. Eventually one of us would have had to call Mekyla, and the longer we put it off, the angrier she would have become with us, Christy."

"Well, I'm sorry for the confusion and the scare I may have caused everyone." Christy said slowly, trying to keep the saliva to a minimum. Her throat was too sore to keep having to swallow.

"Baby, please, don't talk too much right now," said her mom. "We'll see you tomorrow and we're just thankful everything turned out to be okay with no permanent damage done. Besides, I really can't hear you and it's driving me crazy trying to read your lips."

Schonda smirked at her mom. "See you later, Christy," she said.

"Schonda, don't let this interrupt your wedding plans."

"Christy, the wedding is a couple of months away. You'll be home in a couple of days. So, for now, we'll just say we love you and get some rest. Bye."

The women left the room, waving and blowing kisses to Christy, and started down the hall.

"Mama," said Schonda, drawing her hand along the wall to steady her self. "I didn't want to say anything while we were in Christy's room, but I think I'm going into labor."

"What?"

"Oh," said Tere. "Then this means I'm going to get to coach you through this one, because you said if Deon or Mekyla weren't available, I would be next in line."

"Yes, I did, Tere, but Mekyla is on her way here."

Tere raised her eyebrows. "If you don't really want me to be your coaching partner just say it."

"I don't want you to be my coaching partner if Deon or Mekyla are available. I promised Mekyla she could help deliver this one and you know Deon will override Mekyla, if he makes it back in town in time for the delivery."

"So does this mean we have to stay at the hospital because you're checking yourself in?" said Kimberly.

"You can go home and do whatever it is you do," said Tere. "Because you're after me in the coaching thing. Actually, I don't even think you're on the list. It's not like anybody ever sees you anyway, you're so caught up in your own little fantasy world."

"Whatever, Tere. You're so dramatic. I don't *want* to be on the coaching list, and if I did, I'm sure I would have been ahead of you."

As they approached the nurse's station, Kimberly ran ahead a few steps. "Excuse me nurse," she said, pointed at Schonda with her thumb. "It's possible she's gone into labor. Where do we go to have her admitted into the hospital for delivery?"

The nurse nodded toward the elevator. "Go to the second floor for admitting and they'll direct you from there."

"Thank you very much."

"Okay, girls," said their mother. "I'm going to go with Schonda to have her admitted. Are you coming?"

"Yes, we're coming," said Tere. "Why not make a night of it?"

"Schonda, I'll call Termaine and have him pick up your kids from school and bring them up here," Tere said, as she scrambled for Termaine's cell phone number.

"What time is Mekyla's flight getting in, and who's picking her up?" said their mom.

"She said she would allow Ian to pick her up," said Schonda.

"Allow Ian?" said Kimberly furrowing her brow. "So is everything okay with them now?"

"I don't know, Kimberly," said Schonda.

"You probably know, Schonda, you're just not telling me. And why am I the last person to know everything?"

"Like somebody said before, you're not in the loop as much. You can find all of the good gossip at Mama's house. Somehow, she always seems to find the latest information on all of us."

"That's right, Mama knows all," said Tere. "Schonda, how close are the contractions?"

"Maybe about thirty-minutes apart."

"Yes, we're in for a long night. I heard Mama ask what time Mekyla was getting in, but I didn't hear an answer."

"Her flight is scheduled to arrive around six o'clock this afternoon."

"And Ian is going to be the one to pick her up," Kimberly said again in case everyone in the room didn't hear her the first time.

"What's so unusual about Ian picking her up?" said Mama. "Are they not together anymore?"

"No, I didn't mean it that way. Sure they're still together. I'm just playing off the way Schonda said allow Ian."

"Coffee anybody?" said Tere. "I'd like to go get the coffee this time."

"Hold on, Tere. I'm coming with you," Kimberly said, nearly tripping over the waiting area chair as she hurried to follow her sister.

"Mekyla should be getting in about two hours from now," said Mama. "Schonda, you think I should call Ian to make sure he remembers to pick her up?"

"No, Mama, I'm sure he's probably already at the airport. They haven't seen each other in a few days."

"That's right. She has been gone for a while. You would have thought she wouldn't leave so much. The man does have needs."

"I don't know, Mama. I'm sure she has her reasons."

"As soon as we get you checked in, and since I'm still in this hospital and will probably be here well into the night, I'm going to go and check on Christy to make sure Trey showed up to sit with her for a while."

"Okay, Mama, but remember, she can't talk that much."

Her mother looked at her, indignant. "I remember. What do think I am, a child?"

"No, I was just saying."

"Saying some stuff I already know about."

"Ooh! I think I'm having another contraction," Schonda called out just to stop the freight train of her mom's mouth.

CHAPTER EIGHTY-NINE
A BITTERSWEET FLIGHT

"Well, this is my stop," said Natocha, as the plane taxied to the gate. "Dallas Ft. Worth airport, you just gotta love it." She patted the manuscript she still had in her lap. "Mekyla, this was some good reading. "I didn't have a chance to finish it, but here's my card. Please give me a call."

Mekyla took the card from Natocha and read it. Her jaw dropped into her lap. "You're with Random House?"

"Yes, and it was a pleasure meeting you. Don't forget to give me a call."

Mekyla grinned from ear to ear. "I will, and thank you for the compliment. I'm glad you didn't tell me before. I would have been out of my mind with anxiety."

"Send a copy to the address on my card, and we'll talk further. And I hope everything goes well with your family."

"Thank you for that," Mekyla said, as she sat back in her chair with her eyes closed, remembering why she was called back home in the first place.

As the plane took off again, Mekyla's heart pounded. This was the last leg of the trip. She'd be home shortly.

'I guess I should have listened to my little sister when she was obviously trying to tell me something,' she thought. 'But no, I was so tied up in my own little web of problems. I wonder what's going on with Jennifer as well. She sounded very hyper on my voice mail. I'll just deal with all of this when I get home. Home, huh. Now that's probably going to be odd.

What am I going to do when this plane lands? I have so many decisions to make. I need more time to myself, is what I need. But, Christy needs me more right now." She stared out the window at the fluffy white clouds in the clear blue sky.

CHAPTER NINETY
A MOTHER'S LOVE

Mrs. Brinkley stood over her daughter's hospital bed and smiled down at her. "Christy, baby, it's Mama. How are you feeling?"

"I'm okay, Mama."

"I didn't want to say anything in front of the other girls, but the doctor said you may have caused more damage to the other thing you're sick with. What is it he's referring to?"

"Mama, I don't want to talk about it right now."

"I'm just very concerned Christy. It didn't sound like it was something small."

"Can I just talk with you about it at a later date?"

Mrs. Brinkley paused. "Yes, of course, but I . . .. You know what? I'm just going to let it alone for now. Because I believe there's a lot we need to talk about. At first I thought you accidentally took too many pills, but now I'm thinking you *purposely* took all of those pills. But it will keep. But, best believe, I'll be back with those same questions. Does any of this have anything to do with Trey or those kids?"

"Mama, the kids have nothing to do with this, okay?"

"Well, have you heard anything from Trey?"

"No. Not since last night."

"Is that a bruise on your arm?"

"It's nothing."

"Nothing' doesn't leave a mark. Well, I tell you what I'm going to do. I'm going to sit right here and wait on nothing." Mrs. Brinkley sat down in the chair with her arms crossed.

"Mama, please, just let me handle this."

"What, by trying to take your own life? I think not."

CHAPTER NINETY-ONE
THE BEGINNING TO WHAT END

"Excuse me. I'm sorry," Mekyla said as she made her way to the baggage claim area. "What time is it?" she said aloud. She looked down at her watch, and then scanned the baggage claim area. 'Ian should be here somewhere.'

"Mekyla, I'm over here," Ian said in soft whisper, as he was stood up against a wall.

"Hello, Ian."

"Hello." Ian came toward her and grabbed her carryon.

"Thanks for picking me up. I know this has to be hard for you. But, I also want you to know it's hard for me as well."

"First, I would like to start out by apologizing to you. The accusation I made was very insensitive. I don't know what steps to take next, but we're going to have to sit down and decide together." Ian reached out to take Mekyla's hand.

TO BE CONTINUED WITH
WHEN MY TEARS CRY

Book Notes:

Mekyla

Christy

Jennifer

AUTHOR'S AUTOGRAPH